I0736248

SWORDSMAN OF THE RIFT

Volume 2

Written by Brandon Varnell
Illustrations by DanteWontDie

This book is a work of fiction. Names, characters, places, and incidents are the products of the author's imagination or are used fictitiously. Any resemblance to actual events, locales, or persons, living or dead, is coincidental.

Swordsman of the Rift 2
Copyright © 2020 Brandon Varnell
Illustration Copyright © 2020 DantWontDie
All rights reserved.

Brandon Varnell and Kitsune Incorporated supports the right to free expression and the value of copyright. The purpose of copyright is to encourage writers and artists to produce creative works that enrich our culture.

The scanning, uploading, and distribution of this book without permission is a theft of the author's intellectual property. If you would like permission to use the material from the book (other than for review purposes), please contact the publisher. Thank you for your support of the author's rights.

To see Brandon Varnell's other works, or to ask for permission to use his works, visit him at www.varnell-brandon.com, facebook at www.facebook.com/AmericanKitsune, twitter at www.twitter.com/BrandonbVarnell, Patreon at https://www.patreon.com/BrandonVarnell, and instagram at www.instagram.com/brandonbvarnell.

ISBN: 978-1-951904-04-3

CONTENT

DEDICATION

This page is dedicated to my super awesome Kitsune Patrons. Without them, I would never be able to hire artists to draw super lewd artwork of my characters:

Aaron Harris
Alarinnise
C.L. Holgrahm
Chace Corso
Dominic Q Roddan
Edward Lamar Stephenson
Emery Moore
Feitochan
Forrest Hansen
Jacob Flores
Jacob Wonjo
James Leon-Moore
Kevin
Kevin Aulinger
Lane Watkins
Lucid Fayt
Matthew Wallace
Max A Kramer
Michael Moneymaker
Peter Barton
Rafael Eriksen
Seismic Wolf
Syed Hamdani
ToraLinkley
Travis Cox
William Crew

CHAPTER 1

Back when I was younger—I wanna say ten or eleven—my parents took me to a rodeo. My dad had always been a wild west fanatic. In his office, he had John Wayne posters, an action figure of Wyatt Earp, and an old Winchester Lever Action 1873 that sat on a stand on his desk. He loved western movies, so he always made it a point to take Mom and me to the rodeo at least twice a year.

I never much cared for rodeos. You could say I was something of a neat freak back then. Rodeos were covered in dust, had sweaty men and women crowding together, and none of their shoot-out plays were interesting. That said, the rodeo did have one thing I always liked watching.

Bull riding.

I still remember the first time I saw someone riding on a bull, the man hanging on like his life depended on it, a determined snarl on his face. Unlike everything else at the rodeo, bull riding seemed legitimately dangerous. You tried to stay on a violently bucking creature that was raging mad, and if you fell, the bull would try to skewer you. One of the men I'd watched had actually been impaled through the gut by a bull's horn once. That had caused a panic among the crowd. However, it was watching bull riding that really used to get me pumped. It was bull riding that originally turned me into an adrenaline junkie, and maybe it also played a hand in why I joined the Special Forces.

If anyone could hear my thoughts, I was certain they'd be wondering why I was reminiscing over something that happened years ago. In truth, I'd forgotten all about it until just now. The reason I remembered bull riding was actually because it vaguely resembled what I was doing right now.

I was sitting atop a massive creature.

Well, it was more like I was holding on for dear life.

I was gritting my teeth as I firmly gripped the massive double skull roof. I was sure there was some scientific name for it, but I'd never heard of it if there was. The thing I had grabbed hold of looked like a half-circle that was sticking out of the back of this creature's skull. It was covered in hard leather and tougher than my sword. I'd already tried hacking into it, and not even my level 59 strength could dent this thing.

My sword had actually bent.

A loud and angry roar echoed from the creature's toothless beak, which was large enough to easily swallow me in a single bite. Two horns jutted from the top of its head, and there was a shorter horn near its snout. Large black eyes currently dyed red glared up as though they could see me hiding behind its bones.

My bones rattled as this creature slammed itself into a rock wall. Shattered fragments fell from the sky and pelted my body, but I covered my vitals with one hand, held on for dear life with the other, and glared at the back of this thing's head.

The creature was easily ten times larger than me, and while I wasn't the biggest guy around, six feet was still nothing to scoff at. I didn't even want to guess at how much this thing weighed. Shattering rocks was easy as pie for it. A scream of pain and surprise tore itself from my throat as rock fragments from the wall it broke struck me in the back.

"Bryan!"

Just as I was wondering whether I should risk jumping off this thing, a shout echoed from above me. I looked up to find a woman flying toward me. Her hair was long, blond like the sun, and wavy like rolling ocean waves; her bright blue eyes were open wide with concern for me, and her white pinions flapped frantically, making her look like an angel coming to rescue me.

Well, she was an angel. An honest-to-goodness heavenly being. An archangel even.

Not that this mattered right now.

"Michelle!" I shouted as I reached out toward her.

Michelle grabbed my hand even as she curved back up and took off into the sky. I grunted as my right arm was yanked right from its socket, but I really didn't have time to complain. Once we had traveled a safe distance, Michelle pulled me fully into her arms, embracing me from behind. I wished I could enjoy the sensation, but, well, we were still in trouble.

The creature down below roared at us. I thought I could sense its anger at not being able to reach me.

"Thanks for the save," I said.

"Honestly, Bryan, what were you thinking when you decided to jump on that thing's back?" asked Michelle, her tone scolding.

"I'm pretty sure I wasn't thinking," I admitted. "It just seemed like a good idea at the time."

"Good idea, my butt! Stop being reckless!"

Michelle was a beautiful woman with a body that I would have called sinful if making such a statement wasn't something that would have had me sleeping on the couch. Her breasts were squished against my back, modest but well-formed. They might not have been the same size as our other companion's knockers, but they were still buoyant and squishy.

"Well, do you have any ideas about how we can defeat this thing?" I asked.

"That's a level 80 Trycon," Michelle said. "That means it's at the same level as me, but it has an impeccable defense. I can't penetrate its thick hide with my divine powers."

Trycons were creatures of the earth, which meant they were resistant to powers of the divine. It would be one thing if they were beings of darkness or at least had a less solid defense. However, the

Trycon had one of the sturdiest defenses out of all the monsters we'd hunted.

"Where is Adina?" I asked.

"She should be coming in just a moment," Michelle said, her tone reproving as if to say, *"She would have been with us if you hadn't leapt on ahead,"* but I did my best to ignore that.

As if talking about her had summoned her, a woman appeared from the sky, her wings flapping madly as she accelerated while descending. Her body rotated like a corkscrew. I barely saw her extend a single, long leg before she struck the Trycon on the head.

An explosion of fierce winds erupted from where her foot collided with the Trycon's skull. The force of the explosion pushed the Trycon's head down, while simultaneously blowing Michelle and I off course. Michelle screamed as she clung to me so I wouldn't fall. I could barely hear it over the impossibly loud noise of the sound barrier breaking.

Dust billowed from beneath us, spreading out and engulfing the Trycon, completely masking it to the point where I could see nothing. From within that cloud shot a figure.

Unlike Michelle, who had white wings made from the purest feathers, this woman had deep pink wings that were leathery and reminded me of a dragon. Where Michelle was dressed in a full-bodied toga, she wore skimpy leather straps that covered her breasts and crotch but nothing else. Her full chest was also a good deal larger than Michelle's. Pink horns jutted from her head and curved forward to form a crown. Meanwhile, sticking out from her back and waving back and forth, was a long prehensile tail with a spade at the very end.

She pulled up to us, looked at me, and then let out a relieved smile. Her eyes were a gentle blue that complimented her light skin. The curvature of her ruby red lips was enough to inflame any man. She had the face of an angel—a sinful angel who could deprive a man of any conscious thought with a glance.

"I'm glad you're okay," she said. "I was worried Michelle wouldn't make it in time."

"Who do you take me for?" asked Michelle with a scoff. "Do you think me incapable of protecting my man?"

"Of course not." The woman waved her hand back and forth like she was warding off the woman's words. "That isn't what I was saying at all. I know you are more than capable of protecting our man. I was just worried since it looked like Bryan was getting in over his head."

"Can we not talk about my stupid decision right now?" I asked with a sigh. "We need to figure out how to take that thing down."

I looked back at the ground. The dust had cleared and revealed the massive Trycon as it glared up at us, stomping its front left foot into the cracked ground and roaring like it was challenging us. For some reason, the theme song of an old animated series called "Yu-Gi-Oh" began playing in my head.

"Maybe we should consider retreating," Michelle suggested.

"But if we did that, I wouldn't gain any experience points," I pointed out.

"You can't gain any experience points if you're dead," Michelle countered.

"Don't tell me you and Adina can't give me a hand here," I said. "You're a level 80 archangel and Adina is a level 79 succubus. There's no way you can't come up with something."

"I believe you are underestimating us," Michelle said with a sigh. "We *might* be able to defeat that thing on our own, but we cannot weaken it like you want us to. Even if we could, can you land the finishing blow? I'm not sure you're strong enough to do that."

"Hmmm…" Adina didn't say anything at first as she stared at the Trycon. "What if you attacked it from the inside?"

"The inside?" I asked.

"Are you saying you want him to get swallowed by that thing?!" Michelle shrieked.

"Not quite," Adina said with a shake of her head. "I'm saying I can open this creature's mouth and keep it open long enough for Bryan to get inside of its mouth and stab it through the roof. Trycons have an incredibly thick hide with a high defense. I can't break through it, and neither can you, but every monster has a soft interior."

I didn't think Michelle much cared for the plan, but I was all for it.

"I think it's a good idea. Let's do that."

"Haa…" Michelle released a tired sigh like she'd given up on arguing. "And I suppose there's nothing I can do to convince either of you that this is a bad idea, is there? Very well. I will distract it long enough for you to do what you need to. Adina. Catch."

"Woah!"

I squawked when Michelle tossed me through the air, though the feeling of weightlessness didn't last before Adina caught me in her arms. Unlike how Michelle was hugging me from behind, Adina was carrying me like I was a princess. I didn't want to say it was awkward, but being carried like a princess was, well, awkward—not that she seemed to care.

"Well, hello handsome." She laughed.

I gave her a wry smile. "Hello yourself. You ready?"

"Of course I am."

"Good. Then placed wrap your arms around me. I can't do anything with you in my arms like this."

I wrapped my arms around Adina's neck and shoulders, and she let go of me. Now hanging from her neck, I could do nothing but turn my attention toward Michelle as she fought against the Trycon.

She was brilliant.

Even as I watched, several dozen radiant blades made of golden flames erupted from thin air around her. With a wave of her hand, like an orchestrator conducting a musical performance, she sent the blades forward. They shot through the sky like missiles and slammed into the Trycon. None of them did any damage, however. Several explosions ripped through the air as the golden swords slammed into the Trycon's hide, but none of them did any more than leave a scorch mark behind.

Michelle clicked her tongue when she saw this, but that did not stop her from creating an even larger sword and charging forward. The weapon in her hand right now was two times bigger than the swords she shot at the Trycon. She swung it as hard as she could, her blade slicing into the monster's hide, but all it did was leave a shallow cut.

Her actions not only didn't do much damage, but they only seemed to enrage the Trycon further. The earth shook as it turned toward her. It was probably a good thing we were all airborne. That kind of shaking would have knocked us on their asses.

"Looks like Michelle has it good and distracted. You ready?" asked Adina as she looked at me.

"Ready as I'll ever be." I gripped my sword fiercely in my right hand. "Let's do this."

"That's the spirit! Let's go!"

The wind pushed against my face and watered my eyes as Adina shot down like a bullet fired from an M24 SWS. The world around me seemed to blur as my stomach dropped into my toes. Unlike her and Michelle, I had no flight capabilities to speak of, so aerial combat was not something I could do. The most I'd ever done was drop parachute out of a stealth plane.

Perhaps it was fortunate Adina was moving so fast. The trip ended very shortly. I felt an jolt run through my body as Adina slammed heels first into the Trycon's snout, crushing the creature's head into the ground. Before it could recover, she hopped off its body, landed on the ground, let go of me, and spun on the balls of her feet.

"Haa!"

She launched a crushing upper kick that forced the Trycon's mouth wide open, then stepped forward and grabbed the upper mouth before it could close. Her slender muscles strained, veins appeared on her arms and neck, but the mouth did not close.

"Hurry… up…" Adina grunted.

"I'm on it!"

I raced forward, past Adina, and darted into the creature's massive, cave-like mouth. My body threatened to convulse immediately after entering. The putrid stench from this creature was truly incredible. I'd never smelled anything so disgusting before, so nasty I couldn't even think up a proper analogy to describe it. Every step I took caused a squishing sound that made me realize my boots were getting covered in thick saliva. A warm gust shot up from the Trycon's esophagus and hit me in the face, bringing another wave of that horrid smell.

"Bryan! Hurry! Up!" Adina shouted in a strained voice.

Knowing that I didn't have much time, I slid my feet along the slippery tongue, doing my best not to fall, and activated one of my skills.

Death by Piercing.

Death by Piercing was a skill that I had learned back when I was using an avatar. I had relearned it again after traveling through a Rift in my real body. Any swordsman could learn this skill once they reached level 40, but it required that person's Attack and Agility to be at 80 to learn. This was the fourth skill I had learned after returning to the Rift.

It was a powerful thrusting attack that ignored the defense of my enemy to a certain degree. While it could not break through something like this Trycon's hide, punching clean through the roof of its soft mouth was within the realm of possibility.

My blade sank into the soft flesh of the Trycon's mouth. Blood erupted from the wound, spraying all over me. I ignored the sensation of being drenched, gritted my teeth as I gripped my sword with both hands, and further pushed my blade into this creature's soft insides.

A pitiful groan escaped from the creature as it began thrashing around. Adina screamed as she was shaken free and the thing's mouth closed! I snarled as I realized I needed to finish this fast and activated my second skill, Thousand Cuts, and began slicing the Trycon's mouth apart. More blood sprayed everywhere. The tongue I stood on became even more slippery as the blood mixed with saliva. With a grunt, I activated Death by Piercing again, but this time I reversed my handle on the blade and plunged it into the bottom of the Trycon's mouth. My sword was buried all the way to the hilt. A loud squeal like a dying pig echoed within the mouth and made my ears ring. However, the thrashing weakened, then stopped altogether.

I took several deep, gasping breaths, ignoring the blood covering my body from head to toe. My arms shook from the strain of constant combat, my legs felt like they had turned to jelly, and my body slowly sagged as the adrenaline coursing through me wore off. I felt like I could fall asleep right there despite the rancid stench and being covered in mucus and blood.

"Bryan?!"

The mouth opened. A gust of fresh air blew in, blowing away the stench of blood and this monster's vile odor. Adina peered inside, spotted me, and sighed in relief.

"You're alive! I'm so sorry. This thing bucked me off."

"It's fine," I mumbled with a tired sigh. "This thing is dead… and it looked like we accomplished our mission."

Adina's eyes widened. "You mean…?"

I opened the window containing my level just to be sure. The screen that appeared was the kind of thing I expected to see from a video game, not from real life, but I'd grown used to the weirdness that was the Rift Plains. Blinking several times, I stared intently at the screen and felt a smile work its way onto my face.

Name: Bryan Jenson

Class: Magic Swordsman

Magic: Red

Level: 60

Attack: 140

Agility: 140

Defense: 140

Mana: 130

Total Status Points available: 20

Special Skills:

Thousand Cuts+5

Whirlwind Slash+5

Death by Piercing+5

Fireblade+6

Total Skill Points Available: 2

I'd been in the Rift Plains long enough now to understand how this all worked. Every time I gained a level, I earned 20 status points, which I could put into a specific attribute: Attack, Agility, Defense, and Mana. By placing status points into a specific attribute, I amplified that attribute. If I put my status points into Attack, I would become stronger; Agility, faster, and so on.

Having a specific amount of points in each attribute also let me learn specific skills. For example, I could not learn Fireblade until I reached level 40 and my Mana and Attack attributes were at least both at 60. More than the additional physical boost I received, it was unlocking those special skills that made allocating status points really important.

Once I confirmed my level, I looked up at Adina and grinned.

"I reached level 60."

Adina's eyes widened, but then she also grinned and gave me the victory sign.

✳✳✳

With her holding the Trycon's mouth open, I was able to emerge. A grimace appeared on my face when my boots released a loud squelching sound as I stepped onto dry ground. I was covered from head to toe in red. In fact, I don't think a single part of my skin could be seen.

"Bryan! Adina! Are you two okay?" asked Michelle as she landed on the ground next to us.

"We're fine," Adina said, then paused. "Well, I'm fine. I think Bryan is unhurt, but…"

"I'm fine, if a bit repulsed," I said with a strained smile on my face. "Do you mind if we find a stream or something where I can wash off?"

"You're going to have to. There is no way I'm letting you onto the ship smelling like that."

As if to prove her point, Michelle took several steps back and pinched her nose shut, and if that wasn't bad enough, then Adina followed her example seconds later. It was such a delayed reaction. I wondered if maybe her worry for me had overpowered her ability to smell me. In either event, seeing my two lovers looking at me like I was a rotting piece of meat cut deep like one of Michelle's divine swords.

"Real mature, you two," I growled at them.

"It's not our fault you smell horrendous," Adina said with a smile.

"Whatever." I sighed. "Let's just hurry up and find somewhere I can wash off."

I could have argued more, but it really wasn't worth it.

"I'll take you to a stream," Michelle said. "Adina, do you think you can scavenge this Trycon for parts? You're stronger than either of us."

I looked at the now dead Trycon, which looked like a mountain of gray muscle and hard flesh now. Like most monsters that could be found on this world, Trycons could be scavenged and their parts sold on the open market. In particular, their horns, eyes, blood, tongues, and internal organs were all worth small fortunes.

Horns could be turned into weapons.

Eyes, blood, tongues, and organs were used in the creation of medicine.

I personally didn't want to know how any of those were used to create poultices and healing salves, especially since I'd now been inside of this creature's mouth and smelled how awful it was, but I knew we could earn a good amount of money from it. That was all I cared about.

"Yeah," Adina said, hands on her hips. "Leave it to me."

Since we were leaving this to Adina, Michelle and I traveled away from the corpse and walked through the canyon where we'd attacked our prey. The walls on either side were steep and wide. This canyon was about fifty meters across and maybe two or three hundred deep, though I was just estimating.

After leaving the canyon, we entered a forest. Large trees filled our vision, plants covered every inch of the ground. We had to be careful not to trip on any vines. Some of them were alive and would attack... and while watching Adina get strung up and hung in provocation positions was erotic, I personally did not feel like having that happen to me. We had to be even more careful of venomous snakes.

"Haa!"

I dodged left as a snake lunged from within a bush and swung my blood-coated blade. The sword sliced through the snake's neck. Both head and body flew away from me and Michelle. We continued on.

"You are getting much better," Michelle complimented, though she was still maintaining a safe distance from me. She was also staying upwind. "Your reflexes have improved remarkably since coming to this world."

"Thank you," I said.

It had been about six months since I arrived in the Rift Plains, and maybe five since traveling to the world we were on now. We had spent most of our time grinding. I had only been at level 1 when I arrived, and while my body was in great physical shape, my level was pathetic. Not only did I not have the strength to fight the monsters of this world, I didn't have a single skill to my name.

"Here we are. You can wash off here," Michelle said as we finally walked out from the forest and found a large lake spread out before us. The lake was pretty massive. I could not judge its size, but the end was so far away I could only see blurry shapes on the other shore opposite us. Crystal clear water sparkled in the sun.

"Thanks for guiding me," I said before stripping.

The clothing I wore was a kind of light armor. It was made from gleaming black metal with golden designs along the breast plate, greaves, gauntlets, and pauldrons. The first thing I did was undo the straps to my pauldrons, letting them fall to the ground with a clink of metal. I removed my gauntlets after that, followed by removing my chestplate and greaves.

I wore gray pants and a gray shirt underneath all that. The first thing I removed was my shirt. Then I slid my pants and underwear down my hips. My body was covered in blood, so I could not see my own physique, but I still relished in the freedom of no longer being in smelly and blood-soaked clothes.

Without a thought, I waded into the lake, until I was standing in waist-deep water, and then began washing myself. I scooped handfuls of water and splashed them against my chest and shoulders, scrubbing with my hands to remove the blood. The water around me became a deep red, so I moved further in to avoid washing myself off with diluted blood.

Because I didn't have any soap on me, I probably wouldn't be able to completely get rid of the smell, but I did the best I could. Once my body no longer had any blood on it, I was finally able to see my six-pack abs. This made me smile.

While I would never consider myself the most handsome man in the universe, I liked to think I was a relatively fit and handsome young man. My body was covered in corded muscles from years of difficult training. I had the six-pack men tried to gain with hours spent in the gym, the V-cut figure bodybuilders longed for, and arms and legs that contained explosive power and sculpted muscles. Even if my face wasn't anything to write home about, it wasn't like my face was so ugly only a mother could love it either.

And as I walked back out of the lake to grab my clothes, I noticed Michelle staring at me with longing, her cheeks a lovely shade of pink.

"Would you like to join me?" I asked with a smile.

Flushing red, Michelle looked away. "N-not right now. We are… we're still in danger. I'll, um, just stand guard while you clean your clothes."

Turning around, Michelle stiffly walked away, which caused me to chuckle before I grabbed my clothes and began washing them off. I first began with my armor, which was actually easier to clean because it was all metal. My clothes were much harder to wash off. I had to scrub them against the pebbles near the shore, using them as a makeshift washboard.

Once I finished cleaning my clothes, I wrung out the water and hung each article on a branch to dry. The sun was warm and high in the sky. They should dry in about an hour. However, as I was hanging up my clothes, I noticed there was still blood covering my hands.

"Odd." I frowned.

Shrugging, I knelt before the lake and began washing my hands again. I scrubbed them together to remove the blood, then looked at them again.

There was still blood.

Was it just me, or were my hands covered in more blood than before?

I gritted my teeth and began scrubbing once more, harder this time, but even after scrubbing for a good five minutes, the blood was still there. Why? Why couldn't I remove it?

"Bryan? Bryan?! BRYAN!"

"Huh?"

I heard someone calling my name and jerked backward, startled. I looked up to find Michelle kneeling beside me. She took my hands in hers, pulled them away from the lake, and brought them to her chest.

"Michelle?" I asked, blinking.

"It's okay," Michelle said to me. "There's no blood on your hands."

Her words made me tense, but then I looked at my hands and noticed that she was right. There was no blood. Of course there wasn't. What had I been thinking?

"Ah. You're right." I looked up and smiled at Michelle. "Thank you."

Michelle gave me a compassionate look, the kind I would have expected from an angel under God's grace. Still keeping my hands in her grasp, she stood up and pulled me to my feet.

"Come on," she said in a soft voice. "Your clothes are dry. Get dressed and let us return to Adina. She should be about done scavenging the Trycon for parts."

"You're right. Let's go."

After getting dressed with Michelle's help, the two of us walked hand in hand to our destination.

CHAPTER 2

When we arrived back at the canyon, it was to see a large object situated there, but this object was not the Trycon corpse. It was, instead, a massive vessel.

If I had to compare it to something, I would have said it looked like the kind of ship typically discussed in history books about the time periods before electricity and steam engines were discovered. From stern to bow, the ship was made entirely of gently curved wooden panels. It had a length of about one hundred meters, a width of maybe thirty, and a height of about forty. A large mast jutted from the middle. The flag was currently rolled up. Only one thing differentiated this ship from the ones in my world.

This one had wings.

Like the rest of this ship, they were made from wood, but they looked a lot more flexible and were covered in the thick hide of a monster, though I did not know which kind. Each wing was made of numerous joints that gave it the ability to move. There were also a single wing in the back. It reminded me of the tailfin from some aquatic creatures. Just above the fin was a propeller.

The whole object floated about a meter above the ground, tied down with an anchor and drifting on the breeze. A boarding ramp was extended from the currently grounded ship. As we walked around to that side, I found Adina pushing a trolley up the boarding ramp. Several large wooden barrels sat on it. She was already halfway up, so she didn't see us. I watched as she disappeared, then looked at where the remains of the Trycon were.

There wasn't much left. Some blood was splattered against the ground. A few smaller bones remained. The skull was also still present, though the horns were missing. It looked like she really had taken care of everything while I was washing off the blood.

"Ah! Welcome back!" Adina said as she appeared on top of the boarding ramp. She jumped off, flapping her wings to slow her descent, and landed in front of me. I only had a moment to speak before she lunged forward and pressed her lips to mine.

Adina and Michelle were… well, I guess you'd call them my lovers. We shared a bed, shared affection, and trusted each other to watch our backs. Between the two of them, Adina was a lot more affectionate. I believe that was in her nature. As a succubus, she craved physical contact and intimacy, though she wanted sex more than anything.

Her lips were soft as she pressed them to mine, her tongue the epitome of sin as she pushed it past my teeth and caressed the inside of my mouth. I wrapped my arms around her and pulled the woman close.

The feel of her body pressed to mine sent electric spikes straight to my groin. Even her tail, currently curling around my left leg, was sexy in its own way.

"Ahem." The cough came from Michelle, who did looked quite displeased as she glared at us. "I know you are lascivious by nature, Adina, but can this not wait until we are safely at home?"

"Ugh. Fine. You're such a killjoy," Adina grumbled with a sigh.

"All right, you two. It looks like we're all ready to leave, so let's hop on board and get going," I said after coughing into my hand.

Michelle's glare hardened, but I just smiled and mediated between the two. Even though it sometimes seemed like they didn't get along, that was just their nature as angel and succubus. Michelle was a divine being who served God, an archangel from the Bible, though I thought I'd once read that all angels were male… or at least androgynous. On the other hand, Adina was a succubus, a demon from the Second Circle of Hell. Angels and demons were enemies by nature. They may have overcome that nature, but their clashing ideologies still caused some friction.

It hadn't been that long since the many various mythological beings of the Rift gained sentience. I'd say it had been maybe a few years. Speaking from a technical standpoint, Adina and Michelle had not become sentient until recently, so they were still relatively young when it came to forming their own opinions. They could almost be considered children in that regard.

The scent of wood filled my nose as we boarded our ship. Adina went up to the steering wheel. This ship was just like a traditional ship from the late 1700s design-wise. The steering wheel was located atop the superstructure that led below deck. If there was one thing different about this steering wheel and ones on ships from the time before electricity, it was all the levers and pulleys this one had. They were what Adina used to operate the wings and engine attached to the propellers.

While she stood before the steering wheel, Michelle and I undid the ropes tying the sails and set them loose. As the sails unfurled, the puttering sound of spinning propellers echoed in my ear.

"Are you two ready? I'm lifting off now," Adina called out.

"We're ready," I called back.

"All right then. Here. We. Go."

The ship lurched almost violently as it scraped against the ground, but then it lifted off with a slight rumble. I bent my knees to avoid tumbling. Michelle, on the other hand, released a burbling noise and covered her mouth with her hand the moment we took flight. She looked green.

"I cannot believe you can fly through the air just fine, but you get motion sick on a flying ship," I said as I rubbed her back.

Michelle glared at me, though there was no real heat. "It is one thing to fly under my own power and quite another to fly in a vessel. I simply cannot stand the sense of vertigo I get when it begins moving. I especially hate when the ship shakes like—"

At that moment, the ship shook and Michelle ran to the edge, leaned over the railing, and regurgitated the contents of her stomach. The sound of her spewing bile was... quite something. I was honestly impressed such a horrendous sound could come from such a beautiful pair of lips.

With a soft grimace, I came up behind the woman and held her hair away from her face.

"Th-thank you," she muttered.

"You're welcome," I said simply.

The ride eventually evened out, and Michelle's motion sickness became mere uneasiness. Each of us already had our assigned tasks. Adina was the pilot. She'd already been trained in how to fly this vessel, so we always left it to her. I cleaned the deck and did general maintenance, while Michelle took to the crow's nest and informed us if there were any flying monsters coming our way.

Fortunately, this particular area was usually free of those.

Since my job didn't always leave me busy, I ended up standing beside Adina as she calmly and confidently piloted the ship. She was beaming like a child.

"Do you want to try?" she asked.

"No thanks. Remember what happened last time I tried piloting this?"

As I pointed this out with a wry smile, Adina giggled at me. "You crashed. I remember. Christine was really upset with you for crashing her ship."

"She was indeed quite furious. It's obvious I have no talent for flying this thing. I believe it's better if we leave this to you."

"Well, okay then."

Adina shrugged like it didn't matter to her, and why should it? She actually enjoyed flying this vessel. It had become her third favorite activity after sex and eating.

"Are you okay? You seem troubled," Adina said.

I placed a hand against my face, wondering if perhaps my expression was as haggard as I felt. The blood I'd seen on my hands a few hours ago came back to me. I sighed as I realized there were some problems not even time and love could heal.

"I'm fine. Just a bit tired."

I offered her what I hoped was a reassuring smile, but I don't think she was buying it.

"Why don't you go down to the cabin and rest?" she suggested. "Michelle and I can handle everything up here."

I did briefly consider telling her I was fine and that I didn't need to sleep, but the moment I opened my mouth, a wave of exhaustion hit me. Weakness struck me like a bad cold. I suddenly realized we'd been fighting that Trycon for a good several hours, and while I hadn't been severely injured, the numerous impacts had definitely been a shock to the system.

In short, I'd be very sore tomorrow.

"Yeah. Okay. I'm gonna get some sleep."

"Have a good rest."

With a soft smile, I leaned over and kissed Adina on the lips, then proceeded below deck.

This ship wasn't very large. It only had three rooms. The deckhouse, the storage, and the captain's quarters, which spanned the entire width of the stern.

The captain's quarters was not luxurious, but it did have a few amenities. A table sat in the center, and sitting atop it was an old map of Yggdrasil—the world we were living in. Several swords and axes hung from racks on the walls. An entire portion of this room near the back was taken up by large windows. Finally, there was a nice bed located against one wall—a bed that was nearly two times larger than necessary. It was a new addition since me, Adina, and Michelle had come to live in this world.

I quickly removed my armor and set everything on a stand against the wall. I didn't bother removing my clothes as I flopped face down on the bed, closed my eyes, and fell asleep.

✳✳✳

"Bryan… wake… Bryan… wake up…"

I woke up to the soothing tone of Michelle as she called my name. Opening my eyes, I rolled over in bed and found the woman in question kneeling on the bed close to where I'd been sleeping. My face was quite literally level with her wonderful thighs. What was the word kids used to describe them these days? THICC? Yes, she had very THICC thighs. I could attest that they made a great lap pillow.

"Michelle… we in Valhalla yet?" I asked, voice groggy. I felt like I'd swallowed a toad.

Shaking her head, Michelle smiled as she reached out and brushed my bangs away from my face. "Not yet. We're still a few hours out, but you've been asleep for a while now. I thought it best to wake you up."

Sitting up in bed, I stretched my arms out, groaning as my bones cracked. I felt stiff, but that didn't surprise me. The battle with the Trycon had taken a lot out of me. Now that I was thinking about it, maybe I should call it a bull ride instead of a battle...

With a shake of my head, I dispelled those thoughts and focused on Michelle, still sitting on her haunches before me. When she and I first met, she had been wearing a toga of the purest white. White was still the primary color of her clothes, but the dress she wore now was a lot more revealing. It did nothing to hide her long legs and bare feet. Even her cleavage was exposed as a gap ran from her collar bone all the way to her navel.

I felt my body grow warm.

"Are you sure you woke me up several hours early because you thought it was better if I didn't sleep so much?" I asked, a smile on my face.

My words caused Michelle's cheeks to heat up. She looked away from me, as if maintaining eye contact was embarrassing. I looked down at her hands as she grasped the fabric of the bed between her delicate fingers.

"Well... it has... been awhile... since it was just the two of us," she said in a soft whisper.

I shifted against the bed, until I was sitting face to face with Michelle, and reached out to cup her cheek. Michelle stiffened for but a moment. Then she nuzzled her hand against mine. Her skin was soft and elastic, springy and warm. Babies didn't have softer skin than she did.

"It has been awhile at that," I agreed.

Me, Adina, and Michelle were almost always together these days. Sometimes we were joined by Christine, but most of the time it was just us. I had gotten used to that. However, it did mean we didn't get to spend as much time together one-on-one like this.

I leaned forward and placed a kiss on Michelle's soft, pink lips. They were a little wet. Michelle, perhaps having waited for that moment, kissed me back. Her enthusiasm would have surprised anyone back on Earth. An angel so passionately kissing a human? Absurd. Angels were pure beings that did not debase themselves by succumbing to earthly desires. I'm sure people would think something like that. I was one of the only people who knew better.

The kiss quickly grew heated. Her tongue poked out of her mouth, and I opened mine to suck it in. She moaned as my lips closed around her tongue.

I reached out with my hands and undid the golden clasp that kept her dress together, then pushed it down her shoulders, exposing her breasts. The chilly air caused goosebumps to break out on her skin. Her soft pink nipples grew stiff underneath my ministrations as I cupped her chest and began playing with them.

"Ha… ha… Bryan… your hands… are so big… so warm…"

"They're rough and calloused," I replied.

"They're the hands of the man I love," Michelle shot back. Then she moaned as I pinched her nipples. "D-don't be so rough…"

"Sorry. I'll be gentler."

We didn't talk anymore as I kissed her again, pushing my tongue into her mouth, filling it with my saliva. Michelle didn't mind. I placed my hands on her shoulders and pushed her onto the bed. Now lying on her back, Michelle could only squirm and moan as I left her lips and began kissing her neck. Hands came up behind my head, fingers threading through my hair, nails scraping my scalp. It felt nice.

After leaving several shiny red love bites on Michelle's neck, I finally reached my prize. Her breasts were not as big as Adina's, but they were by no means small—two perfectly formed spheres that sat on her chest like modest hills, their peaks covered in light pink nipples. She had very small areolas and her nipples were beautifully shaped. I leaned down and gave them an experimental lick.

"Ahn! D-don't do that!"

"Don't lick your nipples?" I looked up at Michelle.

Her cheeks were flushed as she looked away. "Y-you know they are sensitive…"

"All the more reason to tease them."

With that reply, I bent back down and took one of them into my mouth. Her skin was salty and a little dirty. Unlike me, she had not washed in the lake, but I did not mind as I swirled my tongue around her nipple.

"Ha… ah… ahn…"

I used Michelle's vocals to guide my actions. She liked it when I was gentle, so I didn't bite her nipples and licked them instead, flicking my tongue back and forth across the stiffened tips. I didn't just pay attention to her chest, however. As I kept my tongue and mouth firmly on her breasts, I slowly trailed my hand across her flat stomach, slipped it past her dress, still bunched up around her hips, and cupped her warm sex.

It probably had to do with how she was an angel, but even after six months of having sex with me, Michelle's vagina was still just a tiny slit. It hadn't changed at all since we'd had sex that first time. I pressed my hand against it, letting my finger get wedged between her warm lips. There were already some juices leaking from her. With a smile, I dragged my finger up her pussy, spread her lips apart, and slowly inserted a single finger.

"Ahn! Ah! Haaa!!"

Michelle's voice reached a higher note as I curled my finger inside of her in a "come hither" gesture and used my thumb to play with her clit. Like everything else, her clit was small and cute. It pulsed against my thumb as I rubbed it. Just like how I was licking her nipples, I was gentle as I massaged the slight bundle of nerves.

"Bryan! Bryan!"

She called my name as she grabbed my head and pulled me into her. Her hips were jerking, thighs quivering. The scent of her sweat filled my nose, addled my brain, and made me want more. I felt a strong desire to conquer the woman beneath me. Just one more push…

"AAAHN!!!"

Michelle lifted her hips off the bed as she squirted her juices all over my hand. I continued to massage her warm mound and soft lips as her body jerked and spasmed several more times, before she fell backward onto the bed.

I removed my mouth from her nipple and sat up, gazing at the dazed woman as she lay on her back, breathing heavy, glistening breasts jiggling with each sharp intake of breath. Michelle looked gorgeous. Beyond gorgeous. There was something enchanting about seeing this angel, her hair spread around her like a halo, fanning across the bed, wings spread out to her sides and even partially sticking off the edge. Even her feathers looked ruffled.

Her dress was still bunched around her hips. Since Michelle was not fully cognizant anymore, I took the liberty of lifting her legs off the bed. Her feet dangled in my grasp as I held them aloft with one hand and set them on my shoulder. I then grabbed her dress, slid it down her hips, and pulled it off her legs, revealing her wet sex dripping with sweat and sexual secretions.

With everything now exposed, Michelle came to. She released an embarrassed squawk as her legs fell back onto the bed and tried to cover her crotch with her hands. The pink dustiness of her cheeks was adorable. This archangel was so innocent despite everything we had done.

It made me want to protect her.

It also made me want to tease her.

"Why are you hiding?" I asked, removing her hands to reveal her beautiful pussy lips. It really was just a mound, like the kind I'd expect from a virgin. "It's nothing I haven't seen before."

"E-even so… this is embarrassing." Michelle turned her head, golden hair shifting and catching the light.

"It's embarrassing to be seen by the man you love?" I asked.

Michelle said nothing, but her cheeks gained an extra tone of color.

I felt something warm spread through my chest as I removed my shirt and pants. It wasn't fair that I was the only one still dressed.

My dick was already at full mast as I spread Michelle's legs, crawled between them, and pressed the hard shaft against her outer labia. With my cock firmly nestled between her lips, I leaned down until Michelle and I were nearly nose to nose. She looked into my eyes with her gorgeous green eyes. They were big and innocent, complimenting her pink lips currently pursed with what almost looked like anguish.

"Michelle… may I?" I asked.

She squirmed between me, biting her lips as my dick rubbed against her. "You may. Be gentle."

"Don't worry. I know how you like it."

I grabbed my dick and lined it up with her small entrance, then slowly pushed my way inside. Michelle's body was quite something. It was warm and tight, clinging to me as though it was both trying to suck me in and keep me from intruding.

I took a deep breath and wiggled around a little before pushing in further. My actions caused Michelle to arc her back and released a strained moan, like pain and pleasure were mixing together, and then I was buried to the hilt inside of her.

Before I began pumping my hips, I reached out and found her hands. Michelle laced her fingers through mine and gripped them tightly as I pressed her hands into the mattress. Like that, I began thrusting myself inside of her, gently rocking back and forth. The sensation as her insides rubbed against me brought an indescribable pleasure like electricity coursing through me. It made me want to go faster, but that was not what Michelle liked.

"Ha… hahn… Bryan… kiss… kiss me…"

Michelle looked up at me with her gorgeous eyes, which were now half-lidded, hooded with desire. Even if she hadn't been looking at me like that, I would not have been able to refuse.

My back twitched as I leaned down and kissed Michelle. It was oddly soft, gentle. There was no tongue involved as we kissed and made love.

Sweat formed on my skin as I continued slowly rocking against her. It dripped down my back and torso. Michelle had also grown pretty slick with her own sweat. The wet coat of lubrication made it easy for our bodies to rub together, creating an intense friction as my chest pressed against hers. Her breasts were a lot more sensitive than mine. As her nipples rubbed against my skin, she released more beautiful music.

All too soon I felt the telltale sign of my impending orgasm. My balls contracted and an intense pressure was boiling inside of me. I still didn't increase the speed of my thrusts, moving slowly, in and out, in and out. My slow and steady rhythm built up Michelle's own orgasm, which I felt when her insides convulsed against me. That stimulus seemed to be what I needed to release my seed inside of her.

"Ha… ha…"

Michelle breathed in through her nose and out her mouth, her small nostrils flaring. She had such a cute nose. It was tiny and pert, making me think of a beautiful princess from a fairy tale.

I pulled my semi-flaccid cock out of Michelle's pussy and watched as a small bit of my seed trickled out.

"I'm so glad we don't have to worry about you getting pregnant," I muttered.

"Hmm?" Michelle didn't seem to understand what I meant.

"Well, if we had kids, it would make things harder, wouldn't it?" I asked.

"I guess so." Michelle blinked several times like she wasn't all there. "I never thought about it… are you already hard again?"

I grinned at her as I stroked my shaft back to full mast. Thanks to constantly having sex with her, Adina, and Christine, I had a lot of stamina these days. My higher level might have also had something to do with it.

"Are you saying you don't want to make love some more?"

Michelle bit her lip like she wasn't sure how to answer that, but she eventually relented. "I… wouldn't mind becoming one with you again."

Now that I had her consent to have more sex, I turned Michelle onto her side, lifted her left leg into the air, my hand underneath the back of her knee. This position seemed to make her embarrassed.

I got behind Michelle and pushed my way back inside of her. She was still tight, but there was a lot of extra lubrication from our mutual orgasm. That made moving easier. I thrust my hips against her from this new position, enjoying the new sensations that came from it. Having sex like this felt different from missionary. It felt like I was reaching new places inside of her.

"Ha. Ahn. Ah. Ah. Hnnn!"

I moved in close until my stomach was touching Michelle's back, allowing me a glance over her shoulder, to view her shaking breasts. The way they jiggled was enticing. I wished I could have fondled them, but I was busy holding up her leg. Michelle's slender calf and small foot bounced to the time of my thrusts.

Because of how I'd already cum, I felt my end quickly coming again. I knew I wouldn't last long. Fortunately, Michelle wasn't going to last much longer either. I bit my lower lip and tried to stave off my orgasm, waiting, waiting, waiting. I did not want to be the only one who came.

My resistance paid off. Barely a second later, Michelle's entire body grew stiff and taut like a drawn bowstring. Her insides tightened around me as an orgasm washed over her. I could no longer stave mine off. My vision went white as pleasure exploded inside of me. When I came to, I was still lying on my side, but I had released Michelle's leg, which now lay on the bed.

Michelle was gasping for breath, her shoulders and back heaving. I placed a hand on her hip and caressed it. In response, she moved back, pressing her firm and pert butt into my crotch, though I could no longer get it up. Too bad.

"Bryan…"

"Let's stay like this for a bit," I said, pulling her close.

"Mmm."

She didn't respond with words, but one of her hands covered mine. The two of us continued to lie on the bed for at least another hour.

CHAPTER 3

Michelle and I emerged onto the deck. A strong gust of wind blew Michelle's air away from her face. She shivered from the cold chill caused by the wind.

It was late evening now. I looked at the sky, painted a myriad of colors—red, gold, purple, all mixing together in streaks of color that blossomed like starbursts. This sort of glorious sight was something I could never see on Earth.

"You two are finally up," Adina said, lips twisted into a smirk. "Did you two have fun breaking in the bed?"

While Michelle blushed bright red and looked away, I smiled back and said, "We did. Thanks for asking."

Michelle squawked at me, embarrassed that I so readily admitted to us having sex, but I didn't see the problem. It wasn't like Adina didn't know about my sex life.

"You are so cute, Michelle," Adina said.

"I just do not like my private life being exposed to others." Michelle huffed and crossed her arms, trying to act tough.

Adina shrugged. "A little late for that, don't you think?"

Michelle said nothing. There was nothing she could say.

While I had never slept with Adina and Michelle at the same time, that did not mean they were ignorant about what the other woman got up to when I was alone with them. Adina was particularly sensitive to when I had sex as well. She was like a bloodhound who could scent out whenever Michelle and I got up to some fun under the sheets.

"We'll be in Valhalla soon. Better get ready," Adina added after having her fun.

Just as she said, it wasn't long before Valhalla appeared before us. It spread out across the sky, a massive floating island that looked like an inverted mountain. Resting upon the flat top was a gigantic city that covered the entire island. Towering spires pierced the sky, numerous streets meandered through the city. Valhalla was a bustling city of many archways, columns, and stone structures.

Adina steered our ship into a dock located at the edge of the city. I did not know how our vessel was able to just float in the air like it did as we stopped at the dock and anchored it down, but I tried my best not to think about it as I extended the boarding ramp.

With her task done, Adina pulled the lever that stopped the ship from traveling forward, locked the steering wheel in place, and walked over to me. It was probably because I had just had sex a few hours ago. However, I could not help but notice how her breasts bounced within the confines of her skimpy clothes.

She smirked when she noticed that. "I'm going to travel below deck and grab our contribution to the city. Would you mind speaking with the dock master until I get back?"

"Not at all," I said. Then I glanced at Michelle, who was in the process of pulling up the sails. "Michelle, I'll be heading off! Think you can tie the sails?"

"Leave it to me," Michelle said, grunting as she pulled on the rope that would bring the first set of sails up. Our ship had three.

Since it sounded like she had everything well in hand, I traveled down the boarding ramp as Adina went below deck. The dock master was already waiting for me. He was a stiff-looking man dressed in a black and white suit. His neatly parted hair and handlebar mustache made him look like a mix between butler and bureaucrat. When he noticed me walking onto the deck, he pulled a quill from his vest pocket, placed it against the clipboard, and came over to me.

"Captain Jenson," the man said. "I see you have returned."

"Dock master," I greeted.

"If you have returned, I hope that means you have brought a good haul with you," he said, writing something down on his clipboard. "You are a few days late on your payment because you were gone for so long. I've held this place for you out of respect for Christine, but we cannot allow late payments."

I nodded and didn't let the man's lecturing tone bother me. "Your payment is coming in just a moment."

The moment I finished speaking, Adina came down, pushing a trolley in front of her. Several barrels were sitting on it. The dock master stared lustfully at Adina for a moment, but he was nothing if not a professional. He only looked for a second before coughing into his hand.

"Is this the payment?"

"Yes, sir."

"I hope you don't mind if I inspect it?"

"Feel free."

The dock master walked up to the barrels and opened one. A pungent odor like iron filled the air, but the dock master did not retch or act disgusted, which just went to show how long he'd been doing this. The man was an old hand. He eyed the dark pool of blood inside of the barrel, then cast his gaze at me.

"Blood?" he asked, eyebrow lifted.

"From a level 80 Trycon," I confirmed.

The dock master's eyes widened. Since Trycons were powerful creatures with a strong defense, it was rare for anyone to kill one, never mind a level 80 Trycon.

The higher the level of monster, the more valuable their parts were. Blood was a particularly valuable commodity because it was used in health potions… which actually made me not want to drink a health potion, though I knew it would be stupid not to if I was in mortal peril or on the verge of dying.

"It looks like there are eight hundred liters' worth of blood here," the dock master said, jotting something down on his clipboard. "That is enough to pay for your dock fee, the late fee, and next month's docking fee."

"So we're good?" I asked.

"Yes, I believe we are," the dock master said.

As we finished our conversation, Michelle walked down the boarding ramp and joined Adina and I. The dock master eyed Michelle like he'd eyed Adina. Then he turned around, grumbled something about how some bastards had all the luck with women, and ambled off to the next newly docked vessel.

This was not the only dock on Valhalla. There were many docks located all throughout the city at various levels, but this one was the cheapest, which was why we docked here. They offered the same amenities as everywhere else. The only difference was the location. It didn't matter to me if we docked closer to the city's center or not, so I had no intention of paying more for what I deemed a pointless extravagance.

I ignored the sight of flying vessels like my own coming and going, having grown used to it, and walked hand in hand with Adina and Michelle. We made our way into the busy city. The moment we did, all sorts of sights, sounds, and smells hit our senses.

There were hundreds of thousands of people living in Valhalla. Not all of them looked human. I watched as a group of children ran through the streets. Two of them were human, like myself, but there was also a boy with angel wings, another boy with black crow-like wings, and a beastman child. She looked like a werewolf, her entire body covered in midnight blue fur. Several meters to my left were a group of chatting women. One of them was a cyclops, a woman several times taller than the others with a single eye in the center of her head.

"It looks like there are some new races," Adina observed as she hugged my arm to her glorious chest. I enjoyed the sensation of my bicep being engulfed by her cleavage.

"I see some dragonfolk and a few elves," I commented.

"Do you think it's because of the Frost Giants?" asked Michelle, brow furrowed. "I heard they were attacking other cities."

"Maybe…"

"Think they'll attack Valhalla?" asked Adina.

"No way." I shook my head. "Valhalla is under the protection of the Valkyries. You'd have to be an idiot to attack us."

"Guess so."

We entered a town square, and my stomach suddenly rumbled as the scent of grilled meat filled my nose. I looked around and saw a stand selling meat skewers. Adina also sniffed the air, her stomach growling to let me know I wasn't the only one hungry. Michelle's didn't growl, but she stared at the meat skewers with a hint of longing.

"Let's get something to eat," I said, pulling them over to the stand.

"Oh ho! Here's a familiar face!" The large man behind the stand guffawed. "It's been awhile since I've seen you. I heard you went out hunting."

"That's right," I said.

"Brought back a good haul?"

"I'd say so. Anyway, I'll have six meat skewers."

"That'll be six eyrir."

Eyrir was a type of currency found on Yggdrasil, a gold coin that was about two times larger than a quarter in my old world. One side of the coin was minted with a warrior dressed in armor and holding a round shield, while the other side showed a boat with a dragon head at the bow. It was one of many different coinages found in use on Valhalla.

"Here."

"Ha ha! Thanks for your business!"

I handed the man his coins and received six meat skewers in return, three of which I handed to Adina, and another that went to Michelle. I got the remaining two.

We began traveling again, eating our meat skewers. Adina ate the fastest, gobbling hers up like they would disappear if she didn't eat them immediately, but Michelle acted far more daintily, nibbling on each slice of meat as if savoring the taste. I was probably a mix between the two. At the very least, I tried to eat with manners, unlike Adina who scarfed her food down in several seconds.

"It's pretty late," Michelle said. "The trading hub will be closed soon. I'm pretty sure the Valkyries aren't doing business at this hour. Let's clean up at the bathhouse, head home, and meet with them tomorrow."

"Good idea," I agreed.

"Sounds good to me. I'm tired anyway," Adina said as she finished off her last skewer. She tossed the sticks with unerring accuracy into a trash can.

Valhalla was an odd combination of ancient and modern. All the buildings looked like something I'd expect to see from ancient Europe during the age of the Vikings, but they also had a good deal of modern amenities like skewer systems, trash cans, and public transit. Of course, the public transit were all beast-drawn carriages and whatnot. Still, I don't remember hearing about the Vikings being very hygienic like this.

There were many bathhouses in Valhalla, but the one we used was close to our home. It was a large building of three-stories that was wider than it was long. There were a variety of different baths, all of which were separated by gender, meaning we could not bathe together —much to Adina's displeasure.

The men's bath was large enough to fit several dozen people. Steam rose from the surface of the bath water. It was hot but not to the point of boiling.

I wasn't the only one lounging in the bath. Numerous other burly men of various species were cleaning themselves off. This bathhouse was communal, so a lot of people used it. From what I understood, the baths had some kind of water magic enchantment or something that kept the water fresh and hot at all times of the day. I hoped that was the case. I didn't want to sit in other people's filth.

"Bryan! It's been some time!"

At the sound of my name being called, I turned my head to find a dragonfolk man standing naked in front of me. He was large. By that, I actually meant huge. I wasn't a shrimp at six feet, but this man was several heads and shoulders taller than myself, his body covered in an utterly ridiculous amount of muscle. Like all dragonfolk, this man had wings sprouting from his shoulder blades and a tail from his hind end.

"Drake," I greeted as the man sat beside me.

"How's the hunting been?" asked Drake.

"Good enough." I shrugged. "I'm more interested in increasing my level than I am earning money, but we should make enough for us to last through the month."

"Ha ha ha! You must have gotten quite the haul this time. With that succubus's eating habits, you'd be lucky to last for a week."

I grimaced at the joke, but it wasn't like I could deny him. Adina was our biggest eater. She ate the same amount as myself, Christine, and Michelle combined. I was always impressed by her rampant appetite.

Drake was a dragonfolk who had come to Valhalla a few months before I did. We met at this bathhouse and just began chatting. I wouldn't call him a friend, but he was a friendly acquaintance and someone who seemed sympathetic to my difficulties. He owned a bar with his wife not far from where I lived. We'd had the pleasure of eating there on occasion.

Drake was what you'd call a refugee. I'd heard his home was destroyed during the chaos when all the various realms located within the Rift gained sentience. As was the case with his home, there were some who believed they should invade other worlds, some who believed they should continue doing what they always had, and some who wanted to leave the Rift and invade Earth. The many different opinions caused everyone to clash and war eventually broke out. His story was not all that different from everyone else's.

I didn't remain in the bath for long, and after climbing out, toweling off, and getting dressed, I met up with Adina and Michelle in the main lobby. They were both drinking a bottle of coffee milk. I leaned against the rail and watched as the two, left hands on their hips, chugged down the milk and released a pair of satisfied sighs.

"Ah. Nothing like a bottle of coffee milk after a hot bath," Adina said with a laugh. "That samurai lady who told us about this tradition was onto something. Um, what was her name again?"

"Her name is Amaterasu, and she isn't a samurai. She's a sun goddess." Michelle sighed like Adina was giving her a slight headache.

"Right. Her." Adina nodded once. "I like her. I wonder when she's coming back."

"Last I heard, Amaterasu went back to her own realm in order to quell the violence there. If she isn't dead, she is probably still fighting."

"Hmm…"

It seemed like their conversation was done, so I walked over and raised my hand in greeting.

"You two ready to leave?"

"You bet we are!" Adina beamed as she latched onto my arm, hugging it to her chest. Michelle was much more reserved as she reached out for my hand.

"I am ready," she said.

"Off we go then." I began moving with the two women. "I can't wait to finally get home."

✳✳✳

"We're home," I called out as we entered our house through the front door. No one answered us, but I didn't expect anyone to. "Guess Christine hasn't returned."

The entrance led into a small hallway, which branched off into a living room, a kitchen, and a staircase. Our house was a two-story building. It wasn't very big. Even though we had two floors, there were only six rooms. The first floor contained the kitchen, living room, and toilet. There were three bedrooms located on the second floor.

It was still a nice place, all things considered. The wooden boards on the floor were clean, if not polished to a shine, the walls on the first floor were made of stone and wood on the second floor, and the red-shingled roof was sturdy and wouldn't collapse in a storm. I couldn't ask for anything more.

"Where do you think Christine is?" asked Adina as she slipped out of her knee-high boots. I watched as one dainty foot slid out. Adina sighed in relief and wiggled her tiny toes as though relishing in the freedom of movement, then slipped out of her other boot.

"She said she was going to look for someone who can give us information on the situation happening in my Heaven," Michelle said. She didn't have nearly as much work to do when removing her footwear since she wore sandals. All she did was slip out of them and set them aside.

I had the same issues removing my boots that Adina had. Stooping over as I lifted one leg, I pried the boot off, set my foot down, lifted my other leg, and pulled that one off as well. It felt nice not wearing shoes. While the boots I wore were kind of cool, being something I'd expect from a fantasy video game, they were not comfortable to wear for long periods of time.

"How long do you think that will take?" Adina asked as we made our way into the living room.

"Who knows." Michelle sighed and began playing with her hair. "There are hundreds if not thousands of Heavens out there. I'm not even sure which portal will take us to my Heaven, so I'm not sure how long it will take her to find someone who does, never mind someone who's been there and actually knows what the situation is like."

The Rift Plains had many portals leading to many different realms. All the realms I knew of were based on various mythologies from Earth, and many of those mythological realms were the same or similar, mirror images of each other.

Heaven and Hell were the greatest examples; there were many different portals that led to a Heaven or a Hell, and each Heaven and Hell was subtly different from the other ones. One Hell might have nine levels, while another might have thirteen, or seven. Similarly, there were some Heavens out there that had seven different Heavens (a number that corresponds to the seven classical planets known to antiquity), while another might only have one.

The Heaven that Michelle came from only had one Heaven.

"Well, at least Bryan is at a level where he can help us now," Adina said with a glance in my direction.

"True." Michelle nodded. "He was very weak when he first came here, but he's done a great job of getting his level up."

"Of course, it helps that he has such strong companions aiding him."

"Very true. If he was on his own, I'm sure he wouldn't have survived."

"Ha ha." I laughed without mirth. "If you two are done teasing me, maybe we should make some plans for what we should do next."

It was true that I had been weak when I first arrived in the Rift Plains, but they didn't need to rub that fact in. It wasn't even my fault to begin with. Every human who entered the Rift Plains started at level 1.

"Tomorrow, we should speak with the Valkyries about selling the materials we scavenged to them," Michelle said, twirling a strand of hair between her fingers. "We managed to get quite a lot this time—at least two times more raw materials than last time. It should fetch a hefty price. I imagine we won't have to go out again for a while yet."

"But I think we should still train some more," Adina added. "We might have reached level 80, but that was the level you were at when you were kicked out of Heaven. That means we should at least be at level 90 if not higher if we want to actually help you." Adina sighed and crossed her arms. "Also, I'm sure Eisheth and Agrat bat Mahlat are at a higher level than us by now. They were around level 80 when they imprisoned my mother."

"There's also Asmodeus," I added. "He was around level 90 if I'm not mistaken. While we managed to beat him back, we didn't kill him, and I'm sure he won't take what happened to him lying down."

Asmodeus had been a monster, taking everything we threw at him and barely flinching. It was honestly luck rather than skill that let us get the upper hand in that fight. If the two succubus queens were of a similar strength to him, then we'd need to be much stronger than we were now.

"That's true." Adina crossed her right leg over her left and began bouncing it up and down, reminding me of a child who had ADHD. "We've got our work cut out for us. We have to become even stronger than we are now."

"You have two new skills, right?" I asked.

Nodding, Adina opened her level screen with a swipe of her fingers. It displayed her name, level, skills, and what her stats looked like.

Name: Adina

Class: Succubus

Magic: Pink

Level: 80

Attack: 210

Agility: 170

Defense: 200

Mana: 200

Total Status Points available: 0

Special Skills:

Seduction+10

Energy Blast+20

Flight+5

One Ton Punch+20

Energy Bombardment+14

StrengthUp+10

Intimidation+1

Total Skill Points Available: 0

"To be honest, Intimidation isn't a very useful skill, but I learned it anyway because it makes enemies below my level wary of attacking me," Adina said. "Energy Blast, One Ton Punch, and Energy Bombardment are my greatest skills right now. Strength Up is also a good skill, but it's passive and increases my strength proportionate to my level."

"My skills have also increased with my level," Michelle added as she opened her own level status screen and showed it to us.

Name: Michelle

Class: Archangel

Magic: White

Level: 80

Attack: 190

Agility: 200

Defense: 200

Mana: 210

Total Status Points available: 0

Special Skills:

Dance of a Thousand Blades+20

Divine Sword+15

Divine Dual Sword+15

Divine Sword Dance+20

Future Sight+10

Total Skill Points Available: 0

"I focused less on acquiring skills and more on raising my current skills," Michelle explained why she didn't have as many skills as Adina. "Each of my skills except Future Sight are in the same category of sword skills. Future Sight is the only passive skill I can gain, but it grants me the ability to look one second in the future. The higher its level is, the further into the future I can look."

"That's a cool skill," Adina gasped.

Michelle puffed out her chest. "Isn't it?"

While Michelle was acting like a peacock trying to catch the attention of a mate, I was busy lamenting my own lower level. I knew it wasn't my fault they were stronger than me. Their levels had already been around 70-ish when I first entered the Rift Plains, but it still sucked that my level was so low compared to theirs. Would I even be able to help them at my current level?

The night wore on and our conversation drifted away from levels and onto when we would leave Valhalla again to do more training. We planned to wait a few days in case Christine decided to return. I think, more than anything else, Michelle wanted to hurry up and gain some news about her home. It had to be nerve-wracking just standing around doing nothing.

I mean, it wasn't like we weren't doing anything, but nothing we did in Valhalla would help her people—at least not directly. Becoming stronger would indirectly help because we'd need that strength when the time came. At the same time, people could be dying right now, and we had no way of knowing about it. I was sure Michelle was frustrated by this. She held it in and didn't complain, but a woman with her sense of duty couldn't sit still knowing her people might be in danger.

Later that night, the three of us went to bed. We ended up sleeping together. While Michelle refused to have sex with me and Adina, she harbored no disgust toward sleeping in the same bed as the succubus. I guessed that was just Michelle's personal preference. She didn't like having sex with another woman.

I wasn't sure how long I slept for, but I woke up after realizing my left side was cold. A single glance revealed the reason. Adina was missing. Raising my head, I found her staring out of the open window, a chill wind blowing her hair as she looked at the city.

Working myself out from Michelle's near ironclad hold, I walked over to the woman, whose pointy ears twitched when she heard the sound of my footsteps.

"Sorry," she said with a smile. "Did I wake you?"

I shook my head. "It's fine. Are you having trouble sleeping?"

"Yeah…"

I said nothing as I walked up and wrapped my arms around her from behind, pulling her close enough that I could feel her warmth and vice versa. Adina sighed as she leaned into me.

"I was just… thinking about Mom," she admitted, her voice soft. "Before the change, she was the only person I really knew. I didn't have many friends because my mom always sheltered me. After the change, Mom was overthrown by the other three succubus queens when they teamed up with Asmodeus, and I was forced into slavery. I was never abused, but I wasn't treated very well either. I think Naamah took twisted pleasure in treating her most hated enemy like a scullery maid."

"Don't worry," I said. "We're going to save your mom."

"But what will come after that?" asked Adina. "What will become of us after we've accomplished all our goals? Will my mom let me continue to be with you? Will she force me back into the sheltered lifestyle I used to have? I don't want that."

So she was thinking about what happened after we rescued her mom and saved Michelle's Heaven from the rebellion taking place there. Adina never struck me as the kind of person who thought too deeply about anything. Her actions were decided intuitively. It was all instinct, or so I believed. However, it seemed even she had moments where she thought of the future.

"While I can't tell you exactly what will happen in the future, I can promise you that I won't leave you." I hugged her tighter, feeling her gorgeous butt bump against my crotch, though I ignored the sensation. I wasn't horny right now. "No matter what happens, I am not giving you up. You're mine."

"Bryan…"

Adina turned around in my arms, her wide eyes gazing into mine as though she was surprised. A smile soon broke out on her face. It reminded me of freshly blooming flowers as they were illuminated by the first rays of light.

"This is why I love you so much. You always know just what to say to make me feel better." She stroked my cheek. "Thank you."

"That's not something you have to thank me for. I'm only doing what I want."

After shaking my head once, I leaned down and claimed Adina's lips for my own. Her lips were much fuller than Michelle's. They were succulent and juicy, which made me want to nibble on them.

As Adina wrapped her arms around my neck and kissed me back, I thought about everything that had happened to me. I had gone from a former Special Forces member running from his past to a rift-traveling magic swordsman with three lovers. I was sure no one back home would believe me if I told them about all this. Fortunately, I had no intention of returning to Earth.

This was my home now.

CHAPTER 4

Valhalla was but one floating island located in Aasgard, home of the Aesir and Asynjur, which were kind of like gods, but not really. They were certainly godly beings with incredible powers, but they weren't actually gods. At the very least, these beings calling themselves Aesir were not the gods as I knew them, the ones pertaining to Norse mythology.

Granted, I knew little about Norse mythology, but still.

There were many other cities located within Aasgard, but Valhalla was the home of the Valkyries. These warrior maidens armed themselves with spears and swords, clad themselves in steel raiments, and fought on winged beasts like that reminded me of the Pegasus. I'd never found a more fearsome bunch. Meeting them for the first time made me understand why Christine was such a fierce lady herself.

Valkyries were frightening.

However, they were not unreasonable.

In fact, they could be downright friendly outside of the battlefield.

The Valkyries were the owners and operators of this city, which I suppose meant they were like lords or maybe government officials. You could often find groups patrolling the city, keeping the peace. Very few people would ever pick a fight in this city because of them.

That was not to say there weren't some people who did. However, all those people were newbies who had arrived and didn't understand the terror of the Valkyries… and those people soon learned after they were beaten black and blue, then thrown into jail with their injuries unattended for the night.

While they were generally all over the city, their main base of operations was a building located at the very heart of Valhalla. It looked like nothing more than a large hall. The building was only a single story, but behind the building was a large complex of structures where the Valkyries made their homes—the barracks, in other words. The hall, known as the Hall of Warriors, was where the Valkyries did their business.

I entered the Hall of Warriors to find that it was as busy as ever. I didn't have Adina and Michelle with me today. Adina was double checking our inventory and Michelle was shopping for tonight's dinner. My task was to speak with the Valkyries about selling the monster parts we had salvaged.

There was a long line of people in the hall, which was really just a vast space with several support pillars holding up a vaulted ceiling. A long table sat on one side, and behind that table, several women dressed in white togas stood and dealt with other men and women who came to do business.

Don't let the togas fool you. Each one of those women was a Valkyrie, and lord have mercy on anyone dumb enough to try something.

I waited in line for my turn, and since I knew it would take a while, I imagined stripping Adina and Michelle, then having my way with them in my mind. What? I wasn't the most perverse man around, but I was still a man. I'd always wondered what it would be like if I could sleep with them both at the same time. It was too bad Michelle had an adamant "no threesome" policy. She said she was already bending her personal policies as far as she could by accepting my polyamorous relationship.

Of course, I planned to respect her wishes, but surely there was nothing wrong with imagining it.

It was finally my turn to speak with a Valkyrie. The woman I ended up standing before was a cute little gal with short blonde hair, glowing blue eyes, and triceps that would put any bodybuilder to shame. I barely found myself containing a whistle of appreciation.

"Can I help you, warrior?" asked the woman.

"Yeah. I've got some monster parts I'd like to sell." I reached into a small satchel hanging from my shoulders, pulled out a scroll, and handed them to her. "Here's a manifest of everything I'd like to sell."

"Certainly. Just give me one moment to take a look at what you're selling. I can tally up a total for you in short order."

I nodded and waited patiently as the woman looked at the list. She seemed a tad surprised to discover this parchment was actually longer than it appeared when rolled up. It was about two feet long, all told.

Our manifest this time was quite extensive since we had been battling monsters for about a month now.

As she read over the list, the Valkyrie's eyes gradually grew wider, until it looked like they might fall out of their sockets. I wondered if something was wrong.

"Could you… please excuse me for one moment?" she asked. "Your list is pretty extensive and full of rare ingredients. I'm unable to properly give you an estimate on how much all of this will be since its net worth is outside my current authority."

In other words, she needed someone who possessed a higher authority to look this over and determine a fair price. That made me wonder how much all this cost…

"That's fine," I said.

"Thank you. Please wait over there. Someone will come for you shortly."

The woman indicated for me to stand at a spot away from the lines, against the far wall, which I complied with. This particular area allowed me to observe all the people present. I looked at all the men and women dressed in armor. There were many different variations. Some wore platemail, others chainmail, and still others wore leather and even no armor. One barbarian pair, a young man and woman, wore what looked like a loincloth and bikini respectively.

I wasn't sure that was very safe…

"I should have guessed the one giving me a headache would be you, Bryan," a voice suddenly said to me.

Turning around, I faced the source of the voice. A gorgeous woman who was tall and leggy stood about half a meter from me, a hand on her cocked hip, an exasperated smile on her face. She didn't look a day past twenty. At the same time, there was an air of maturity about her that I'd never seen in a twenty year old woman.

Perhaps it was all that armor? This Valkyrie was clad from head to toe in glistening silver armor. A chestplate, pauldrons, gauntlets, greaves, and a pleated skirt. The whole shebang. She looked like a gallant hero, the kind I'd often read about in stories and played in video games. Very few people I knew, men or women, could strike a pose as heroic as this war maiden.

"Brynhildr," I greeted with a grin.

"It's been a while," she said. "Have you been hunting all this time?"

Brynhildr was the undisputed leader of the Valkyries. The leader among this group was not selected by blood. Heredity meant shit to these women. Strength was everything. Every ten years, a tournament was held to decide who would be the next leader. I myself had not seen the tournament yet since one already happened six years ago, but Brynhildr had won that tournament… and the previous six others.

That made me wonder how old she was. She had won seven tournaments in a row, which meant she was at least seventy years old. She was quite beautiful for a grandma…

"Yeah," I answered as I rubbed the back of my head. "Adina, Michelle, and I were training, trying to get me up to level 70. We decided there was no point in just letting the monster parts go to waste, you know?"

"I do know," Brynhildr said. "Still, with a manifest this large, I cannot make a decision right away. I hope you don't mind if I inspect the cargo?"

"Feel free." I shrugged. "Adina should be at the ship right now. I'll escort you there."

✳✳✳

The Hall of Warriors was located in the center of Valhalla. My ship was docked at the cheapest dock located on the very edge of the city. In most cases, it would have taken several hours of walking to reach.

We reached it in fifteen minutes.

If there was one benefit to tagging along with a Valkyrie, it was definitely the transportation. Valkyries always had several methods of transportation available. The first was their flying steeds. The second was a small airship that reminded me of a zeppelin, only it was meant for just two people. It did not have the maneuverability of the steeds, but it could move very fast linearly.

"I'm always amazed by the strange technology you people have," I muttered as I stared at the mini-zeppelin (my name for it) in awe.

"That is quite the compliment, coming from an Earthling," Brynhildr said.

Earthling was the generic title given to people like me, people who had arrived in this world from Earth by traveling through a rift. Turns out I wasn't the only one to have done so. I didn't know how many people had traveled through a rift like me, but I'd met a few others aside from Christine. Some were people who had accidentally stumbled into one, others were people who had done so on purpose.

"Well, let's check the cargo," I said and, with a jaunty whistle, I led Brynhildr onto the ship.

The cargo hold was located below deck. We traveled down a flight of stairs and reached the door that would lead into the cargo hold. It was locked with a magic device that could only be unlocked by myself, Adina, Christine, or Michelle. I placed my thumb against the device, watched it light up, and then heard the click to signify it was unlocked.

"Come on," I gestured for her to follow me as I opened the door.

I think I mentioned before how technology in this world was strange. That was because this world had a lot of technology that seemed far more advanced than anything in my world, but it was so primitive in other ways.

I think I could thank magic for that. A lot of the technology in the Rift Plains and its various realms revolved around magic. That mini-zeppelin, this ship, the toilets… heck, even stoves and lights were magical devices.

The cargo hold of my ship was one such magical device that seemed decades ahead of my world. It could be called a cold storage shed, but I think calling it a stasis room would be more accurate. Everything placed inside of this room would remain in stasis until the door was opened. This meant we could store numerous spoilable items inside without having to worry about them spoiling.

Lined up in several rows were a number of square boxes stacked atop each other and barrels sitting in front of them. There were a total of six rows, and each one spanned the entire cargo hold.

"This is… very impressive," Brynhildr murmured.

"Thanks," I said. "Should I let you get started?"

"Yes, that would be good."

Even though I said that, we did not get started immediately, but that was because Adina had walked around the corner, a clipboard in one hand and a quill in the other. She looked like she was checking off marks on a list. However, the moment she saw us, she stopped.

"Bryan. And Brynhildr." Adina walked over to us, grabbing my arm as she stared warily at the woman accompanying me. "What are you doing here?"

"Our supply list was apparently too large for the standard procedure," I said, hitching a thumb at Brynhildr. "So she had to come and personally catalog all the items we're selling them to create an accurate price."

"Oh. Well, I just got finished double checking our cargo manifest, if you want to have a look."

Adina handed the clipboard to Brynhildr, who looked over all the items listed before nodding several times.

"This matches the list Bryan gave me, though I would like to check your cargo myself." She looked up from the checklist and at me. "Is that okay?"

"Knock yourself out," I said with a shrug.

It took around two hours for Brynhildr to properly look through all of our salvage, but she was not just seeing what we had available. She was also checking things like quality instead of just quantity. Trycon blood sold for a lot. However, the higher the level of Trycon the blood came from, the more expensive it would be. It was that way for all parts salvaged from monsters.

"This really is an impressive haul," Brynhildr said. She looked legitimately impressed. "I don't think I have ever seen someone who managed to salvage so much monster parts."

"How much do you think all of this will sell for?" I asked.

Brynhildr bit her lip, which struck me as oddly feminine. She might have been a woman, but this was a woman who could kill bears barehanded, who wielded a sword as she dove into battle, and whose fierceness was so legendary stories were told about her in taverns. I never expected her to perform such a girlish act.

"With this many parts collected, not to mention the blood, I believe I can buy it from you for twenty thousand eyrir. How does that sound?"

I sucked in a deep breath. It had been five months since I came to Yggdrasil with Adina, Christine, and Michelle. By this point, I was perfectly aware of how much everything around here cost.

The house we lived in cost 1,000 eyrir, though I did not have to pay for it because Christine had already been living there. It generally cost only 60 eyrir to buy enough food to feed a single person for a month if you were careful. The bathhouse we used cost 10 eyrir per use, which was on the cheap side compared to other bathhouses. When

I combined the cost of clothes, supplies, the docking fee, and everything else, it only cost maybe 400 eyrir a month to live.

Cheap, I know.

"If we had twenty-thousand eyrir, we could live comfortably for over two years without worry!" Adina exclaimed in shock.

"You can." Brynhildr admitted with a wry smile. Her eyes were locked onto mine. "So, how about it? Twenty thousand eyrir for all this."

It didn't sound like a bad deal, but I needed to think about it for a moment. Twenty thousand did sound like a lot—it was a lot—but I also knew we weren't getting the best deal we could. I could probably go to another dealer and get a better deal. On the other hand, that would mean having to deal with a middle man and I didn't much care for that. The reason we always brought our salvage to the Hall of Warriors was because the Valkyries were easy to work with and straightforward. I didn't have to worry about them trying to con me. Their warrior pride wouldn't let them.

A middleman on the other hand…

"We'll take the deal," I said, extending my hand.

"Good." Brynhildr smiled as she reached out and grabbed my hand in a firm shake.

***

Because twenty thousand was a large sum, Brynhildr planned to pay us in installments. We'd get one thousand eyrir each month for twenty months. That would give us more than enough to live off of every month. If we wanted, our group could stay holed up in Valhalla for the next twenty months without ever once going back to Midgard.

Of course, I don't think any of us were all right sitting on our laurels. We'd definitely go back soon. Aside from money, we really needed to train and grow stronger.

Michelle had already finished her shopping by the time Adina and I arrived home. She was just putting everything away inside of the cooler, which was like a fridge that used ice magic instead of electricity. I didn't know how it worked. I only knew the Nordic runes inscribed on the surface were somehow responsible for its operation.

Our group always took turns on who was cooking dinner, and tonight was my turn. I had asked the other two what they wanted. Adina said she didn't care, but Michelle had asked me to cook a hamburger.

I had introduced Earth food to the pair some time ago. They'd both taken a shine to it. The techniques used to create the food in my world were vastly different from the ones in this world. Hamburgers were a good example. No one seemed to have thought of grinding meat and turning it into a patty. Most meats were grilled, roasted, dried, or smoked.

Because there was no machine to grind meat with, I had to get creative, but it wasn't so hard once you knew how to do it. I ground up the meat in a bowl. Once it was ground, I added eggs and mixed it into the meat, then added other spices like salt, pepper, cayenne pepper, garlic powder, and brown sugar.

We didn't have a grill. Because of that, I put the meat patties onto the skillet and let them cook. The kitchen we used had a vent above us that let out smoke, so I didn't need to worry about the place filling with smoke and choking us to death.

As I was making the food, the door to the kitchen opened and Adina walked in. She was wearing the same skimpy outfit as always. Unlike Michelle, who had bought herself some armor after we began living in Valhalla, Adina did not wear any armor. Her clothing made from strips of strategically placed fabric was her preferred outfit.

"That smells good," Adina said as she walked up to me.

"Thanks," I said. "It should be ready in just a bit." I paused for a moment before turning to gaze at the woman. "What are you doing in the kitchen? I thought you were helping Michelle."

"She's sleeping right now," Adina said. "I think shopping on her own exhausted her."

Shopping didn't sound like a particularly exhausting task, and Michelle was a level 80 Archangel, so her strength and stamina were far greater than the average person's. Something seemed fishy here. I wasn't given time to think on it, however, because Adina came up to me with a smile and wrapped her arms around my waist.

"What are you doing?"

"What's it look like I'm doing?"

"It looks like you're trying to distract me from my cooking."

"Hmm. Perhaps I am. What are you going to do about it?"

What was I going to do? I tried to think about that, but Adina was pressing her full breasts into my back. Those straps really did nothing to hide her body at all. I could even feel her nipples poking through the fabric. As if that wasn't bad enough, Adina had placed her hand over my crotch and was rubbing me through my clothes. It took everything I had to stifle a groan.

"It's not fair that Michelle got to have sex with you while I didn't," Adina whispered into my ear before taking a nibble. The feeling of her warm mouth engulfing my ear was… quite something. Very distracting.

"Can't we do this… after dinner?" I asked, trying to retain my hold on my sanity.

"If we wait until after dinner, it will be me, you, and Michelle once again," Adina said. "I can't do anything with Michelle present. You know how she gets."

I did know how she got. While the three of us did have sex in each other's presence before, the circumstances at the time had been extenuating, to say the least. We'd been trapped in a dungeon within the First Circle of Hell, our levels were weak, and we needed a fast method of leveling up. We'd used a method known only to succubus. It was a sex method. I wasn't sure how it worked, but succubus could increase their levels by having sex with people more powerful than themselves.

In either case, that was the one and only time all three of us had sex in the same room. After that, Michelle expressly forbade it from happening again, stating that a virtuous archangel such as herself could not abide by such crass behavior.

While I had been remembering the past, Adina had already fished my dick from my pants. It was already standing straight up thanks to her gentle ministrations. Her hand felt divine. It was warm, soft, and above all, tender. She stroked my veiny shaft from the base all the way to the head, which she teased with her index finger.

"Oh, my. Looks like you're leaking," she murmured as precum escaped from my piss slit.

She released me from behind, walked around me, and knelt on her haunches. By this point, I had forgotten completely about dinner. All that I could see was Adina as she stared at my cock like it was a gourmet meal.

"Heh heh. Now this is a meal I can dig into," she said, looking up at me with a grin.

"Getting in your protein?" I asked with an amused smile.

"Oh, yes."

Adina didn't hesitate as she engulfed the tip of my head with her mouth. I gritted my teeth to keep from grunting as she went lower, taking in more and more. The feeling of her tongue as she rubbed the underside of my shaft with it made my knees weak. I could only gaze in awe as my dick went right down her throat. This was something Michelle could never do, not because she was an archangel, but because she had a gag reflex.

With a hum, Adina began bobbing her head back and forth. An electric sensation raced through me. My body felt like a livewire. I placed my hands against the counter and leaned over as Adina gave me the best blow job in the history of blow jobs, but of course, she wasn't anywhere near finished.

Adina pulled back until just the tip of my head was still in her mouth, undid the clasp on her clothes, and grabbed her large breasts. I felt the warmth of her tits as they engulfed my shaft. When she began moving them, I was almost certain I'd gone to Heaven… or should I say Hell? Given that she was a succubus, that seemed a more appropriate word, but I couldn't think of the pleasure she was giving me as hellish.

It really didn't take long for Adina to get what she wanted. I felt my balls tighten several minutes after she began, and then I exploded inside of her. Even though I hadn't given any warning, Adina had no trouble swallowing everything. Not a single drop escaped her mouth. The sight turned me on so much that I was hard again in moments.

"You really do have a lot of vigor." Adina admired my still fully erect penis. "I've always heard the other succubus complain about how hard it is to keep a man up after he cums, but you're just as stiff now as you were when we began."

"Maybe you're just that sexy," I suggested.

Adina laughed as she stood up, slipped her underwear-like bottoms down her hips, and smiled at me. Her exposed pussy was already dripping. Unlike Michelle, her nethers was not a little slit like the kind I'd expect from a virgin, but that didn't mean it looked used either. She had very plump lips. They looked soft and squishy, like they would suck a man in and give him incredible comfort. Her clit was also larger than Michelle's little bud.

Adina turned around, placed her hands on the counter, and wiggled her perfectly rounded ass at me.

"Well? Are you going to come over, or would you like an invitation?" she asked.

"Who needs an invitation?" I said as I grabbed her hips and lined myself up with her dripping sex.

Unlike with Michelle, I thrust myself inside Adina in one go and began pounding her from behind. I did not start slow, did not go gently. It was fast and furious. The sound of my hips slapping against her asscheeks mixed with the sounds of sizzling meat and Adina's wanton moans.

"Yes! Oh, fuck yes! Harder! Haaa! Haaa! Harder!"

Because she had asked for it, I lifted her left leg off the ground, turning the woman so she was on her side, and placed her foot on my shoulder as I increased my pace. My thrusts became faster, more powerful. Adina screamed deliriously. Her tongue was lolling out of her mouth and her eyes had gone crossed. More than the look of immeasurable pleasure on her face, however, what really caught my attention was the way her tits bounced and slapped against each other with each vigorous thrust of my hips.

Sweat formed on our skin as we continued to fuck like this. Had anyone else seen us, I was sure they'd be reminded of animals rutting as they went into heat. You couldn't call this loving. At the same time, I felt an immense wellspring of affection for this woman mixing with the primal urges she invoked in me. It was a different feeling from what I felt for Michelle. Different, but no less powerful.

I couldn't tell you how long we went at it, but Adina's body shook and heaved as she experienced two orgasms, and I eventually shot my own load inside of her. We didn't stop just once. After my first orgasm, I picked her up, placed her on the counter, and began plunging into her like that. We shared a sloppy kiss filled with tongue as I took her in this new position, her legs wrapped around my waist, body heaving as her breasts squished against my chest.

"Ha… ha… oh… that was good… so good… Bryan, I love you so much…"

Adina was shaking with exhaustion after what I think was her third or fourth orgasm. I had lost track of time, so I wasn't sure how long we'd been at it, or how many times we'd done it.

"Mmm. I love you too."

Adina smiled at me as she leaned forward and pressed our lips together. Unlike our passionate and sloppy kisses when we were fucking, this one actually was tender and loving. It was like the kisses shared between lovers during their post-sex cuddling.

The door to the kitchen slammed open just as we were sharing this loving moment, and a very irate Michelle stormed in.

"How dare you lock me in the bedroom! What were you thinking?!"

"Oh, come on. I just wanted some time alone with Bryan," Adina complained. "What's the harm? You got to have sex with him the other day, but I haven't done anything for over a month."

It was only after Adina had spoken that Michelle seemed to realize the position we were in. Her cheeks burned with savage fierceness, but she tried her best to maintain a stern demeanor.

"You locked me in the bedroom just to have sex?"

"Yes."

"And what about dinner? Look at it! Dinner is ruined! Do you know how long I spent shopping for ingredients?"

Adina looked at the hamburgers, which could no longer be called such. They looked more like charcoal. The six meat patties were black, burned, and shriveled. Now that I had noticed them myself, the stench of burning meat had mixed in with the smell of sex. I couldn't call it pleasant by any stretch of the imagination.

"Uh… we could always eat out," Adina suggested.

Michelle's response was to grab her hair out of frustration.

CHAPTER 5

Valhalla had a lot of taverns. A lot of taverns. I think it was something like for every street, there were at least two or three taverns present.

Taverns served a multitude of purposes in Valhalla, and while sharing a stiff drink with comrades after a day's hard work was one of them, it wasn't the only one.

It likely had something to do with how Valhalla was home to a myriad of races from all across the Rift Plains. This place had become a major stopping point for weary refugees searching for a new place to call home. The taverns also seconded as inns, which many displaced beings took temporary residence at until they were ready to move on.

Taverns were also a great place to find jobs. There was a job board in every tavern, where people who needed something done posted it on a sheet of paper. People who wanted to take a job merely needed to pluck the appropriate sheet from the board and meet up with the client for further details. I myself had never taken a job before, but that was because I didn't need to.

The tavern we had selected to eat at was called the Silver Deer, which could be considered a higher end tavern.

When people in my world typically thought of taverns, I was sure they imagined a grimy place with loud people who drank themselves stupid, beer sloshing out of their mugs and spilling onto the floor, barmaids being sexually harassed by patrons, and barroom brawls happening at the drop of a hat. That was how traditional media portrayed bars in fantasy novels and movies.

The Silver Deer was nothing like that. The lighting was warm and the atmosphere sophisticated. Tables sat arrayed in the center of a large room composed of polished wood floorboards and booths lined the walls, but there weren't that many tables or booths, almost like they didn't want too many people crowding their space. This also meant there was more space for patrons to sit and enjoy their meals.

Of course, the Silver Deer was also a lot more expensive than other taverns. It didn't cater to the kind of patron typically found in low-end bars.

When Adina, Michelle, and I entered, we spotted the few patrons who were already sitting at tables. Everyone was decked out to the nines. Colorful doublets made of silk. Beautiful dresses that sparkled in the light. Ruffled sleeves and high-collared capes. The people present looked like members of high society. While Valhalla did not have a noble class, it did have a number of successful men and women who'd made a name for themselves. A faux noble class, if you will.

I felt underdressed in my black pants, collared shirt, and jacket.

If I looked underdressed, then Adina looked completely out of place. Despite Michelle attempting to convince the succubus to dress in an outfit that was less revealing, she wore the same thing she always had. Her breasts were exposed. Everything except her nipples was visible. Her underwear-like bottoms covered her naughty bits, but I could see cameltoe as her nether lips pressed against the fabric of her underwear. She struck a sexy figure with her succubus wings, horns, and spaded tail, but I understood why Michelle didn't want her wearing something like this in a high-end eatery like the Silver Deer.

On the other hand, Michelle had dressed herself up nicely, though she still lagged behind these sophisticated snobs. Her dress was pure white and shimmered as she walked. It reached all the way down to her ankles. A small hint of her chest was exposed, while the back had a dip that revealed a good deal of her wonderfully soft skin. Her angel wings were sticking out of two slits that had been sown into the dress for her. They complimented her outfit, or perhaps I should say her outfit complimented her wings? Either way, she looked divine.

"Excuse me," someone said. He was a young man with black hair, dark skin, and wearing a black and white suit. "Do you three… have a reservation?"

I noticed the pause in his words and sighed when I saw him giving Adina an unrepentantly lustful gaze. Some protective instincts came over me, but I shunted them aside. It wasn't like I could blame this boy for being a boy. Any straight male would have drooled at the sight of my lover.

"We do not." Michelle gave the boy a bit of a scornful look, jealous that he was focusing on Adina instead of her. "However, I'm sure you can accommodate us."

Even as the boy frowned at her, Michelle produced a larger than average eyrir. If the ones I'd used with the vender were the size of two quarters, then the coin she had now was the size of my fist.

Eyrir were gold minted coins. Their value depended on the composition and size. The one I had used was sort of like a penny. It was worth one eyrir. The one Michelle just handed to the boy would probably constitute a hundred dollar bill in my world, which explained the flabbergasted expression the boy wore.

The boy discreetly pocketed the gold coin, coughed into his hand, and tried to discreetly look at Adina as she hung off my arm before replying to Michelle.

"We can definitely accommodate such generous patrons. Right this way, please."

We were led to a booth located near the back of the room. I had the feeling the boy did this so we wouldn't be in the spotlight. On the way to this table, I noticed the many eyes glancing in our direction, some disdainful, others curious, and some full of lust. Everyone present knew we didn't fit in. If it wasn't for the fact that Michelle demanded we eat here as recompense for destroying dinner, I would have never been caught dead in this place.

The booth was big enough to seat all three of us easily. I sat in between Adina and Michelle.

"You're spending awfully exorbitantly," Adina said as the young man left, though not before getting another eyeful of Adina's figure.

Michelle huffed. "I just didn't want to deal with the hassle of not having a reservation. Even I know that money talks."

"That is true, but we could have just eaten at a regular tavern and spent less."

"Ugh. I am not going to some establishment filled with drunkards and idiots."

"Why not? It's fun."

"How is dealing with buffoons fun?"

I let the two talk and thought about the differences between them. Adina was definitely the more outgoing of the two, always up for trying new things and meeting new people. She wasn't afraid of getting down and dirty. We'd actually been to one of those taverns they were speaking of before. She had immediately drunk herself stupid, began singing and dancing with everyone else, and then blasted a man through a wall when he touched her butt. Not only that, but she had the nerve to laugh at the man who she punched through a wall for being a loser.

On the other hand, Michelle had hid herself in the booth we'd been using and curled her lips at the many patrons laughed and drank themselves into a stupor. She was definitely the more reserved of the two. She also preferred the finer things in life, an example being how she wanted to eat at the Silver Deer instead of a more affordable tavern like the Prancing Pegasus. Michelle enjoyed shopping, wearing jewelry, and dressing up. She was more girlish than Adina, who I'd probably consider something of a roughneck.

While I think my taste in taverns aligned more with Adina's, I couldn't deny the food at the Silver Deer was much better than standard tavern fare. Rather than a simple meal, they served food in courses. There was the four course, the six course, and the five course meals.

We ended up getting the five course meal, which came with pistachio soup (first course), aged AZ beef carpaccio (second course), potato gnocchi (third course), seared duck breast (fourth course), and brioche bread pudding as the dessert course. While Adina complained about how much all this cost, she immediately shut up when the pudding arrived.

Adina had a sweet tooth.

As the three of us enjoyed our dinner, a group of young men and women dressed in outfits that made me peg them all as snobs wandered up to our table. Their outfits consisted of gorgeous silk, fine leather, and they were carrying weapons that looked like they were more decorative than functional. I was surprised. Most people who ate here seemed more interested in ignoring us, but this group was sneering down at us like we'd committed a personal crime against them.

"You three dregs have a lot of nerve to besmirch our restaurant with your presence. Begone, foul ruffians."

I blinked several times as the man in the lead spoke using words that didn't help alleviate his snobbish image. He had blond hair, blue eyes, and white skin. He looked German… but that wasn't so unusual.

Most people—Valkyries included—either had blond and blue eyes just like this man. Only a few Valkyries had red hair and green eyes, and rare was the Valkyrie with brown hair.

"Sorry," I said as I set down my fork and smiled politely. "But I'm afraid I don't speak buffoon. Try using English please."

Adina snorted into her wine while Michelle's lips trembled. She tried to give me a displeased look, but I could tell she felt vindicated by my words as well.

The spokesperson of their group turned red. "H-how dare you insult me! Do you not know who I am?!"

"No. No, I don't. And I don't care either."

"You—"

"You're the one who waltzed over and interrupted our meal to insult us," I interrupted the man before he could begin. "If you think I'm just going to lie down and take it because you're dressed in fancy clothes, then you're obviously an idiot and not worth my time. Get lost."

I knew this type of man well enough. There were plenty like him back on Earth. He was the kind of man who reveled in his own sense of superiority and wealth and looked down on those who weren't rich, never mind the fact that he probably only had money because his daddy was wealthy. This wasn't the first time I had to deal with asshats like him.

The man's face grew an even darker shade of red as all the blood rushed to it. He looked like a volcano ready to explode. However, I didn't think he would attack us. This man was not a rough and tumble mercenary like the men I associated with at taverns.

"I hope you remember those words of yours, pissant, for I certainly will."

With a final sneer, the man turned around and left. His companions looked back and forth between us uncertainly, but then they left as well. I hoped this meant I would be able to finish my meal in peace.

"Are you sure that was a good idea?" asked Michelle as she gazed at me.

"I personally think it was a great idea." Adina took a swig of her wine like it was ale, then grinned at me. "I love how you talked him down. It was hot."

"I'm glad you enjoyed the show," I said with a grin of my own.

"I'll say. I'm all wet now. I hope you'll take responsibility for this later tonight." Adina winked at me.

"Would you two be serious?!" Michelle hissed.

"We are being serious," I said. "I seriously do not care about that man at all."

"You should," Michelle said gravely. "I understand that you do not pay attention to people who aren't of interest to you, but that man really isn't someone we should casually offend."

"Why not?" I asked. "Is he that big of a threat?"

"Maybe not on his own, but he is in charge of a rather powerful group." Michelle sighed and tucked a strand of hair behind her ears. Meanwhile, Adina was sipping some more wine. I think she'd downed an entire bottle herself. Michelle bit her lower lip before leaning forward and explaining who that man was. "His name is Randy Sexton. He runs the largest mercenary group operating in Valhalla. They call themselves Red Vengeance, a name they created to symbolize their desire to get revenge on the people who forced them out of their homes. From what I understand, he's gathered thousands of people across the Rift Plains together and formed this mercenary company for that purpose."

"Really?" I took a sip of wine when Adina poured some in my half-empty glass. It was good wine. "Sure didn't seem like it."

Michelle shrugged. "I'm sure Randy himself doesn't care about revenge and just wants to live luxuriously, but it doesn't change the fact that his group is large and dangerous. I've also heard that Randy is the kind of man who holds a grudge and isn't afraid to break the law in his quest for revenge."

"Maybe that's the real reason his group is called Red Vengeance," Adina quipped.

"It's possible," Michelle agreed.

I thought about what Michelle told me, not dismissing it out of hand just because that man pissed me off. If he really was as dangerous as she suggested, I would need to stay on my toes.

"Well, we'll keep our eyes open just in case he tries something, but I don't think we should live in fear either," I decided. "Nothing good ever comes from backing down when someone like that confronts you."

"That is true," Michelle admitted, though she sounded reluctant.

"What should we do if he tries something?" asked Adina.

"Isn't that obvious?" I asked, smiling. "If he tries anything, we'll teach him why acting against us is a bad idea."

∗∗∗

It only took two days for the Valkyries to unload all the cargo our ship was holding. I also received my first payment, which we used to buy some equipment needed to maintain our weapons and armor. It was important to consistently clean our armor at least once a week with oil, though we needed to do it more if we entered combat and our armor got bloodied. Blood stains decreased the armor's efficiency. It was the same with my sword. If I wasn't constantly sharpening mine after using it, the sword would rust, the edges would grow dull, and it would become useless.

So much for this being like a video game.

I sometimes wished I had a magical sword, one that never rusted or grew dull. Brynhildr had such a weapon. However, swords like hers were legendary artifacts, which wasn't something just anyone could acquire.

After our cargo was removed by the Valkyries, Adina, Michelle, and I took our ship back to Midgard.

Midgard was what everyone called the world below the floating islands where people lived. It was infested with all kinds of monsters. Some of the areas had weaker monsters, but none of them were below level 40. Definitely not the kind of place you'd go for a picnic.

The area we had turned into our hunting ground was an old forest located near some ancient ruins. Twisted tree roots sprouted from the ground like the tentacles of an eldritch horror. Only sparse amounts of light penetrated the thick canopy above us. The scent of earth and bark filled our noses as we marched, careful not to step on a root. There was no telling if one of them might be a treant until it was too late. They loved waiting for their prey to step on their roots, then acted faster than most humans could hope to track them, wrapping their prey up and crushing their bones to make devouring them easier.

"This place gives me the creeps," Adina muttered.

"You are not the only one who feels that way," Michelle assured the woman. "I can sense the vile magic from those ruins. I've no idea what kind of people built it or why, but the repulsive magic emanating from that place has perverted the nature of this forest, tainted it."

"Mmmm."

"Can you sense anything?" I asked Michelle.

She nodded. "There is a rather large group of monsters up ahead. They are a few levels above your own, so be careful."

"I'll stick close to Adina," I assured her.

"That's right." Adina grabbed my arm and hugged it to her chest, grinning at me. "Stay right next to me."

"Could you please not get so close to him while we're out on a job?" asked an irate Michelle. "It's dangerous."

"Sorry." Adina stuck out her tongue as she let go of my arm.

We eventually came upon a group of small humanoid creatures traveling through the forest. They weren't much bigger than a human child, but their features were reptilian, with sharp yellow eyes, scales covering every inch of their bodies, and gangly arms and legs. Each one was dressed in armor, though all of the armor was mismatched. One might be wearing a steel chestplate and leather gauntlets. Another might have a pleated skirt and iron chainmail.

"Kobolds," Adina muttered. "Nasty creatures."

"How should we do this?" asked Michelle.

I thought for a moment, then nodded.

"Michelle will start us off. Launch a ranged attack at them. After that, Adina and I will rush in. You follow behind us and protect our flanks."

Both of them agreed to my basic plan, which was simple because complex plans never remained intact after first contact with the enemy. Better to not have a complicated plan that will fail and instead go with something we can adapt to suit any change in circumstances as the fight progresses.

Michelle stepped away from us and narrowed her eyes. Energy seeped from her skin, a golden aura that made me think of divine flames of retribution. She raised her hand, and several hundred swords suddenly appeared in thin air. With a wave of her hand, she sent the swords flying into the horde of kobolds, causing all of them to squawk, shriek, and howl in surprise and pain. Some died when they were impaled through the throat or chest, but most avoided heavy injuries.

"Let's go!" I shouted, running toward the kobolds, unsheathing my sword.

"Time to party!" Adina added as she raced after me.

While our attack had definitely surprised them, kobolds were an intelligent race and quick to adapt. They brandished their own makeshift weapons the moment they spotted us. Reptilian hisses and roars tore from their throats as they charged at us.

I sidestepped the first attacking kobold, swinging my sword upward to bisect him, though I didn't hit. Instead, the clang of metal against metal echoed around us. The kobold had been fast enough to block my attack. My arms jolted as the clash of our blades rang out, muscles straining as I tried to push the shorter creature back with little success. The bastard had dug his heels in to keep himself from moving.

I guess this creature really was a level or two higher than me.

Adina and I fought back to back, to help us avoid being struck from behind. While this limited our ability to dodge, neither of us was really the dodging type. We were both power fighters. We attacked with powerful swings and shielded ourselves as best we could. I guess you could call us tanks. Michelle was the finesse fighter among us.

As Adina and I defended each other, Michelle swooped through the battlefield, her vibrantly glowing twin blades cleaving through kobolds like they were butter. Heads flew, bodies were sliced apart, and the screams of the dying kobolds echoed around us. There were a lot too. I couldn't count how many there were, but there must have been at least a few dozen.

One of the kobolds I was fighting overextended its attack. I took advantage, swinging my sword hard enough to cleave through armor and bone, severing an arm at the elbow. The creature fell back with a startled scream as blood sprayed from the missing stump. I silenced its scream by slicing through its neck.

Adina was much more powerful than I was. While I relied on my sword to get the job done, she relied on her fists. Because she was behind me, I couldn't see what she was doing, but I could hear it, the loud detonation that rang out every time her fist struck an enemy. It mingled with the dying squeals of whoever she hit.

Succubi were often known for how they seduced men, but that wasn't all they had to them. A succubus could train other powers and become abnormally strong. Lilith was the perfect example. According to Adina, her mother was one of the most powerful beings of Hell, easily ranked within the top ten strongest, which was why Naamah, Agrat bat Mahlat, and Eisheth needed to team up with Asmodeus to defeat her. Even then, all they had managed to do was seal her away.

I wasn't sure how Lilith trained, but Adina had trained her body to contain explosive power, putting most of her status points into her strength and learning skills that utilized strength more than anything else. I'd once seen the woman punch a hole clean through a fifteen meter tall treant. These kobolds wouldn't stand a chance against her fists.

Several more kobolds rushed in. I narrowed my eyes and channeled mana through my blade, activating Whirlwind Slash. I didn't spin around. I couldn't with Adina at my back, but I performed a half spin that created a blade of compressed air, which cut through the bodies of the kobolds racing toward me, though it sadly didn't kill them. The injuries they suffered were light.

As the injured and now angry kobolds tried to rush me, I activated Fireblade. The sword in my hand ignited in a brilliant orange haze. I swung the sword without pause, my blade tearing through the face of one unlucky kobold. Another tried to block my return swing, but they met their end when my sword cleaved through theirs like it was made of paper. No blood spurted from their wounds. The fire cauterized all their injuries instantly.

While I was fending for myself and protecting Adina's back, I spotted Michelle as she flitted through the kobolds like a bolt of lightning. Her feet barely seemed to touch the ground as she twirled around like a dancer. She swung both swords to her own rhythm, and each time she did, she cut off something from her enemies. An arm. A leg. A head. The ground around her was strewn with bodies of the dead and dying.

Several kobolds attacked her at once, surrounding her on all sides, but Michelle merely flapped her wings and took flight, resulting in all the kobolds crashing into each other. She came back down behind one of them and swung her sword. There was a spray of blood as the kobold's head was removed from its shoulder.

I was unable to keep watching her as a kobold swung its sword at me. I parried its attack with a deft flick of my wrist, then impaled it with my blade. Blood ran down my sword as the blade went through its throat. The creature released a death croak and tried to grab my weapon, but I planted a boot on its chest and kicked it off my sword as I turned to the next one.

The fighting seemed to last for a long time, though I was sure that was just my perception of time playing tricks on me. Time seemed to slow down when adrenaline was involved. At some point in the battle, I realized there were no more enemies nearby and released a weary sigh.

"Looks like that did them in." Adina wiped the sweat from her forehead as she turned to me. "So, how's it look? How much more experience points do you need to level up?"

"Let me check."

I opened my status screen as Michelle walked over to us and looked at the information listed on—specifically, I was looking at the area that showed how many more experience points I needed to reach level 71.

"It looks like I need another two hundred thousand experience points, give or take," I said.

"So you still have a long way to go," Adina muttered with a sigh.

I could only offer her a bitter smile. The higher a person's level was, the more experience points they needed to level up. I was pretty sure Adina and Michelle needed around one million points to reach a higher level.

"These Kobolds don't look like they have anything really good on them. Let's find more monsters to kill," Michelle said, already turning around and walking away from the sight of the battle.

We followed her and used Michelle's ability to sense monsters to find several more groups. We ran across more than just kobolds. There were also a few orcs, which didn't quite look like the creatures

Earthlings like myself had come to know through books, movies, and video games. They were another humanoid race, but they were all hideously malformed, with prominent fangs and grotesque facial features. Their skin was traditionally green, but sometimes they would have gray, black, brown, or even red skin.

Orcs were violent by nature and didn't get along with anyone, not even their brethren. That said, they still traveled in groups. It wasn't unusual to run into a tribe of orcs in Midgard. During my five months in Yggdrasil, I had destroyed a number of tribes alongside Adina, Christine, and Michelle.

Most of the orcs we fought were levels 75 to 80. We ended up wiping out a few orc tribes, which ended up bringing my level to 71. Since I was trying to keep my stats balanced, I added my status points into Attack, Defense, and Mana. I added my skill points to Thousand Cuts and Fireblade.

Name: Bryan Jenson

Class: Magic Swordsman

Magic: Red

Level: 71

Attack: 200

Agility: 180

Defense: 200

Mana: 200

Total Status Points available: 0

Special Skills:

Thousand Cuts+17

Whirlwind Slash+7

Death by Piercing+7

Fireblade+16

Total Skill Points Available: 0

Now that all of my stats had risen exponentially, a new set of skills became available to me, though I was only allowed to choose one. I opened up the menu showing what skills I could learn and studied each one to see which would be best suited for my style of combat.

Available Special Skills:

Dual Whirlwind Slash: This is a double attack. You spin around and create one Whirlwind Slash that softens your enemies' defenses. Upon completing a full 360 degree spin, you spin once more counterclockwise and attack again. This attack does twice the damage as Whirlwind Slash. Effects multiple enemies.

Berserk: This is a skill only someone who has Soul Bound to a red planet can use. It turns the user into a raging berserker, amplifying their strength several times over at the cost of their sanity. Berserkers will attack friend and foe alike. The effects last for 60 seconds. Can last longer if you put more skill points into it.

Double Jump: When your Attack and Agility reach 180, you can learn the Double Jump skill, which lets people jump on thin air as though you were standing on solid ground.

Flame Whirlwind Slash: Someone who is Soul Bound to a red planet can infuse their sword with fire and perform a Whirlwind Slash. This extends the range of your attack and adds fire damage.

It looked like I only had four new skills to choose from. Berserk was out immediately. I had no desire to become a raging idiot who attacked friend and foe alike, which left Double Whirlwind Slash, Flame Whirlwind Slash, and Double Jump. Truth be told, Double Whirlwind Slash and Flame Whirlwind Slash sounded like they would be useful to me since I was interested in attacks that did a lot of damage, but I also thought Double Jump would be a good skill to have handy. It sounded like I could use this skill to perform attacks from another angle. I also wouldn't be surprised if this skill branched off into other useful special skills that I could learn.

Well, selecting a skill was something that I could think about later. For now, I joined up with Adina and Michelle as we went out in search of bigger prey.

CHAPTER 6

I ended up choosing Double Jump as the skill I learned. I thought it would be useful to have an ability that let me jump in the air twice. Say I was jumping along the roofs of Valhalla, either because I was chasing someone or being chased myself, and some of the buildings were spaced too far apart for me to reach under my own power. Double Jump would help me close that gap.

Not that I ever planned on running along the roofs of Valhalla, but you never know what the future might hold.

The skill Double Jump also opened several other skills that I could learn. They were called branch skills because after learning the initial skill, the skill tree branched out into other skills that could be learned by spending skill points. When I looked at my skill tree now, there were five skills branching off from Double Jump: Avenging Angel, Falling Flame Cutter, Destitution, Cushioning, and Triple Jump.

Avenging Angel was a falling attack. You used double jump to reach an impressive height of several dozen meters, then fell back to the ground and impaled your enemy with your sword. This attack was great for attacking trolls, ogres, and similarly large monsters that had fallen to the ground, but it could also be used as a surprise attack.

Falling Flame Cutter was similar to Avenging Angel, but it was a slashing attack. As you fell toward the ground, you channeled mana through the blade, igniting it with flames and cutting your opponent by using the resulting gravity to increase your attack power. This was a deadly attack that could slice through anything that wasn't enchanted with defensive magic. It might even be able to cut through a Trycon, though I was not going to test that.

Destitution was an odd skill. It wasn't quite an attack so much as an empowerment skill. After using double jump, the user hung in the air and gathered energy from the surroundings, channeling it into their own body and using it to increase their physical strength by several times. I wasn't sure why one needed to leap into the air to use Destitution.

Cushioning was another non-attack skill, a passive ability that let someone falling from a great height cushion their fall to avoid injury. It was a useful skill for people who were constantly jumping from high places. I personally did not think I had much use for it.

Triple Jump was a self-explanatory skill. It allowed someone to jump three times instead of two like Double Jump. I didn't think I'd be learning that one either. Honestly, I couldn't see the point in it.

Each skill required one skill point to learn, but I didn't know if I would learn any of them right now. I'd learned from Adina and Michelle that knowing a lot of skills was not better than mastering a few skills. A jack of all trades might have a great many abilities, but they would always be countered by someone who had mastered their abilities to the greatest extent possible.

In short, I planned on mastering the skills I had now before even thinking about gaining new skills.

We had been traveling through Midgard for about a week now, fighting monsters during the day and returning to our ship at night. We had moored our ship on a lake that was free of monsters. It was important to be careful when docking a ship since some lakes might have a serpent sleeping at the bottom.

"Michelle! Pull back! Adina! You're up!"

At the moment, sweat was pouring down my back as the three of us stood inside of some ancient ruins we had decided to explore. There were many such ruins scattered across Midgard. According to Christine, these ruins belonged to the race of humans who had lived here under the protection of the gods, but they had long since been abandoned by the people after the great change.

These ruins were all infested with monsters known as draugr.

At present we were fighting against a draugr priest located deep within the ancient ruins. This creature was tall and gangly, with rotten flesh sloughing off its skin and ragged robes covering its body. Glowing crimson eyes sat inside of its eye sockets. As I stared into the gaunt face that reminded me of a mummified corpse, I could not help but shudder just a little.

It was one thing to see a creature like this in a video game. Quite another to see it in real life.

The draugr priest raised its staff, light flashing from the black gem situated on the crown. I knew it was getting ready to charge up one of its spells. It had several powerful spells that it could use, some of which could kill a person in a single attack, but Adina did not let that happen. As Michelle moved back, she moved forward, feet sliding along the ground as she bent her knees, tucked her fist into her side, and released a powerful punch.

An attack like this wouldn't normally reach the draugr priest, who was floating in the air several meters from us. This attack was not normal, however. The moment she thrust out her fist, a powerful explosion of energy erupted from it and slammed into the draugr priest, disrupting the spell it was going to use. The draugr sailed through the air in an uncontrolled spin.

"Let's go, Michelle!"

With the draugr priest tumbling about above us, I leapt into the air as Michelle blasted off the ground, flying just a few centimeters above the floor. I used Double Jump to reach a height that let me easily close the distance between me and the draugr priest, body soaring in a parabolic arc.

Michelle reached the draugr priest first. Two golden swords had appeared in her hands. Even I could feel the divine energy pouring from her weapons, which she swung forward to attack the draugr priest. One of them was blocked by the staff gripped in the priest's decrepit hand, but the other drew a line across its body. Light exploded from the creature as the holy energy from Michelle's attack purified the dark energy keeping it alive. It released a terrifying screech as black mist poured from the wound. This was not enough to kill it, however.

As the draugr priest was releasing a pained scream, I finally descended and swung my blade. The sword split the draugr priest's head clean open. Black blood sprayed from the wound, splattering against the floor. Michelle and I avoided the blood by leaping backward. The draugr priest lurched forward as if it would still try to attack us, but then, like a puppet with no strings attached, it tumbled to the floor and remained still.

"Phew. We did it," I muttered, wiping the sweat from my brow.

"It took a very long time to clean out these ruins," Michelle said. "There were a lot more draugr than I anticipated. A vile and dark energy is permeating this place. It brought nearly all those buried here back to life."

The ruins we were exploring had once been a crypt, the burial site for warriors who had fallen in battle long ago. We had been attacked nearly the moment we arrived in this ancient burial ground by the draugrs who'd been resurrected.

Draugrs were humans who had been resurrected into undead monsters. They roamed crypts and other ruins, guarding the places where they had been buried. I'd heard a rumor that draugrs were created via necromancy, but there was another rumor stating they were created when the magic of a specific place was perverted with negative energy. I didn't know which was true. Maybe they both were.

"It looks like I gained a level!" Adina said with a cheerful smile as she walked up to us. "I'm now at level 84!"

"As am I," Michelle said.

When the two mentioned gaining a level, I checked my stats to see that I had also gained a level during this fight, though mine was still much lower than theirs. I decided to allocate my status points into my Attack stat.

Name: Bryan Jenson

Class: Magic Swordsman

Magic: Red

Level: 72

Attack: 220

Agility: 180

Defense: 200

Mana: 200

Total Status Points available: 0

Special Skills:

Thousand Cuts+17

Whirlwind Slash+7

Death by Piercing+7

Fireblade+17

Total Skill Points Available: 0

My level had risen quite a bit this past week. If I were to face those kobolds we had battled when we first came down to Midgard, I could probably kill an entire horde of them by myself. Well, maybe not. I might be feeling overconfident, but I was sure I could at least hold my own.

"Since we've cleared out these ruins, why don't we head back up?" I suggested.

"Good idea." Adina agreed immediately. "This place gives me the creeps."

"I'm not too fond of these ruins either," Michelle added. "There is dark and vile magic at work here. It is difficult for an angel like myself to stand in a place that has been tainted like this. I feel like it might cause me to fall."

"You mean to fall from grace, right?" I asked.

"Exactly."

"Angels can fall from grace?" asked Adina.

"Of course we can," Michelle said. "There have been many angels that have fallen from God's grace. There are the Grigori, rebellious angels who fell from grace because they became enamored with human women and had intercourse with them. Their leader is Shemyaza. He is known for fathering two half-breed sons. There is also Azazel, the angel who fell for giving humans forbidden knowledge."

"Hmmm…"

Adina hummed and stared at Michelle, who turned away.

"W-what are you staring at?"

"If those angels fell because they slept with human women, then doesn't that mean you've also fallen because you're sleeping with a human man?"

Michelle said nothing as they ascended a flight of old stairs. The spiral staircase made from cold stone seemed desolate and decrepit, like it could fall apart at any moment. This place had suffered the vicissitudes of time and disuse. None of us paid attention to the old bloodstains covering the walls.

"You… may be right," Michelle admitted with a sad smile. "It is quite possible I have become a fallen angel as well. Angels who fall in love with humans are cast out of Heaven. I wonder what will happen when I return to aid my fellow brethren and they find out that I have bedded a human."

Neither Adina nor I knew what to say in response to Michelle's sadness. We could both sense her sudden uncertainty. Her walking had slowed, face morphing into something resembling a pained grimace.

Adina looked away, her own expression regretful. I didn't think she meant to make Michelle feel so worried and uncertain. Her words had been said in jest, but upon thinking about it, everything she said was true. Michelle had been sleeping with me for months now. If sleeping with a human caused angels to fall, then she had fallen a long time ago.

I did have to wonder, though. In most media, when an angel fell from God's grace, their wings turned black to symbolize their fall, but Michelle's remained as pristine now as they always had. Did that mean she hadn't fallen? Or did that simply mean I shouldn't trust the media as a reliable source of information?

Those were the thoughts I had as we traveled outside of the ruins and made our way back to our ship.

Our ship was about a kilometer from our current location. While I had originally been worried about people trying to steal it, I learned a long time ago that ships like this required a key to activate. So long as someone didn't have the key, they couldn't activate the ship.

Because of Adina's careless comment, none of us spoke as we traveled through the forest. I focused on trying to extend my senses. Unlike Michelle, who had the ability to sense monsters thanks to her divine nature, I had no such powers.

While I couldn't sense anything, as I concentrated on the area around me, I was able to enhance my five senses. The scent of the forest filled my nose. The earthen scent of wood and dirt was strong enough that I felt like I could actually taste it. My vision became sharp enough that I could count the number of leaves on a tree. Everything seemed so much clearer to me.

I wondered if this was the result of leveling up. Whenever I gained more levels, my body became stronger and my abilities better. It wouldn't surprise me if leveling up brought other benefits as well.

And perhaps it was because my senses were currently so strong, but I was able to pick up on the smell of metal. I thought it was coming from us at first. Michelle and I were both wearing armor, after all, but then I realized this smelled different from us. It was also coming from further away.

I stopped walking.

"Bryan?" Adina called out to me.

"We're surrounded," I said.

At those words, Adina and Michelle became a lot more cautious. The three of us moved so we were standing back to back, eyeing our surroundings. Adina readied her fists, Michelle created golden swords from her divine energy, and I unsheathed my sword.

A bush to my left rustled, drawing my attention. I stared at it, wondering if something would come out, but nothing did. Several seconds passed. Nothing happened. I relaxed my guard.

And that was when they struck.

A whizzing sound pierced the air, pain exploded in my shoulder, and I looked down to find an arrow penetrating the area where shoulder pauldron met chestplate. It was an incredible shot. Whoever had fired the arrow must have been a master archer, but I didn't have time to admire it.

"Adina! Michelle!"

"I'm on it!"

Adina was the first one to respond. She traded places with me and used the trajectory of the arrow that struck me to unleash a powerful Energy Blast that slammed into a tree not far from where we were standing. Bark exploded as the trunk was destroyed. It tilted back, falling, and a figure was forced to leap from the tree before it struck the ground with a loud crash.

The person who landed on the ground several meters from us was... he looked like an elf. Silvery blond hair. Long and pointy ears.

Fair skin. A beauty that defied logic. He was a classic example of an elf from old fantasy stories. He held a bow in his left hand and there was a quiver full of arrows behind his back. This guy was obviously the jerk who shot me.

With a grunt, I yanked the arrow from my shoulder, ignoring the pain as I reached into the pouch at my waist. I pulled a healing potion from my pouch and downed it in a single go. While I couldn't see it, I could certainly feel the wound on my shoulder healing, the skin knitting back together to create new flesh.

While I downed a healing potion, Michelle raised her hand, divine energy pouring from her body as she attempted to create several dozen swords for her skill, Dance of a Thousand Blades. It was unfortunate that she would never get the chance to launch her attack.

A loud noise echoed around the clearing, one that I was familiar with. It was the bang of a gunshot.

Michelle gasped as blood spurt from her stomach. Her armor only covered her chest. Then again, I wasn't sure her armor would be able to protect her from a bullet since it wasn't enchanted with defensive magic. She fell to a knee, her skill dissipating as she lost concentration. Pressing a hand to her stomach, she tried to staunch the bleeding, but even I could see that wasn't going to help. A large, red stain was expanding on her pure white clothing.

Adina was now the only one who hadn't been injured. Her fists were glowing with brilliant wisps of energy as she thrust them out like a raging berserker. Blast after blast of pure energy exploded from her fists, slamming into trees, making them detonate and fall. She didn't just attack one area, but turned a full 360 degrees to damage all of our surroundings.

Her attacks had the desired effect. Several figures fell from the trees and even more stepped out from a variety of hiding places. I counted at least a dozen people. Most of them seemed human, but there was also a dwarf, the elf who shot me, and a couple of lizardmen. All of them were wearing armor.

"Who the hell are you people?" asked Adina, holding her fists at the ready.

"Hmph."

One of the men snorted. I turned to look at him. He was a tall man with dark brown hair, brown eyes, and a scar traveling across the left side of his face. The armor he wore was made of leather instead of metal and looked like it was designed to blend into forests. A sheath was strapped to his waist, the sword it normally contained held within his left hand.

"You don't need to know who we are," the man said. "Just know that Randy sends his regards."

Now I understood. Thinking about it in hindsight, it should have been obvious that the people attacking us were sent here by Randy Sexton, the man who had begun insulting us and only left after we insulted him right back. There was an unspoken rule among the people who made Valhalla their home, and that was to not interfere or attack each other while traveling through Midgard. Only someone like Randy would dare go against this rule. These mercenaries must be working for him.

"I knew we should have killed that jerk when we had the chance," Adina grumbled.

Neither me or Michelle said anything. Michelle had downed a health potion and was busy recovering. I had already recovered by this point, but I didn't attack right away. If we attacked carelessly, we could leave ourselves open to attack from the others. There were only two long-range attackers, the bowman and the person with the gun, but I didn't like our chances of getting out of this unscathed if we attacked recklessly.

I quickly confirmed that none of these people could fly. All of them except the axe-wielding dwarf and the elf were human. Good.

"Adina! Strike the ground!"

I leapt into the air as I shouted, activating Double Jump to reach that extra height I needed. Michelle also followed me into the air, wings flapping, ascending even higher than me. At the same time, Adina raised a fist into the air, then brought it down, striking the ground with such force that the earth around her exploded like a bomb planted under the soil had gone off. Cracks spread across the ground. The many people who had been surrounding us were knocked off balance, some falling, others barely managing to steady themselves by bending their knees.

As I descended back to the ground, I raised my blade and swung it down, my attack slicing through the face of the scarred man. I was careful not to kill him. My attack slid through his eye, but it was a relatively shallow cut. I wanted him alive.

From high above us, Michelle was finally able to use Dance of a Thousand Blades. Dozens of golden swords appeared out of thin air and flew toward the ground. Her targets were the elf bowman and the gunman. Neither of them were able to dodge as the numerous swords fell upon them, piercing their bodies. They died underneath the hail of falling swords.

I kicked the man I'd attacked in the face, knocking him out cold. By this point, our enemies had recovered and were getting ready to attack, but I wanted to get rid of a few people before that happened. I rushed toward the nearest human, a man in silver armor, and thrust my blade into his neck.

His death was near instantaneous.

Ignoring the blood on my sword as I kicked the corpse off it, I spun around upon hearing footsteps behind me. Two people were coming up like they'd been planning to attack while my back was turned. One of them wielded a sword and the other had two daggers in his hands. I couldn't backpedal because there was a large crack spreading across the ground, so I decided to push forward.

I took a step toward my enemies and spun around, swinging my sword as I activated Whirlwind Slash. My attack should have carved these people open or at least damaged their armor. That wasn't what happened. The one with the daggers leapt over my attack, while the other one raised his sword to block it. Our blades met in a clash of sparks.

While the swordsman blocked my attack, the dagger wielder landed behind me. I snarled as I launched a kick at my back.

Something impacted against my leg, which I knew was the dagger wielder. A grunt echoed behind me when my kick connected. However, I couldn't focus fully on the dagger wielder yet because I needed to take care of the swordsman first.

Since our swords were still locked, I kicked at the man's leg, striking his shin to throw him off balance. Then I activated Fireblade. Intense flames wrapped around my sword as I slashed it down, and this time, my attack cut straight through the man's armor and flesh. I had put in so much force that the swordsman spun like a dreidel before hitting the ground, a puddle of blood spreading out beneath him.

With the swordsman dead, I was able to turn my attention to the dagger wielder.

The dagger wielder didn't seem bothered that I had killed his comrade. His eyes contained a hard glint as he advanced on me. Now that I was paying more attention, I could see that his armor was actually all black clothing, which made me think of an assassin. His class must have been related to assassination. I'd run across a number of people with classes like Assassin, Thief, Rogue, and Ninja.

I think my belief that this man was an assassin had been right on the money. Just as he was charging at me, the man disappeared. Vanished. I was startled, but I tried my best to remain calm as I listened for him. It was hard to hear anything over the sound of explosions, the clashing steel, and the roars of combat. Adina and Michelle were also fighting against several enemies. However, I still tried to tune everything out and focus on my own battle.

Instincts screamed at me that danger was approaching, and I leapt away from where I'd been standing as several sharp objects penetrated the soft ground. They were throwing stars. I was shocked at seeing legit ninja throwing stars. This man was obviously of the Ninja Class.

My thoughts were interrupted when I spotted the man descending from above. It looked like his special skill had allowed him to ascend into the air so quickly it merely looked like he vanished from my sight. I didn't know what kind of skill he used, but I decided not to worry about that as I used Double Jump to meet him halfway. After jumping into the air, I activated Fireblade once more and swung my weapon as hard as I could.

Because he was in midair, the assassin could not dodge, which meant his only option was to block my attack. However, trying to block a sword covered in white hot flames with a pair of flimsy daggers was never a good idea. My sword sliced through his daggers and into his flesh. The scent of burning flesh filled my nose as a thick line was carved from his left shoulder to his right hip.

We both hit the ground at nearly the same time, but he was dead. His body crumbled and didn't get up.

I ignored him and moved to help Adina, who was fighting the most opponents out of all of us. It was pretty impressive actually. She had her knees bent and was standing in a boxing stance. Several people attacked her, but Adina was light on her feet as she dodged their swings, then came in with a series of punches that broke their swords. She used her incredible perceptions and reflexes to hit the flat of their blades. The force of her punches was enough to snap their swords like they were twigs.

Since several of them were unarmed, I came in and used Thousand Cuts. It was an attack that increased the speed of my swings, allowing me to swing my sword one thousand times in the blink of an eye. Since they were unarmed, none of them stood a chance against my attack. I cut into them with blindingly swift strikes. I aimed for the unarmored parts of their bodies—the head, the throat, the arms, the thighs. Blood sprayed out of hundreds of wounds as I ran through the group attacking Adina.

Six of the eight men who were attacking her died by my blade.

Adina finished the remaining two.

"Thanks for the assist," Adina said.

"Anytime. Let's help Michelle now."

Like Adina, Michelle was fighting several opponents at once. Four men were surrounding her on all sides. One of them was the dwarf with the massive battleaxe.

Dwarves originated from Germanic myth. They were human-shaped entities that dwelled within mountains and were often associated with wisdom, smithing, mining, and crafting. Often depicted as comically short in modern culture, the dwarf Michelle was fighting against looked like a smaller than average human. He was stout, body covered in thick muscles and heavy plate armor.

The four enemies surged forward and attacked her with swords, spears, and axe. Michelle, wielding two golden swords, did her best to fend off the attacks. She evaded the axe by sidestepping it, blocked a spear that came in from her left, and also managed to block a sword from in front of her. However, the attack from behind struck true. Michelle let out a scream as the blade tore into her back.

I rushed over with Adina and slammed into the dwarf as he was lifting his axe back up. I didn't give him a chance to attack as I activated Fireblade and severed his head from his neck. As his body fell to the ground, I turned to find Adina slamming her fist so hard into a human's face that his head exploded. Paying no attention to that, I used Death by Piercing to impale another enemy through the chest.

Because Death by Piercing was a skill that allowed me to ignore the armor and defense of an enemy to some extent, my sword went straight through this human's armor. The man coughed up blood as my attack punctured his lung. He looked at the sword in his chest in shock, but I just kicked him off and turned to Michelle.

The battle was over. All of the men who attacked us, except their leader, were now dead. I knelt beside the injured Michelle and removed a health potion from my pouch, feeding it to her and watching as the wound on her back sealed shut, not even leaving a scar behind. These health potions really were amazing. They would have been useful during my time in the Special Forces. If I'd had these at the time, then maybe Chris wouldn't have died.

Shaking my head, I focused on Michelle. "Are you okay?"

"I'm fine." Michelle smiled at me. "Thank you."

I smiled back before standing up and offering her my hand, which she took, allowing me to pull her up. Once she was standing, I took a look at my weapon and grimaced. The metal was beginning to melt. I'd have to spend several hours with a whetstone smoothing it out and sharpening it, but that was only a temporary solution. I'd eventually have to buy a new sword.

Adina was already in the process of piling up the bodies. We would need to burn them, not only to hide what happened here, but also because people who died in Midgard became infected with whatever dark magic permeated this land. If they weren't cremated, they would become draugrs like the ones we fought in those ruins.

While she did that, I wandered over to the leader of this group. He was still alive and just waking up. A groan escaped his lips as his eyes fluttered. Before he could fully come to, I stomped on his face so hard it created an imprint in the ground. It also knocked him out again.

"Let's take him with us," I decided. "We already know he was sent here by Randy, but we need to know more before we can make any plans against him."

"I agree," Adina said with a nod.

"I am not fond of taking prisoners," Michelle sighed. "But I do agree with you. We need information if we want to confront Randy."

We didn't have any rope on us, so I stripped some of the men we'd fought of their clothes, turned it into a makeshift rope, and bound his arms and legs. I also covered his mouth with cloth as a makeshift gag. I didn't want him screaming if he woke up before we arrived at our ship.

CHAPTER 7

Reaching our ship required using a small boat to row across the lake. Our ship was located in the center of the small lake. We had hidden a tiny raft within some bushes so no one would discover it.

Getting to the ship was harder than leaving because of our new cargo—the man who had attacked us—but we made do. After climbing aboard, I had Adina tie the man against the mast with several ropes. Now bound up, we waited for him to awaken.

It didn't take too long.

"Ugh… what… where…?"

"I'm glad you're finally awake," I said to the still groggy man.

"You…" The man stared at me for several seconds before his eyes widened. "You fucking bastard! Let me out of here! Untie me right now so I can fucking kill you!"

"Why would I untie someone who wanted to kill me?" I asked with a sigh. "Are you stupid?"

People who found themselves captured always fell into one of three categories. There were the ones who became frightened, promising to do whatever their capturer wanted in exchange for their freedom. Then there were the belligerent types who acted arrogant and violent. They threatened their captors with death and spewed insults. Last among them were the ones who kept silent and observed the situation before acting.

I liked to think I was the third one, but this man was definitely the second type.

"You fucking shitstain! You think this fucking rope is going to hold me?! I'm a level 65 Ranger, fucker! I can break these ropes no problem, and when I do, I'm gonna cut your fucking legs and arms off, and then I'm gonna force you to watch as I rape those—"

"Shut up."

Blood shot from his mouth as I stomped on his face. It wasn't hard enough to knock him out, but he'd definitely get a concussion since his head knocked back against the mast. The loud cracking noise was satisfying. But it wasn't enough. Because I was angry, I dug my boot into his face, feeling only a little satisfied as the man whimpered.

"Every time you talk out of turn, I'm going to hurt you. A lot. You'd better think about your words carefully."

"Fuck you!!!" the man screamed. "You think I'm fucking afraid of a little bitch like you?! You're just a fucking pansy! Once I'm outta this rope, I'm gonna—"

Stomp!

"G-Goddamn it! Don't fucking stomp on me like—"

Stomp!

"S-shit… you think I'm gonna fucking put up with—"

Stomp!

Every time this man said something vulgar—which was basically every time he opened his mouth—I stomped on his face. The first attack merely drew blood. The second broke his nose. My third stomp knocked out several teeth. Bruises soon began forming on his skin after my fifth time stomping on his face. One of them had formed over his left eye, nearly covering it entirely.

It wasn't until I had stomped on him ten times that he grew quiet. Even if he was a hardass and stubborn, there was only so much pain a person could take before they would do anything to make it stop. Had Meliperum tortured me enough times back when she had imprisoned me, I would have broken too.

This man was not a soldier like me, had not gone through the training to resist torture and interrogation that I had, so his threshold for pain was much smaller. All it took was slamming my foot into his face ten times.

"So, you about ready to answer my questions?" I asked, kneeling so he and I were face to face. "If not, I could always begin actually torturing you."

The man was quiet for a time, but he eventually spoke, though it was not the words I wanted to hear.

"I ain't telling you shit."

"I see. That is unfortunate."

I stood back up and turned to Adina and Michelle, asking them to leave this man to me. Neither of them looked very pleased. However, I didn't want them to see what I was about to do.

While I had been mostly trained to resist torture, that didn't mean I couldn't apply everything I'd learned on resisting to inflict torture onto others. We didn't have a whole lot of time on our hands. I wanted to head back to Valhalla soon, so my options were a bit limited, but I didn't think I'd need more advanced torture methods for this man.

Since he already said he wouldn't talk, I decided not to hold back, activating Fireblade and impaling him through the shoulder. A scream tore from his throat. He tried to thrash, but there was no way he could with his body bound like that. The most he could do was kick his legs, for all the good that did him.

I waited for ten seconds before removing the sword. The wound had cauterized. The scent of burning flesh filled the air, but I didn't wrinkle my nose or give any hint that I was uncomfortable with the smell.

"Ready to talk now?" I asked.

"Ha… ha… fuck… I don't get fucking paid enough for this…"

"What was that? Did you just say 'stab me again because I haven't learned my lesson'? Well, if you insist."

"I'll talk! I'll fucking talk!"

It was just like I thought. This man was no soldier, no warrior. That could only mean one thing.

"First, are you from Earth?"

My question caught the man off guard. He stared at me in shock, but then seemed to realize something.

"Fuck, you too? Yeah, I'm fucking from Earth. What of it?"

"How did you get here?" I asked.

The man was silent for a moment, but he began singing when I moved my sword. "A-a friend of mine got his hands on some swanky VR systems! He said they could take us to a magical place where we could be lords! Where we could rule the entire universe! And he was right. With our high levels, we were kings… or we should have been." He glared at me as if suggesting that it was my fault he wasn't a king.

I moved onto the next question. "And is the one who bought those VR systems Randy Sexton?"

"Th-that's right. He bought several dozen VR systems for us all to use. Heh. Randy's a pretty rich dude. The man's got so much fucking money, he doesn't know what to do with it all."

"I see."

So Randy was a man who was rich on Earth, bought some virtual reality systems like the one Brad used to bring us into the Rift Plains, and now he and his group were here in Valhalla. That did make me wonder how many people had entered the Rift Plains through this method. Also, how was the rest of the world, my world, responding to all this?

"Tell me about Randy's forces," I ordered. "How many are there? Are they all from Earth?"

The man looked like he was about to get stubborn, but then he eyed the blade. Despite having stabbed him, the sword wasn't dripping with his blood, but that was because Fireblade cauterized all wounds and caused blood to evaporate.

"N-not all of them are from Earth. The dwarf and elf who were with me were natives to this plain. We have around a hundred that come from Yggdrasil, but the rest of us are from Earth."

"And how many are there in total?" I asked.

The man licked his lips. "I don't got exact numbers... but it's probably something like a thousand people."

So Randy's forces was a thousand strong mercenary unit? That wasn't good. I didn't think there was any way Adina, Michelle, and I could defeat a force that strong, even if we added the still absent Christine. That meant we couldn't just launch a frontal assault. It would be suicide.

"Do you know how strong everyone is?" I asked.

The man shook his head. "I think most of us are around level 50 and 60, but some of his stronger members are even higher. I know his Four Generals are all at level 80, but that's about it."

I nodded and thought about what he was telling me. Level 80 meant they were close to the level Michelle and Adina were at, and there were four of them. That was not good. While I was confident in our combat prowess, I wasn't so overconfident that I thought we could defeat four level 80 individuals on our own. We'd have to take them down one by one.

"What about Randy? What level is he at?"

"No one knows," the man admitted. "But everyone believes his level is higher than his generals. Rumor has it he's at level 90."

I sucked in a deep breath. Level 90 was the same level that Lilith was at, meaning we could not defeat him right now even if he wanted to.

I rubbed my forehead and tried to think about what our next step should be. I felt like we couldn't just this leave this Randy to his own devices, but we also lacked the strength to deal with this ourselves. Should we get the Valkyries involved? I didn't know if they would be willing to aid us, especially since we didn't really have proof of Randy's wrongdoings. Not even bringing this man to Brynhildr would yield results since we couldn't just go off the word of a man who randomly attacked us in Midgard.

In short, we might have to wait for him to make a move before we could move ourselves.

I didn't like this.

Not one bit.

***

Because I wasn't the kind of cold-blooded murderer who could kill someone no longer capable of defending themselves, I decided to take this man to the Valkyries and have them deal with him. After docking our ship, we led the man, now bound in chains instead of rope, off our ship and toward the Hall of Warriors.

We got many strange looks from the citizens of Valhalla. I was sure it wasn't every day people saw a group leading a chained man through the streets. In all the time I had been living here, this hadn't happened at least. Valhalla was traditionally well-run and the city's crime rate was low. There probably weren't many people who'd cause enough trouble to be bound like this.

The Hall of Warriors was crowded when we arrived, the hustle and bustle of life filling the interior, but our appearance caused enough of a stir that one of the Valkyries came up to inquire about the man who was bound. He, of course, could not talk because I'd shoved some cloth in his mouth. I did all the talking.

"This man led a group of mercenaries to attack us while we were in Midgard," I explained. "We're not sure what he wanted, but I believe he was hired by someone to kill us."

"Is that so?" The woman looked at the man, her eyes sharp enough to make our prisoner look away, then glanced back at me. "I understand. If you'll hand him over to us, we can deal with him."

"Thank you," I said.

Once we handed the prisoner off to the Valkyrie, Adina, Michelle, and I left for our home. We were tired from our training on Midgard, the ambush, and really wanted to relax. Of course, a hot bath would also be nice.

When we arrived home, however, we discovered that someone who hadn't been around for over a month now had returned.

"Welcome home, you three," Christine said as she walked into the entrance hall.

Christine Douval was a woman with short blonde hair and boobs bigger than her head. Okay. That was an exaggeration, but they were still really large, easily the largest among the three women I lived with.

Her skin had a light orange tint to it that gave her a somewhat alien vibe, and her eyes were a glowing green with no sclera.

At the moment, Christine was wearing plain clothes. The booty shorts were so small her asscheeks were hanging out, her sleeveless shirt showed off her muscular stomach, and her breasts were straining against the fabric. I worried it might tear and cause her chest to burst free, though the thought of her boobs springing out was not the least bit unpleasant. She wasn't wearing shoes.

Between the three women, Christine was definitely the most fit. Adina might have the strength to destroy boulders with a single punch, but her body still retained the softness of a woman. Christine's body was all muscle. Her stomach had abs even more defined than my own, her arms were covered in hard muscles, and even her lower back, shoulder blades, and legs looked like something I'd see on a bodybuilder.

"Christine," I said in surprise.

I planned on saying more, like asking when she got back, but she pounced on me before I could speak again. My arms were pinned to my sides as she hugged me. Her lips hampered mine, making it impossible to speak.

Someone whistled behind me. It was probably Adina. Michelle wasn't the type to whistle or catcall like that.

While Christine's body was covered in powerful muscles, her lips were just as soft as any woman's, and I couldn't say I didn't enjoy the enthusiasm of her kiss… or the way she manhandled me. It was different than how Adina and Michelle treated me. I know I technically had a harem, but there were times I felt like the three of us were actually part of this woman's harem.

"How long are you planning to kiss him?!" Michelle demanded to know.

Christine grinned as she pulled back, let go of me, and looked at Michelle. "I'm sorry. Did you also want a kiss?"

"D-don't be ridiculous!" Michelle shouted scornfully, her cheeks burning with either anger or embarrassment, or both. "I would never want to kiss another woman!"

"I want a kiss!" Adina raised her hand like she was a student in a classroom.

"All right." Christine grinned. "Come here, you."

While Michelle scowled and looked away, I had no trouble watching as Christine pulled the succubus into a passionate kiss. It was a mesmerizing sight. Adina and Christine were holding each other close, bust to bust, their hips pressed together as though they might start grinding against each other. Christine grabbed a handful of Adina's butt as they kissed, which made the succubus moan into her mouth. I was witness to how Christine slipped her tongue inside of the succubus' mouth and began ravaging her.

"This is immoral!" Michelle screamed.

I kind of agreed. I mean, I could see where Michelle was coming from. Gay relationships were, from my understand, a sin according to the Bible. At the same time, I was a guy. Seeing two gorgeous women making out aroused me too much to care about sin. I also wasn't religious enough to care.

Fortunately for Michelle's peace of mind, Adina's and Christine's kiss didn't last any longer than mine, and I was certain the "show" they put on had also been for my benefit. Once our greetings were done, the four of us adjourned to the living room.

"So when did you get back?" I asked Christine as the four of us sat together.

The living room contained two couches and a coffee table. There was also a fireplace situated against the far wall. It was currently crackling merrily with a fire that warmed up the entire room. Our group was sitting on the couch. I sat with Michelle, while Adina and Christine sat together on the other couch.

"Yesterday," she answered, crossing one leg over the other. "I arrived home early in the afternoon, but none of you were here, so I've been bored out of my mind."

"If you're back, does that mean… you found out something about my home?" asked Michelle.

Christine shook her head, which made Michelle's shoulders droop, but the woman's next words caused hope to swell within the archangel's eyes.

"While I didn't discover anything about your home, I did find someone who can point us in the right direction."

"Who?" asked Adina.

"A man known as the Information Broker," Christine answered. "He's a strange man who never reveals himself to others, so nobody knows what he looks like. However, this man has a large-scale information network that spans across several different realms in the Rift Plain."

"So he deals in trading information?" I asked.

"That's right." Nodding, Christine crossed her right leg over her left, bouncing her bare foot up and down as she spoke. "I don't know if he has any information on your Heaven, but if anyone in the Rift Plains knows about your realm, then it would be him."

I wondered who the Information Broker was. Was he a person from Earth who had somehow managed to establish a wide-scale information network, or was he someone from one of the many realms out there who had decided to take advantage of his new situation?

"If he never reveals himself to others, how do we get any information from him? How do we contact him?" asked Adina.

Christine shook her head. "That's the tricky part. We don't contact him. He contacts us."

"I'm not sure I understand," I admitted.

"It's a bit hard to explain..." Christine paused for a moment, closed her eyes as if reviewing the information in her head, and opened them again. "First of all, the Information Broker never meets with anyone. He does everything through intermediaries who basically act as his mouthpieces. I'm not sure how, but he has an odd way of knowing when people are looking for him, and he only sends his intermediaries to people he thinks he can benefit from."

"So he contacts people who are looking for him through other people, and then has them pay him for information?" I asked for clarification.

"That's more or less how it goes, yes." Christine nodded once. "However, the payments he asks for are not in any form of currency. From my understanding, he usually asks for a favor. The person I spoke to was someone who had been contacted by the Information Broker because he was looking for his lost child. The Information Broker had him deliver a parcel of some kind to someone living in a different Yggdrasil."

A different Yggdrasil, meaning an Yggdrasil that was not the one we were currently living in. Just how many Yggdrasils, Heavens, and Hells existed in the Rift Plains was something I was unaware of. It sometimes felt like there were hundreds of thousands, or maybe even millions, of realms based on the same mythology, all of them slightly different from the others.

"Then where should we go to meet with one of the Information Broker's middle men?" I asked.

"A space station," Christine said.

"A… a space station?" I parroted with what I was sure was a surprised gawk. "Like… a station sitting in outer space?"

"Yes," Christine answered with a vague but amused smile.

While I was gawking in surprise, Adina and Michelle merely looked confused. Space was a non-existent concept for them. Neither of them grew up on science fiction stories about people sailing through the stars in ships that could travel faster than light like we had. I wished I could explain it to them, but I honestly wasn't sure how to explain the concept of space to someone who'd never heard of it before.

The idea that there was a realm out there that didn't exist based on a pre-existing mythology was something I found odd, but I guessed the Rift Plains were just like that. Maybe it didn't take mythology into account so much as concepts.

Yggdrasil was founded on concepts found in Norse mythology, but it wasn't like the Yggdrasil we lived in was the one from Norse myth. It was just a loosely based replica—no, it was not even a replica. There was only one Yggdrasil in Norse mythology, but there were hundreds or even thousands of Yggdrasils in the Rift Plains.

Taking that into account, this could mean any concept that existed within the collective mind of humanity existed within the Rift Plains. There was still so much I didn't know about it. I'd probably never discover what exactly the Rift Plains were.

"I'm guessing there is a rift that will take us there?" I asked, swallowing hard.

"You guessed right," Christine said. "The rift is about one month's travel from here. It will require us going back to the Rift Plains, traveling several thousand kilometers across it, and finding the appropriate Rift. I marked the one we can use to get there on a map, so there are no worries there."

We spoke for a little while longer, and it was decided we would gather some supplies tomorrow and leave the next day. I only hoped we would find the information we were looking for on this space station.

✳✳✳

Our revenge on Randy Sexton would have to be put on hold. The day after Christine arrived was spent shopping for supplies. Our journey was going to be a long one, and while we'd be able to bring our ship through the Rift with us, that would only cut our travel time down by maybe two weeks. Ships like ours could travel at the same speed as a horse. They weren't like plains in my world, which traveled a couple hundred miles per hour.

Valhalla fortunately had a wide selection of shops, everything from clothing stores to apothecaries. There was even a newer shop that sold guns. I guessed someone from a more advanced realm had come here and set the store up. It looked like that particular shop had quite a few patrons too.

The store we spent the most time in was the apothecary. Health and mana potions were the bread and butter for magic wielding warriors like ourselves. We bought a total of one thousand health potions and another one thousand mana potions.

Food was another item we needed an abundant supply of. We didn't know how long we would be gone, nor did we know if there would be any place to restock our supplies during the journey, but since it would take at least two or three weeks minimum to reach the appropriate Rift, we bought enough food to last for one month. We believed that would be enough food to last the trip to the space station.

Most of the food we bought was stuff that could easily be stored for long periods of time like dried meat, but since we did have a cargo hold that put items in stasis, we also bought fresher meat and some spices that could be used to create various dishes. The dried meats were our emergency rations in case something went wrong during our journey and we found ourselves without food.

Another thing we needed was weapon and armor maintenance. This included whetstones, cleaning oil, scrubs, and rags. I also wanted to get a weapon that would last longer than the traditional sword. The one I already had was nearing its end, covered in dings, scratches, and somewhat melted.

Swords weren't really made to withstand intense fire.

"Do you have any magic swords?" I asked the weapon shop owner, a beefy man with a thick neck. He didn't look at all like a blacksmith with his incredible girth, but I knew he was considered one of the better blacksmiths in town.

"I do have a few magic swords. I even have one legendary sword. But let me warn you, boy, these swords are expensive," he said. "Not just anyone can afford them. If you don't have the money, I can't help you."

Thanks to all the hunting we did, I wasn't strapped for cash, and I'd made sure to save up money for the past six months so I could buy a stronger sword. I was sure I had enough. I hoped I had enough.

"How much do they cost?"

"The legendary sword Dainsleif is a cursed sword made by the dwarves. Once drawn, it must kill someone before being returned to its sheath. A single swing from this sword will never fail to kill someone and even a scratch will cause a wound that can never heal. The cost of this legendary weapon is 50,000 eyrir."

I nearly flinched at the number. 50,000 eyrir?! My house didn't cost even a fifth of that! This kind of price was a complete rip-off, at least in my mind. Maybe there were some people out there who'd be fine paying that much for a magical cursed sword, but I was not one of those people.

"And how much are the magic swords?" I asked.

"Depends on the sword," he admitted. "I've got several."

"I want one with an immunity to fire," I said.

"I do have one of those. Hold on for just a moment."

The big man went into the backroom and came back after several minutes with a double-bladed sword made from a type of red metal. The surface was glossy and smooth. I could see my reflection in the sword's surface as he presented it to me. Aside from the red metal used for the blade, the crossguard was made to look like flames. It was about the size of a standard broadsword, maybe a little bigger.

"This here is the Meteorite Sword," the man said. "It got its name because the sword was forged from a strange material found inside of a meteor that struck the ground the gods know how many years ago. This material can absorb and amplify fire magic. It's also very sharp. While it can't cut through everything, there are very few materials outside of mithril that can withstand a swing from it."

I was already interested in buying this weapon. Having spent so many months around swords now, I could tell when a weapon was good, and the one this man was holding in his hands was probably the best sword I'd ever seen.

"How much?" I asked.

"20,000."

The reply was immediate, and I grimaced at the cost. So even a non-legendary weapon like this one was stupid expensive.

"If you don't have the money, then don't bother," the shop owner said.

"I have the money!" I snapped. "I just don't know if it's worth that much."

"Don't know if it's worth that much? Ha! This is one of the best weapons in my store! Do you think I'd give it such a high price if it wasn't worth that much?"

"I… I guess not."

"Listen here, boy. A great warrior needs a great weapon, and there's no better weapon for a magical swordsman with a red element than this sword. It's fine if you don't got the money, but if you're a powerful warrior, then you're gonna need a sword like this eventually."

Listening to the man speak made me feel more and more like I needed to get this sword. It was true. I really did need a good weapon. All my previous weapons melted after a couple dozen battles. It was impossible to maintain a sword if it melted down to the hilt. This magic sword would go a long way toward fixing this problem.

"I don't know…"

"What is there to think about? You don't want it? Fine. I'm sure someone else will come along and buy this from me."

The shop owner turned around and began walking toward the backroom where this sword was stored. I bit my lip. Could I really just leave like this without getting a proper weapon? No. No, I could not. I needed something.

So I bought the sword.

CHAPTER 8

"Ha ha ha! I can't believe you bought that sword just because a shop owner said you would need one!"

"Sh-shut up! It's true that I needed a better sword! All the ones I've been using keep melting on me!"

I came home after shopping for supplies and showed my new sword to Adina, Christine, and Michelle. It wasn't like I expected them to be excited for me or anything, but, you know, I hadn't quite expected the reaction I got. Namely, I didn't expect Christine to begin laughing at me.

At present, Christine was on the floor, her arms wrapped around her stomach, legs kicking in the air… laughing. She was laughing so hard tears came to her eyes. I wanted to scowl at her, but I was so embarrassed that I didn't think a scowl would do anything.

Adina and Michelle weren't making me feel any better. They were giving me these pitying smiles like I'd just been duped. I didn't need any pity.

"W-well… that is true." Christine snorted as she sat up, wiping the tears of mirth from her cheeks. The grin on her face wouldn't go away. "But, you know, you could just buy a mithril sword. Those are expensive, but they aren't half as costly as a magic sword, and they are still made from one of the strongest metals in all the realms. Buying a magical sword is just going overboard."

"Ugh…"

Thinking about what she said made me realize that she was correct. It was wasteful to buy a magic sword when I didn't have a need for one. The shop owner had made it sound like I needed to buy this sword, like not buying it now while I had the chance could lead to some dangers somewhere down the road. Now that I was really thinking about it, a mithril sword would have done just as well. Hadn't my last weapon when I was using an avatar been a mithril sword?

"Well, what's done is done," Michelle said as if that would settle this issue. "While I agree that it might be a tad wasteful, it is also true that you needed a good sword. You've already gone through several normal swords. To be perfectly frank, I am surprised you haven't considered buying a better weapon until now."

I sighed as I sat down on the couch beside Adina, who immediately cuddled into my side. Her warm body was pleasant, the somewhat spicy scent coming from her mind-addling, and I couldn't stop the instinct to wrap my arm around her shoulder and pull her closer. I also took guilty pleasure in the way her magnificent bosom pressed into me. She was quite squishy.

"I had thought about it when we first arrived in Valhalla… but we didn't have enough money at the time." I ran my free hand through my hair and released a slow breath. "While a number of our living expenses were made easier thanks to you, we still needed to pay for a lot. Food, clothing, armor, and the docking fees. I bought normal steel swords because they're cheap. I guess it just became a habit. By the time we had the money to buy a better sword, I never thought about it."

"I guess that's what happens when you become used to something," Adina said from her place in my side. She was rubbing my chest through my clothes, and it felt quite pleasant. "I think I once heard someone say it takes thirty days to form a habit, and once the habit is there, it's hard to break. Speaking of, I've also formed a bad habit."

"What's that?" I asked.

"It's a sex addiction habit," Adina said with utmost seriousness. "Specifically, a threesome habit."

"Not this again," Michelle groaned.

"Yes, this again." Adina stuck her tongue out at Michelle.

"You haven't even had a threesome in months," Michelle fired back. "If anything, you kicked the habit already."

"Then I want to form it again." Adina pouted as she reached down to my pants and rubbed me through them. "What do you say, Bryan? Let's have a threesome tonight? Please? It's been so long, and the last one was amazing. We could even make it a foursome if a certain archangel is interested."

"Absolutely not," Michelle said sternly, arms crossed. "If you are going to have a threesome, then you may count me out. I have already… broken quite a few of Heaven's laws, and while I do not regret it, there are some things I just won't do. Have your threesome if you wish, but leave me out of it."

I thought back to when we had first moved to Valhalla. Back then, Christine hadn't quite been a part of our group, though she did help us a great deal. I couldn't quite remember when she joined us. It might have been when Adina and I caught her masturbating while peeping on us having sex.

At some point, Adina had convinced her to join us in bed… or maybe Christine had convinced Adina? I was never clear on that, but either way, I still remembered the first night we had a threesome. It had been stimulating, passionate, and probably one of the best nights of my life. I'd been exhausted afterward, completely spent, but it had been worth it. So worth it.

"Well, I don't mind if Christine doesn't," I said, looking at the woman as she finally picked herself off the floor.

"You know I never have a problem bedding you two." Christine licked her lips as she sat on the couch with Michelle, who scooted away like the woman had germs. "That said, we should probably get all the important matters out of the way first."

After saying this, Christine pulled a map out of a satchel she was carrying with her, unrolling the map and setting it on the coffee table in front of us. The parchment looked brand new, the ink fresh. Many parts of the map was missing, but that wasn't because this was an incomplete map. It was because no one had explored those areas yet.

This was the most current map of the Rift Plains.

"This is the rift that leads to Valhalla," Christine said, pointing at a spot on the map. "We're going to be traveling this way, through the Rusty Mountains, past the Desert of Snakes, and up to Blue Haven." She dragged her finger across the map, taking it through a mountain range, a desert, and then a port town at the end of the desert. "The rift that leads to Station 13—that's the space station we'll appear on—is right around here." She pointed at a spot on the map that was about two or three kilometers from Blue Haven. "It's located in the sky, so we'll have to fly through the rift like we do when entering Valhalla."

Rifts could form anywhere. On land. In the sky. Under the ground. Under the ocean. Every day new rifts were being discovered by a variety of explorers from both Earth and the various realms that had begun appearing. It was both exciting and scary to think about, especially since there were many hostile races that wanted to invade Earth.

"And the trip will take three weeks?" I asked.

"Three weeks minimum." Christine shrugged. "It could take longer… like if we get attacked on the way and our ship is damaged, we'll have to repair the ship. Depending on where we land, we might even have to trek across the Rift Plains to a town or something. Did I tell you? Several Earthlings like us have created towns in the Rift Plains now. They're being turned into fortifications against invasions from other realms."

"I was aware," I confirmed.

The numerous hostile forces threatening to invade Earth had instigated a few of the more renown Earthlings to create defensive measures against invasion. I didn't know much about that since I was busy helping Adina and Michelle fulfill their tasks. I wondered if Brad was a part of those defensive measures?

Well, either way, I was hoping this would be a smooth journey.

✳✳✳

As the night wore on, our group of four traveled into our bedrooms.

Michelle, already knowing what was in store for me, traveled into one of the unused bedrooms. The last I saw of her, the angelic woman was huffing at us with a bit of disdain in her eyes. And perhaps a bit of melancholy.

I was the last one to enter the master bedroom. From the moment I shut the door, Adina was on me, ravishing my mouth with her experienced tongue. She'd been a boiling pot of anticipation all night. At this moment, all the desires she'd built up flooded through her, causing her to act on her succubus instincts.

As a man who'd slept with a number of women in my life, I wasn't inexperienced. In fact, I had more experience than Adina, who'd only ever slept with me. That meant nothing in the face of a succubus' natural inclinations. Succubi were creatures of lust and sex. They lived for it. Sex empowered them, and while Adina was slightly different from what I traditionally thought of as a succubus, it did not change what she was.

Her hands slipped underneath my shirt, mapping out the grooves of my abs and chest. I thought I heard her purring as she moaned into my mouth.

A second set of hands undid my belt and pulled down my pants. That was not Adina. Neither was the mouth that suddenly engulfed the head of my cock, or the tongue that flicked my piss slit.

I would have looked down, but I could do nothing as Adina orally ravaged me. Her hands had gone from my chest and stomach to my head, hands making a mess of my hair. I did manage to fondle her breasts, but I was so busy just trying to keep up with her passionate kissing that I could barely do anything else.

Matters weren't helped by the mouth wrapped around my cock. Christine could not deepthroat me like Adina could, but she still had talent. Her experienced tongue worked the underside of my shaft, hand fondling my balls. The warmth of her moist mouth was enough to drive me up the wall.

My end came all too soon, and as I shot my load into Christine's mouth, Adina pulled back and stared up into my eyes, her own lidded with desire.

I fell backward, my back hitting the door. Gasping to catch my breath, I watched as a satisfied Christine stood up, licking her lips.

"Tasty," she murmured.

That wasn't something most women said about a man's cum, which I was told often tasted bitter, but the words were appreciated nonetheless.

"I want some too," Adina said with a pout.

"Don't worry." Christine smiled as she pulled the succubus close. She scooped some of the cum that had gotten on her chest up with a finger and stuck it in Adina's mouth. "I saved some for you."

I think I might have had a mini-orgasm as I watched Adina and Christine share my cum between them. Adina was sucking on Christine's finger with such fervor that my heart skipped several beats. Once she had thoroughly cleaned the woman's finger, she pulled back the woman's button-up shirt, popping the buttons, and dove into her cleavage, licking up the rest of my seed. Christine moaned as she caressed Adina's hair.

Even though this was an amazing sight, I hated that I was the only one not doing anything. That needed to change.

I walked behind Christine, slid my arms around her waist, and undid the buckles for her pants. Like what she did with me, I slid them and her underwear down her legs. Now kneeling, I had a perfect glimpse of the woman's nether lips situated between her firm thighs and below her impressively muscled buttocks. She had larger labia than either Adina or Michelle. That might have been because she was human. Her lips were also puffier.

Leaning over, I pressed my mouth against her cunt and my nose between her asscheeks. Christine released a moan my tongue darted out. I first licked around her outer labia, but I knew that wouldn't do much. What I really needed was to hit her sweet spot. I went for her clit, which was harder to reach from behind than it sounded. It required pressing my face further into her butt. My nose was practically wedged into her ass by now.

It was a good thing Christine was so hygienic.

"Ha… ahn… ha… hrrn! Haaanh!!"

The sound of Christine's cries let me know she was feeling it, and the flood of juices on my tongue let me know she orgasmed. Her powerful thighs shook and even her butt seemed to flex as she came. Part of me was afraid my nose might get crushed, but then she relaxed, and her body fell almost completely limp.

"Whoa there." I caught the woman underneath her armpits before she could fall. "Can't have you falling quite yet. You're still needed."

"Ugh… was that revenge for the blowjob?" asked Christine, her breathing labored and her body covered in sweat.

"I have no idea what you're talking about," I said with a straight face.

"Are we gonna make a Christine sandwich?" asked Adina.

"We are."

I reached around Christine once I was sure she could stand on her own power and placed my hand on Adina's hips. She helped by squishing herself against Christine, until their tits were smashed together, nipples rubbing against each other. It was a wondrous sight. However, I was focusing mostly on rubbing my shaft between Christine's thighs. Her lips were engulfing me in their warmth.

"Are you ready?" I asked as I licked Christine's ear. "You were the one who asked for this."

"Of course I'm ready," Christine whispered in a husky voice. "Give it to me."

"All right. Here it cums."

"That was lame—ahn!"

Christine let out a loud groan as I spread her vaginal lips apart, stuffing her with my cock. Her arms went around Adina, who began making out with her, and giving me a front row seat to their session. The sight of their tongues swirling around each other made me hornier than I'd been in a while. It also spurred me on to start off powerful.

So many sounds were mixed into the music we made. Adina's and Christine's groans accompanied the slapping sound of my hips hitting Christine's toned butt. It was a mighty fine ass, if I did say so myself. Lewd noises echoed from our conjoined hips as I stirred her insides.

Christine was different from Adina and Michelle. Adina felt like I was being lovingly milked by a tender seductress, Michelle was always virginally tight, but Christine... her pussy was like a wall of muscle. I mean, technically, it was a muscle, but she knew how to flex it. Sometimes tight, sometimes soft. It was like she had trained every part of her body and not just the muscles I could see.

Because I didn't want to lose, I added some gyrations to my hip thrusts, and I also may have brought my arms around, stuffed them between her and Adina, and rubbed her clit. Christine screamed into Adina's mouth as her entire body shuddered from head to toes. Once I'd felt her orgasm, I shot my own seed inside of her.

Christine went limp. Adina and I had to catch the woman to keep her from falling. I never said anything, but she was really heavy. All that muscle meant her body probably weighed several times more than a woman of the same height and size.

Because of her weight, Adina and I needed to lift her together to get her to the bed. I got her shoulders and Adina took her feet. We set her on the bed, then gazed at each other and smiled.

"Christine is such a good sport," Adina said.

"She is at that," I agreed.

"I really like her."

"Me too."

"I wish Michelle would join us."

I paused, not quite sure what to say, though I eventually shook my head. "I know you do, but I think we need to respect her wishes. Michelle is still an angel. Having a threesome probably goes against her precepts."

Because I wasn't religious, I didn't really know what the precepts were for Catholicism or Christianity, but I did know the religion practiced monogamy. They did not believe in having multiple partners. Even I was a little leery of polyamory because it was illegal on Earth, but I had slept around a lot, so adapting to the dynamics of this new relationship was easier for me.

"I know." Adina smiled sadly at me. "I don't plan on pushing her. It doesn't stop me from wishing she would join us."

With an indulgent smile on my face, I brought up my hand to caress Adina's cheek. She leaned into it, bringing her hand up as though to keep mine in place as she rubbed her face against it. She reminded me of an abnormally affectionate cat.

"Let's get you out of those clothes," I said.

Removing her clothes was easy. She wore so little that there wasn't much to remove. Once I had her stark naked, Adina removed the rest of my clothes.

Adina was a gorgeous woman by any standards of the word. While everyone had a different standard for beauty, some things were universal, and I believed she fit the definition of universal beauty to a T. Her large breasts sat perkily against her chest, two large hills that fit her proportions perfectly. She had a thin waist that I could wrap my hands around. On the other hand, her hips were wide, and her asscheeks rose to form a perfect heart. Combined with her pure white skin, gorgeous blue eyes, and dark hair, and you had a perfect woman.

The succubus wings, spaded tail, and horns only added to her allure.

"God, you're beautiful."

"I'm not sure you should be talking about 'God' in my presence, but thanks for the compliment."

Adina smiled at me before we were kissing again. Now our bodies were pressed together without the clothes, and I could feel her warm skin, so soft, so perfect, like rubbing against chiffon.

She quickly trapped my dick between her thighs, letting it become wedged in her pussy lips. I groaned into her mouth as I ground my hips. I didn't push myself inside of her, instead building up the anticipation by trying to make this moment last.

We eventually took our activities to the bed. Christine was still a little out of it, but we straddled her body anyway and began making out on top of her. She would come to eventually and join in. She always did.

It was hard to tell which of us grew more impatient first, but one of us eventually snapped, and it wasn't long after this happened that I found myself thrusting inside of her. We were still on top of Christine. It was a little awkward having sex with someone while straddling someone else, but it was also pretty kinky. I think Adina liked that part of this whole affair the most. The kinkiness.

Adina was the first one to orgasm. She cried out and leaned forward as her vagina convulsed around my dick. A flood of juices leaked around my cock and dribbled down her thighs. As her lips sought out mine, I came inside of her, thrusting several times before pulling out.

Even though my dick had grown flaccid, Adina dove down and began licking it like a lollipop, quickly bringing it to full mast again. I wondered if this was some kind of succubus magic. I'd already shot my load three times. However, I was somehow rearing to go again.

"I'm not letting you sleep tonight," Adina said, looking up as she pressed my cock against her cheek and rubbed it.

I groaned, but managed to say, "I'm not sure that's a good thing since we're going on a journey tomorrow."

"Too bad. I need this."

With those words, Adina began deepthroating me. Her throat seemed to expand, or the muscles loosened, as she took all of me into her mouth. I could only stare in awe as she pressed her nose against my hairless pelvis. I actually used to have pubic hair, but the girls didn't like it and told me to shave it.

Christine woke up as Adina began giving me one of her amazing blowjobs. She saw what was happening, spotted Adina fingering herself as she sucked me off, and then raised her head and began licking the succubus' honeypot. It was easy enough for her to reach since it was literally right in her face. This caused Adina to moan around my dick, which further stimulated me. It felt like someone had shot a lightning bolt through my brain. The pleasure was explosive.

I ended up exploding inside of her, but unlike Christine, Adina did not let a drop escape. She pressed her nose back up against my pelvis and let my cum shoot straight down her throat.

"This would have made a good dessert," she commented with a grin after letting me go with a wet pop.

"Would it really?" I asked.

"I think so," Adina said with a nod. "Maybe it's your diet, but it's kinda got this salty sweet flavor."

"Really?" I found this hard to believe.

"Really." Adina nodded, looking quite serious.

I still wasn't sure I believed her, but I did appreciate the sentiment.

With Christine now awake and ready for more, Adina turned around until she and Christine were lying bust to bust, their pussies pressed together. Both of them were covered in sweat as well. The sight of their glistening bodies rubbing against each other would have made any straight man hard. I was no exception.

Since I had just been sexing it up with Adina, I thrust inside of Christine first. The woman's moan was muffled by Adina's mouth. I set a steady pace, mixing fast and slow thrusts, listening to her verbal cues, and then I pulled out. While Christine made a muffled moan of complaint, Adina squealed when I speared her pussy without warning.

I kept at it, switching between Adina and Christine, trying to keep both of them on the edge of a climax for as long as I could. It was harder than it sounded. Their bodies were so different, but oh so stimulating. I wanted to cum more than ever. I think it was only willpower that kept me from shooting my load seconds after we began.

The scent of sex hung heavily in the air. I was sure we'd need to freshen this out tomorrow. For right now, however, it was an addictive scent that made me continued.

Christine was the first to orgasm, and what an orgasm it was. She bucked her hips hard enough to startle Adina, who was nearly thrown off, and her juices squirted from her like a hose. She sprayed my front, particularly my crotch. I didn't mind.

Once Christine settled back onto the bed, I plunged into Adina until she also began shaking as an orgasm rocked her body. That was as long as I could last. With a grunt, I pulled out and thrust my dick between the two, enjoying the sensation of both their pussies as I sprayed my white cum onto their stomachs and chests.

Adina rolled over onto her side, heavy breasts jiggling. She took several gasping breaths before bringing her hand up and rubbing the cum I'd shot into her skin. After a moment, she brought it to her mouth and sucked her fingers clean.

"You're an animal," she complimented.

"Th-thank you…" I said through my pants.

I was exhausted. I loved threesomes, but I wasn't sure I could do this all the time. It might actually kill me.

Adina made some space for me, and I laid down between her and Christine, who immediately nestled herself against me. She was awfully cuddly for such a powerful woman, like a super buff teddy bear. I held her close as Adina set her head on my chest and rubbed my legs with her own. I also felt her tail coil around my thigh.

I wanted to say something, like, you know, "good night" or "I love you," but I think my exhaustion had finally gotten the best of me. With a tired sigh, I shut my eyes and fell asleep.

CHAPTER 9

We began our journey the next day, waking up early, boarding our ship, and setting off. It took a bit longer than normal because Christine wanted to set her ship in the cargo hold. Her ship was a tiny skiff—a one-man vehicle that could travel through the air at higher speeds than our large vessel. It looked like a bird with wooden wings and propellers near the back. The cockpit was but a bulbous protrusion covered in a glass capsule.

Once Christine flew her skiff into the cargo hold via the top entrance, we began our journey.

Flying through the air on what was essentially an old-school boat with wings never failed to be an interesting experience, even six months after coming to Valhalla. The wind in my face, the sky high above, the ground far below. I remembered once thinking the helicopter rides I went on during missions were exciting, but this might actually beat out that experience.

Just a little.

We didn't run into a single problem on the way to the Rift—this time. In the past six months, we'd sometimes get attacked by griffins, harpies, and even dragons if we were unlucky. The dragons were the worst. They had scales harder than tungsten, could breathe fire, and were highly intelligent. Fighting them was always a pain.

It was fortunate we didn't have to deal with one this time.

The rift looked the same as most rifts did. It looked a lot like a ripple in space, or maybe a tear. This particular rift was large and pretty well-known, evident by how other ships were constantly traveling through it. Even now, two ships sailing side by side flew into the rift and disappeared.

"Is everyone ready?" Adina called out. "We're entering the rift!"

No one said anything, but we all braced ourselves.

A sensation like something crawling over my skin came over me as we passed through the rift. It was over in a second, and then the world on the other side lay before us. I wandered over to the bow of the ship with Michelle and looked at the Rift Plains.

"How long has it been since we came here?" I wondered out loud.

"About three months, I believe," Michelle said.

I glanced at the woman standing over half a meter away with a frown. She normally stood much closer, close enough that I could hold her hand or wrap my arm around her waist. That she hadn't meant something was wrong. I fortunately had a good idea as to what that something might be.

"I am sorry," I apologized. "I know you dislike it when we have threesomes."

Michelle looked startled at first, but then her lips trembled, like she wasn't sure whether to smile or look guilty. She eventually settled on guilty. Turning her head, she gazed at the vast Rift Plains as Adina steered us through the air and Christine gave her directions.

"It is true that I do not approve of sleeping with more than one partner at the same time…" she began. "But that's like saying I approve of a man having multiple partners to begin with."

"Do you… think I shouldn't?" I asked carefully.

Michelle bit her lip. "That is a very hard question to answer. As you know, our religion does not allow for polyamorous relationships. They are considered a sin in the eyes of God. Marriage is an intimate connection between a man and woman who pledge themselves to each other under God's watchful eye. However… it's not as if this rule has been followed to the letter by humans. King Solomon, the son of David, had a large harem of a thousand wives and concubines, and many monarchs would have mistresses on the side. They still went to Heaven despite their sin. And also… I like Adina. She's a succubus and we should be enemies, but she's such a pure and honest girl that I cannot help but like her. I do not want you to discard your relationship with her, just like I do not want you to discard our relationship. It does go against the precepts I have always believed in, but this is perhaps the one precept I am willing to break."

I couldn't think of what to say to her words, which I understood to mean she was not only willing to break one of her laws but also that she wanted me to remain with her and Adina. I noticed she said nothing about Christine. While Adina, Michelle, and I had bonded in the First Circle of Hell, Christine came much later. Michelle did not have the same emotional connection to her that she did us.

"The truth is," Michelle continued in a much softer voice, "I am simply jealous."

"Jealous?" I gawked for a moment before recovering enough to ask, "Do you want to have a threesome with us?"

Michelle shook her head. "No, the idea of having a threesome does not appeal to me in the least. I've no desire for it. And yet, I cannot deny that I am jealous all the same." She placed a hand against her chest. "It's awful, isn't it? I don't want to have a threesome with you and Adina, but I also hate the fact that you two are having threesomes without me. I feel... very guilty, I guess, for being so envious."

I think I understood the situation now, or at least some part of it. Smiling, I closed the distance between us and slipped an arm around Michelle's waist before she could move away. She tensed. However, as I pulled her close, her body relaxed and she leaned into me.

"You've never been envious before now, have you?" I asked. Michelle shook her head, causing me to nod. "I thought so. You and the other angels didn't begin to experience emotions like I have until just recently, so it makes sense that you might be feeling guilty about this, that you aren't sure what to do with these feelings. Let me tell you: you have nothing to feel guilty over. What you feel right now is perfectly natural."

"Is it?" Michelle bit her lower lip. "I feel like it's not something I should feel good about, like it's unnatural and may taint me if I keep experiencing it. This jealousy, this envy, it's a very black emotion."

I sometimes forgot that Michelle and Adina had only gained the ability to think for themselves and experience emotions like this recently. Because they had never felt this way before, they did not know how to deal with the emotions they currently felt. Like a child who'd been scolded for the first time by their parents.

Well, Adina might, but she was the type to act first and think never. She didn't have the moral quandaries that Michelle had.

"It might be unnatural for someone who has only gained true sentience recently, but I can assure you that it's a perfectly natural feeling." I looked out at the Rift Plains. We were passing over an open field right now. I could see little specks down below that looked like monsters of some kind. "Being a creature who can think, feel, and make decisions for yourself means experiencing both positive and negative emotions. You take in the good with the bad and accept them for what they are."

It was a bit odd being the one to give Michelle advice. She always seemed so wise and all-knowing, but that only came to certain matters. She could look at most issues objectively and come to her own, usually correct, conclusions, but her own emotions were something she was still muddling through.

"I guess… this is a part of being human." Michelle gave me a sardonic grin.

I smiled back. "Something like that."

We stayed there for a few more minutes, but it wasn't like we could just stand around. There was a lot that needed to get done on a ship this big.

Because we didn't have a full crew, we often had multiple jobs, and while Michelle's was watching for enemies and trouble (like storms) from the crow's nest, mine was cleaning the deck, checking the magic engine, and helping Adina maintain her course. Fortunately, we had Christine with us today, so that task was being performed by her.

I first checked the engine. It was located in the very back, in a room that required me to move past the cargo hold. The engine was not large. In fact, I was not sure I could properly call it an engine. It was more like a magic core placed inside of a cylinder that was attached to the propellers via a cable. The core had a vibrant glow, meaning it had quite a bit of mana stored up. We probably wouldn't have to worry about recharging it for another month or so. Everything seemed in working order, so I left it at that.

I scrubbed the deck afterward. It was backbreaking, mind-numbing labor, but someone had to do it.

Something interesting about the Rift Plain was that it was impossible to tell time in this place. There was no day or night—or rather, it was constantly daytime no matter how much time past. I didn't know how that worked, but it made telling the passage of time difficult.

"How are we looking?" I asked as I walked up to where Adina and Christine were.

Adina had been steering the ship this entire time; her feet stood shoulder width apart, hands on the wheel, a dauntless look on her face. I could tell she was having fun getting into character.

"We're on course," Christine answered. "If we keep going at this speed, we should reach the rift to Station 13 in three weeks. Fortunately, with me and Adina here, we can travel through without stopping."

"Is that safe?" I asked.

Christine shrugged. "Yes. We'll just fly the ship in shifts. Speaking of, I think I'm gonna get some sleep." She glanced at me with a suggestive smile. "Care to join me?"

"So long as we're only sleeping," I said with a serious look on my face. I didn't believe in having sex during a mission—and I didn't count the time I got kidnapped. Those were extenuating circumstances.

"Well, that's no fun," Christine muttered with a sigh.

Despite saying that, she still dragged me into the captain's cabin and used me as a body pillow.

The first few days of our trip were easy enough. While it was difficult to figure out the passage of time because there was no night, that didn't slow down our progress, and it made spotting enemies and trouble easier. If night actually existed in the Rift Plains, our progress might have been slowed. We could not travel if our vision was hampered, after all.

While I spent a lot of my time doing the tasks that were a part of my duty, I also spent a good amount of time sparring with Michelle and Christine. Adina wanted to spar, but she was destructive, so we didn't let her.

Sparring did not increase my level at all, but it was a great way of keeping our skills sharp. I'd been doing this ever since I arrived in Valhalla. Michelle had said it would be a good way to get a better foundation—that while my level was important, it was not everything, and I shouldn't neglect my sword skills. Christine had agreed.

I was not a swordsman by nature. I knew which end of a sword to stick into an enemy. That was all. It was only thanks to my military training, which taught me how to wield a combat knife, that my sword fighting could barely be considered passable. Christine and Michelle were both sword wielders and worked me over, polishing my talent until it shone.

At the moment, Christine and I were in the middle of intense sparring session.

Christine was a far different beast than Michelle. Where Michelle was elegant, Christine was brutal. Where Michelle fought with refined grace, Christine fought with the grace of a barroom brawler. However, while her style might not look as pretty as the archangel's, there was no denying this woman was an incredible combatant.

My breathing had already grown labored as I leapt backward, avoiding the woman's upward swing. I'd already learned not to block her sword. My arms still felt numb from the last time I'd tried that, but constantly retreating also meant I couldn't attack.

Christine came in with several quick slashes that seemed deceptively soft. I didn't need to be a genius to know they were feints, and I was proven right when the woman suddenly attacked with a vicious overhand swing. I avoided it by traveling to the left. Her attack cut through the air, producing a whistling sound.

I thought that would be the end of it, that maybe I'd get a chance to strike back after avoiding her last swing, but then she stomped hard on the ground and used the kinetic energy to swing at me even faster than before. Left with no choice, I angled my blade to block her incoming swing. Sparks flew. My arms shook. Even though it was only a glancing blow, I was still sent stumbling backward.

"You're getting better," Christine said as I straightened. "You can avoid most of my attacks now."

"Th-thank you," I rasped, my shoulders slumping. My body ached. I was more tired after fifteen minutes of sparring with her than I had been after having three hours of sex with her and Adina.

"That bit at the end where you angled your sword to deflect my attack was particularly impressive," she added. "You should remember to fight like that from now on. When you can't dodge an attack, deflecting it so you no longer take the full brunt is often the best method of avoiding injury, especially if your opponent is even stronger than you are."

"I'll remember that," I said.

"Good." With a pleased smile, Christine yawned and stretched her arms above her head. "Ah… it's so good to be able to get some exercise in. Don't you agree?"

"You exercise a lot, huh?" I said.

"Damn right I do." Christine grinned at me. "I used to be a professional bodybuilder back on Earth."

"Really?"

"Really. Did I not tell you that?"

"No, you didn't."

"Oh. Oops. Well, now you know. Pretty cool, right?"

"I don't know that many women bodybuilders, that's for sure."

"Yeah... most women don't want to be ripped like me. A lot of them complain about not wanting bulging muscles or how they could lose their breasts... which is a valid concern."

"And how did you avoid that? Losing your breasts, I mean."

"I think I was just blessed by nature at birth." Christine grinned as she looked down and grabbed her own chest. She squeezed and hefted her tits for me. "Most people think I got implants, but these sweater stuffers are all natural. Of course, there's nothing wrong with getting breast enhancements. I have a number of friends who've done it. I just had no need to."

That explained why this woman was so ripped. I was a former spec-ops in the US military, but I did not have muscles like this woman did.

"I guess that means I should thank nature for giving me such a bountiful harvest," I said. "Or should I thank your parents for that?"

"Thank whoever you want." Christine chuckled. "You know, I like you a lot better than your friend Elric."

I tilted my head. "That came out of nowhere."

"Ah… I guess you wouldn't know, but I've seen him a few times while I was on a mission," Christine said. "He was part of a few teams who'd been traveling to some of the other realms. I was on his team twice."

"How's he doing?" I asked curiously.

"Same as always."

"Constantly hitting on you, then?"

"Yup."

"I'm sorry about that. He's a perv, but I promise you he's harmless."

"Oh, I know that. And he fortunately backed off when I told him I was already in a relationship with you."

"Glad I can become your shield from the unwanted advances of men."

"As you should be. It is quite the honor."

My conversations with Christine were oddly familiar to me. Unlike when I spoke to Adina and Michelle, with her I sometimes felt like I was shooting the shit back with my old military buddies, like I was talking to "one of the guys" and all that… except Christine was a hot babe with muscles on her muscles. Our talks always left me with an odd sense of nostalgia and awkwardness. They were enjoyable, though. I couldn't deny that.

"There's something coming!" Michelle suddenly shouted from the crow's nest. "It's coming from our starboard side! Looks like a roc!"

Christine and I rushed over to the starboard side. Christine brought out a telescope and brought it to her eyes, cursed, and passed it to me. When I looked through the telescope, I understood why she was cursing.

Appearing in the telescope was a bird coming our way. I couldn't tell how big it was, but the fact that I could see it so clearly when I could barely see a speck without the telescope meant it was probably huge. As the bird drew closer, it grew in my field of vision, revealing more features that made identifying it easier.

This creature had the appearance of an eagle, with a body coated in brown feathers, a head of white feathers, and massive, talon-like claws. Its beak was the color of the sun. Meanwhile, vicious red eyes seemed to peer right at us. While I could not judge its size, I wagered it was possibly comparable to our ship.

"Shit," I muttered as I handed the telescope to Christine.

"Shit is right. I can't believe we'd run into something like this. Talk about bad luck."

I studied the ground below and noticed the mountains we were traveling over. We actually weren't far from the peaks. I'd say the nearest peak was maybe twenty kilometers below.

"I guess we entered its territory," I said.

"Maybe, but this creature wasn't here before, which means it probably came from one of the realms. There might be a rift somewhere out here," Christine said.

"Either way, we need to prepare for combat."

✳✳✳

It was unfortunate, but our ship did not have any long-range weapons. Those cost money, and until recently, we did not have the money to buy weapons or have people install them. That meant we would not be weakening this from a distance before engaging in close-range combat.

I was not looking forward to this battle.

You couldn't tell from a distance, but as the roc got closer, it became readily apparent that this thing was massive. It must have had a wingspan of at least 30 meters. Just one of its feathers was at least the size of my torso. With every flap of its wings, powerful gusts of wind blasted our ship and set it rocking.

I already did not enjoy the prospect of fighting this thing.

Christine took the wheel from Adina, who leapt off the ship and spread her wings. She and Michelle closed in on the roc before it could reach our ship.

Michelle raised her hand and summoned golden swords of light that appeared around her as if from thin air. She sent them toward the roc at speeds I could barely follow with my eyes. Because of its massive body, it could not move fast enough to dodge, but that hardly meant it was defenseless. It swept its wings forward. A blast of wind slammed into the swords and forcefully dispersed them like a gust snuffing out a candle.

While Michelle's flashy attack didn't damage the roc, it did prevent the great creature from noticing Adina as she came in and slammed a foot into its underbelly. The creature screeched in anger and pain as it was sent skyward. Its body tumbled in an out-of-control spin, but it righted itself, locked onto Adina, and shot forward, large claws outstretched.

Adina was able to dodge the claw with some impressive aerial maneuvers, but then she was struck by a powerful tornado the roc generated from its beak.

"Adina!!!" I screamed as the tornado slammed into a mountain several kilometers below.

I wanted to jump out of the ship, but I knew that would not be a good idea since I couldn't fly. Sadly, Adina's fall meant Michelle was fighting the creature alone.

The archangel soared through the air with the grace afforded to her species. She dove in close to avoid being hit by its wind attacks and buried her golden sword into its flank, but sadly, the creature's feathers must have been harder than they looked. While her sword broke through, it didn't appear to injure the roc much.

After shaking her off with an impressive bucking maneuver, the roc screeched again, but this time airwaves spread from its mouth. I screamed and grabbed my ears. My brain felt like it was being rattled. Even the boat was vibrating as if it might shake apart at the seams.

Michelle had it worse. She was much closer to the roc than I was. I couldn't see what sort of damage the attack did, but Michelle had no choice but to cover ears, and even that didn't seem to work. Her wings folded on themselves as if they were trying to protect her. However, without her wings, Michelle quickly began plummeting.

And the roc went after her.

"Damn it!!"

I swore as I raced to the opposite side of the ship, ran across the deck, and leapt without hesitation. It was only after I'd jumped that I realized this was a stupid idea.

The wind whipped around me as I soared through the air. I was nowhere near Michelle and the roc, my stomach was flipping around, and I thought I might vomit, but that didn't stop me from straightening my body like a missile and surging forward. I gritted my teeth and fought through the tears as the wind slapped my face and I plummeted down.

After a moment, I activated my ability, Double Jump, and blasted forward even faster. Michelle and the roc were below me now, so I angled myself until I was plummeting nearly headfirst. With a snarl on my mouth, I unsheathed my sword and used Whirlwind Slash behind me to increase my speed.

I reached the roc. My blade tried to slip from my grasp as I reached out and grabbed a handful of its hard feathers. Activating Fireblade, I plunged the weapon into the roc's back. The creature screeched and went into a bizarre aerial maneuver that left me dizzy. The ground and the sky flashed by in an interchanging blur. I thought I was going to be sick, but I forced myself to look for Michelle.

I found her. She was falling several meters away. With a grimace, I kicked off the roc, then quickly used Double Jump to increase my speed again.

I could see her more clearly now. Michelle was unconscious, her body falling fast. At this rate, she'd be a splat on the ground.

Terminal velocity is the maximum velocity attainable by an object as it falls, the constant speed that a freely falling object eventually reached when the resistance of the medium through which it was falling prevented further acceleration. I remembered learning about this in middle school. Technically, I'd forgotten until this moment, but freefalling without a parachute made me remember.

I caught up to Michelle, slamming into her and grabbing her tight. I had no idea what I should do now, however, except maybe die together with her. I had no tricks to play. Jumping off the ship had been stupid, but I didn't know what else I should have done. Adina had been slammed into a mountain, and Michelle was plummeting unconscious to the ground. If I did nothing, she would die.

I looked ahead of us as we fell. It looked like we were falling toward a mountain. Was there anything I could do to slow our descent? Anything that would help us survive this?

I was beginning to feel light-headed. I wasn't sure how high up we were, but the air was so thin that I couldn't breathe, and I was falling, who knew how fast. My vision was fading in and out. Damn it. Now was not the time to pass out!

I think I must have blacked out, because the ground was much closer when I came to. We were still falling, and Michelle was still unconscious. If she woke up, then maybe she could have done something. Shit. What I wouldn't give for a pair of wings. Why didn't magic swordsman have a Wing of Flight special skill?

A thought occurred to me. Maybe I could create an updraft with fire? I remembered another science lesson about how heat rises. It made the molecules in the air move faster… something like that, I think. It was worth a shot.

I was fortunate I hadn't somehow lost my sword when I passed out. It was still in my hands, my grip firm. Trying to ignore the rising sense of panic inside of me, I channeled mana through my sword, activating Fireblade. Flames engulfed the weapon, which I swung down, over and over and over and over. I kept swinging with reckless abandon, and I think it was working. It felt like my speed was slowing down bit by bit, but I also didn't think it would be enough. The ground was maybe a hundred meters below us now.

The ground was covered in a thick layer of snow, which was good. I really hoped the snow would help break our fall… and I also really hoped it wasn't hard snow, because that would be no different from hitting concrete.

My arm was getting tired now. I wasn't thinking straight anymore. I continued swinging my sword, even though the effects of Fireblade had passed and it was just a regular sword now. The ground was still rising to meet us. No. Wait. Did that kind of phrase even work? The ground wasn't rising. We were falling. What would you call that?

I couldn't think of an answer. Seconds before we reached the ground, the world went dark.

CHAPTER 10

I knew I wasn't dead when I woke up. Granted, I wasn't sure what happened to people when they died, but I imagine feeling like your entire body had turned into a bruise wasn't one of them. My aches had aches, and my aches' aches were also aching. Unpleasant was not the word I'd have used to describe how I felt. It didn't even come close to the hellish pain echoing deep within my bones.

Opening my eyes, which was a task in and of itself, the first thing I discovered was an orange ceiling—oh. No, wait. The ceiling wasn't orange, I realized. An orange hue had been cast over the ceiling, but that was because of the fire some half a meter or so to my left. Now that I was waking up more, I could feel the heat on my side and hear the crackle of wood popping.

I wondered where I was. The last thing I remembered was falling to my death—or thinking I had fallen to my death. I didn't think that had been an illusion either. The feeling of the air whistling around me, of passing out from a lack of oxygen, of the ground coming closer with every second—all of it had been so vivid. There was simply no way it could only be my imagination.

Because I wanted to study my surroundings, I tried to sit up, but that turned out to be a mistake. My body groaned in protest. My arms gave out the moment I tried to push myself up. I ended up falling flat on my face, stars exploding in my vision, pain racking my head, causing my brain to rattle.

"It's been a long time since I felt this bad," I muttered. "I don't think I've felt this shitty since being caught by Maliperum."

Since it didn't look like I'd be going anywhere, I decided to just lay there. It was boring. Dreadfully dull. However, it wasn't like I could do anything else.

I wasn't sure how long I waited, but footsteps eventually reached the cave I was in, and I craned my neck to look at who was entering.

Her silver breastplate was dented and dinged. The white clothing underneath it was covered in dirt. However, she walked with her back straight, spine erect, and bearing confident despite not being in the best of shape. Blonde hair cascaded down her head, framing a gorgeous face with two beautiful eyes. She was slender in all the right places, with shapely hips and a modest bust.

She was also carrying a line of fish and a satchel over her shoulder.

"Michelle," I muttered.

"Bryan!"

Michelle dropped the satchel and fish on the floor, forgetting about them as she raced over to me. She knelt at my side and pressed her hands against my face. Tears sprang to her eyes as she stared into mine.

"I'm glad… you're okay," I said with a smile.

"I should be the one saying that," Michelle muttered, tears now pouring down her cheeks. "What possessed you to jump out of the ship like that?"

"You saw?" I asked.

"No, but I can guess. I know you."

"Mmm. Then you should know why I did it." I stared into her eyes without faltering. "I was not gonna leave you to die."

Michelle choked back a sob, but then she smiled and leaned down, pressing her lips together. I sensed her desperation in her kiss, her worry. It probably should have made me feel guilty, but I would have made the same choice over again if given the chance, so guilt was useless.

"Where are we?" I asked once she removed her lips from mine.

"We're in a cave I found underneath the mountain," Michelle said, then extrapolated further. "I woke up just as we were about to crash into the mountainside and managed to adjust our flight. We still hit pretty hard, but we survived. However, the ground collapsed beneath us. This underground cavern is part of a network. Fortunately, there is an underground lake not far from here that has some fish for us, or we might starve to death."

"Good to know. Can you help me sit up please?"

"Just be careful. Don't strain yourself. I healed your wounds, but I cannot heal overused muscles."

Michelle helped me sit up, and I realized my muscles were feeling a little better. I placed my hands behind my back as the archangel went back over to her satchel and fish. I realized the satchel was actually made of reeds. Several twigs rested inside of it.

I watched Michelle as she gutted the fish, stuck them on the twigs, and placed them by the fire to cook. She'd probably never done this back in heaven. Now she was an expert survivalist.

The scent of cooked fish soon caused my stomach to growl. I didn't know how long I'd been out, but it must have been a while. Michelle handed me one of the fish and sat next to me with one of her own. We ate in comfortable silence, neither feeling the need to break it.

I thought about Adina during this time, about how my last sight of her was when she'd been swept up in that tornado and slammed into a mountainside. Was she okay? Had she survived? My blood chilled at the thought of her dying. Adina was a part of me now, a member of my family, and I didn't think I'd want to live in a world where she didn't exist.

"I'm certain Adina is fine," Michelle said with a smile, as if she could read my thoughts. "You know how strong she is. How durable."

"I do," I said in agreement, though just because I agreed didn't mean I wasn't worried. This sense of unease would continue to eat at me until I saw Adina alive and well with my own eyes.

Michelle had caught six fish, and I consumed four of them while she only ate two. I had offered the last one but she claimed to not be hungry. She might have been acting polite to make me feel better about eating it myself, but I did know Michelle was not a big eater, so maybe not.

"I believe we should consider what to do next," I said after a moment of silence.

"I agree." Michelle nodded as she sat with her feet planted on the ground, legs forming a triangle between herself and the floor, arms resting on them. "And I have an idea about what our next move should be."

"Which is?"

"This cave is rather long and twisting. It branches off in many directions. I haven't explored any of them aside from the lake yet, but I am sure one of them will lead to the surface. We just have to find the right one."

"And once we're out, we can see about locating our ship." I nodded slowly. "I'm sure Christine has been circling around this area in the hopes of finding us… though I do hope she hasn't been attacked by that roc again."

Michelle shook her head. "We can't worry about that now. Our first goal has to be getting out of here. We should put everything else out of our minds until we can accomplish it."

"You're right."

"But before we go exploring, you need to heal up, and we could both use more rest."

There was no arguing with a woman when she was right. I was still in bad shape, and while Michelle looked better than me, I could tell from the bags under her eyes that she was exhausted. She must have spent most of her mana healing me. Then she'd gone in search of kindling and wood to build this fire, followed by fishing for food. Lord only knew how exhausted she must be.

I looked around for a place to sleep, but there was nothing present except the hard ground. I made do with the smoothest rock I could find for a pillow. It wasn't going to do my back any favors, but I didn't have much of a choice. Of course, I had no intention of letting Michelle suffer like I was, and so I pulled her into my chest and let use me as a pillow.

"I feel like I should be the one letting you rest on me," Michelle murmured.

"Nope. It's a man's honor and privilege to become his woman's pillow when there is a distinct lack of them in the vicinity."

"Is that how this works?"

"It is."

"Mmm. Well, I suppose if that's how this works, I won't argue." She nuzzled her cheek against my chest and smiled. "You do make a very nice pillow. You're very warm."

"I'm glad I can be of service."

I began running a hand through Michelle's hair, listening as her breathing evened out. Even after she fell asleep, I continued stroking her hair, enjoying the feel of her tresses even though they were greasy and covered in dirt. Despite the pain in my head and neck, it did not take too much longer before I finally fell asleep as well.

✱✱✱

I felt better the next morning, but not by much. The aches from my injuries were gone. Sadly, now I had new aches from sleeping on a hard stone floor and using a rock as a pillow. I wished more than anything for a bed now. I'd even take a pile of straw at this point.

With my body bruised from an uncomfortable sleep, Michelle and I traveled through the cavern. This place was a series of branching underground tunnels that twisted and turned, ascended and descended, with no rhyme or reason. It reminded me a little of the lava tunnels I'd seen as a child, but I didn't think this had formed naturally. The walls were too smooth, too polished. I was certain someone had made this tunnel.

Just what the purpose had been was something I didn't know.

There were monsters in the tunnel. Most of them were level 50 goblins, but there were also a few level 70 ogres. Michelle and I took care of them easily enough. While I was only at level 72, Michelle was at level 85. Her strength alone was enough to kill most of the monsters in this cave.

"I think we're traveling down," I said after a moment.

"We are," Michelle said.

"Are you sure we should be going down?"

"I don't know. I don't even know where we are. However, we can't afford not to explore every region here. Who knows if we might miss our exit because we assumed there was nothing down this way."

"Good point."

We continued traveling. This tunnel was odd. There would occasionally be unusual trees forming from the ground, but they were black instead of brown, like they were made from charcoal. I knew otherwise since Michelle had used them for the fire last night, however.

The tunnel eventually opened into a much larger space, one that was so wide and long I couldn't see the ends. Were we still underneath the mountain? I glanced around as we walked, looking at the dead trees growing from the ground.

"What are these things?" I wondered out loud.

"I'm not sure." Michelle furrowed her brow. "All I know is they're highly flammable and—"

Whatever Michelle had been going to say, she stopped saying it when the earth began rumbling. I also paused and turned my head as the sound of footsteps thundered through the space. We definitely weren't alone.

Michelle and I closed on each other. I pulled my sword from my sheath, while she created a golden sword of light. Standing side by side, our shoulders touching, we watched as something emerged from the darkness. Multiple somethings.

The creatures that came from the darkness were tall, easily towering over Michelle and myself by a good half a meter. Their bodies were covered in fat. Stomachs like jelly rolls wobbled as they walked. Pig-like faces glared at us, their puggish noses snorting, thick jowls quivering. None of these creatures wore clothes. Completely naked, their goods on display, I felt like vomiting at the sight, and Michelle curled her lip in disgust.

"Battle Boars," Michelle murmured.

Battle Boars were a type of humanoid, boar-like monster. They walked on two legs and possessed outstanding strength, but they were also slow and slow-witted. Their lack of intelligence meant they were easy to kill one on one. However, killing them when they were legion like this would be no easy task.

One of the Battle Boars walked over to a tree and grabbed it, thick fingers closing around the trunk before it pulled the thing from the ground. I was astonished to see the trunk transform into a weapon. Now it looked like a massive club.

"Natural weapons?" Michelle gawked. "Just what are these trees?!"

"That's what I'd like to know," I muttered.

There was no more time for conversation. The Battle Boars were all grabbing trees, which transformed into weapons. Several beat their fists against their chest, others roared, and all of them charged toward us like a surge.

Michelle quickly used Dance of a Thousand Blades, creating dozens upon dozens of swords from thin air and launching them at the Battle Boars. Her swords stabbed into the creatures thick hides. Black blood spurt from numerous wounds. Only a few of the Battle Boars fell, however, and the rest continued to charge forward.

Since her attack had softened them, I dashed in front of her and attacked the first one that came in. My blade flashed like a silver streak as I swung it over and over in a relentless barrage. Left. Right. Up. Down. Each swing of my weapon created streaks of light that formed geometric shapes in the air. Ten swings. One hundred swings. One thousand swings. I leapt back after the thousandth swing and watched as the bodies of several Battle Boars fell apart into meaty chunks.

More were coming. It wasn't long before I found myself surrounded.

I bent my knees, held my sword at the ready, and activated Whirlwind Slash. A ripple of energy left my blade and slammed into the Battle Boars surrounding me as I spun a full 360 degrees. I had to ignore the blood spilling from the cuts in their stomachs and used my level gifted strength to leap over the surrounding monsters, twisting my body and slicing through the face of one as I went.

I landed on the ground not far from the encirclement. Turning, my blade ignited as I channeled mana through it, activating Fireblade. I released a battlecry as I charged forward and cut into the back of a Battle Boar, severing its spine. The creature dropped, but this only served to further enrage the others.

Michelle was also fighting not far from me, two golden swords held in both hands as she spun and danced around the Battle Boars attacking her. She was all finesse. Leaping and twirling, she attacked the Battle Boars' weak points instead of just swinging her weapons like I did. One attack slit the throat of an enemy who got too close. She sank her blade into the armpit of another, severing the arm and cutting open a vein so the Battle Boar would bleed out. Each attack came close to being one-hit kills. Sometimes she would miss her target and need to attack again, but her accuracy was such that it rarely happened.

I wasn't sure how many Battle Boars were in this room, but it was large, and they kept coming no matter how many we killed. Despite taking the initiative to attack, I found myself being pushed back by their sheer numbers.

Gritting my teeth, I channeled more mana into my sword. The weapon glowed brightly as I leapt into the air, landed on a Battle Boar's shoulders, and impaled it. Death by Piercing. My sword went straight through the Battle Boar's skull. I pulled my weapon out as the creature tottered back and forth, and leapt off before it plummeted to the ground.

Something appeared in my vision. I ducked just in time to avoid whatever it was, and discovered very quickly that what flew past had been a club. I glared at the Battle Boar who swung at me and darted forward. The creature howled as it raised the club again and swung down, an overhand strike that would bash my skull in, but I sidestepped and moved into its guard, activating Death by Piercing once more to stab my weapon through my enemy's thick hide. As blood leaked from the wound, I pulled the weapon down, opening a large hole in the monster's stomach.

I felt weary as the battle continued, my arms growing tired, my head ringing like someone had struck it. A headache came to me. That was a sign that I'd been using too much mana. Whenever people ran low on mana, they became lethargic. I would have to conserve my mana if I wanted to survive.

Just as this thought crossed my mind, a loud wailing sound echoed around us. It reminded me of something I'd heard a long time ago. It was during a trip to Alaska. We had come across a herd of whales, and they made a sound very similar to this. The Battle Boars all stopped fighting us, looked around in what seemed like fright, and began running away when the noise came again.

Michelle and I stepped closer to each other.

"What do you think that was?" I asked.

"I don't know." Michelle bit her lip. "But whatever made that noise is strong."

I could only agree with her, but I couldn't speak because the earth shook at that moment. We bent our knees to avoid falling. Seconds later, a giant foot emerged from the darkness. It was about the same size as me, shaped kind of like a tree trunk, and clawed at the ends. The foot was followed by a second one, then a third and a fourth as something emerged from the darkness.

The only thing I could think when I saw the creature now standing before us was that it resembled a dinosaur. Its skin was black, it stood on four large legs, and had a long neck with a head that looked vicious and rabid, with a row of sharp teeth. A tail jutted from behind its back, sweeping back and forth. It knocked over dozens of trees without thought. It looked down at us, glowing red eyes containing a malevolence that made me shudder.

"What... is this?" asked Michelle.

"I don't know, but it's coming," I answered.

The creature let out another whale-like roar before stomping toward us. Michelle and I moved out of the way. While I ran, Michelle took to the air, raised her hand, and summoned her numerous golden swords. She sent them at the dinosaur-like monster. I watched in shock as they struck the monster's hide and bounced off. They didn't even leave a mark.

The dinosaur looked in her direction and glared before trying to snap at her, head moving so fast I almost missed it, teeth attempting close around Michelle's leg. She avoided it by soaring backward. Even so, the fact that this thing almost took her leg off was a testament to its speed.

I darted forward, activated Fireblade, and tried to attack this creature's legs. Like Michelle's attacks, my sword bounced harmlessly off the creature's hide. This thing had an incredible defense. It might even have a higher defense than the Trycon.

Before I could attack again, the dinosaur was trying to squash me flat, lifting its feet and bringing them down. I darted out from underneath it and attempted to gain distance. Before I could get far, something fast appeared in my vision like a blur and swatted me in the chest. Vomit and bile spewed from my mouth as pain struck my ribcage. I was thrown back by the force of the attack, hitting the ground hard and rolling across it.

"Bryan!!"

I heard Michelle's shout, but there was nothing I could do to reassure her. I pressed a hand against my chest. It hurt. It felt like my ribs had been crushed by an anvil falling on me.

It took me several seconds before I could move again. I sat up and saw that Michelle was harassing the dinosaur from the air, attempting to keep its attention on her while I recovered. However, it was getting closer to reaching her. I was certain it would eventually take a chunk out of her flesh if something wasn't done soon.

Racing forward, I once more attacked it, this time wary of an attack as I swung my blade hard. Sparks flew as my sword struck a hind leg. It didn't do any damage, but I wasn't worried about that. As my attack struck, the creature finally noticed my presence, and this time I noticed the attack coming for me. It was the tail.

As the tail swung toward me, I leapt into the air, landed on the tail as it passed underneath me, and held on for dear life. My action enraged the beast. Its tail shook fiercely to throw me off, but I wrapped my arms and legs around it and clung on for dear life despite the world around me shaking, my vision growing blurry.

I was eventually flung off when the dinosaur swung its tail upward. I was simply unable to maintain my grip. Now soaring into the air, I could do nothing but wait for myself to fall.

"I've got you!"

Michelle darted forward before I could hit the ground, pulling me into her arms and taking off. The dinosaur released an enraged cry and tried to attack her, but Michelle was faster, flying out of range before it could chomp down on either of us.

"We have to do something," she said. "This thing must have a weakness."

I nodded. Every monster had a weakness, and this one should be no different. The problem was figuring out what that weakness was. Some monsters were weak against a specific element, while others had specific points on the body that were weak. I didn't think this monster had an elemental weakness, which meant…

"Let's go for its eyes," I said at last.

Michelle nodded, having come to the same conclusion. She flew forward as I readied my sword. The dinosaur tried to snap at us, but Michelle pulled up at the last moment, and then let go of me. I landed on the monster's head and swiftly plunged my sword into its left eye. I would have activated Fireblade, but I was almost out of mana.

Black blood spurted from the eye as the Meteor Sword stabbed into it. The dinosaur released a displeased roar of anger and shook its head back and forth. My sword slipped free and I was flung off. I couldn't maintain my grip on my sword and it flew off as I fell, but Michelle swooped in and caught me once more.

"It looks like that worked, but we've only injured it," she said as she flew up. "We need to find a way to finish it."

"I know." I tried to think of something, but my only thought was dealing with this the same way we'd fought the Trycon. "It might be vulnerable inside, but…"

"So you're suggesting we go for the mouth?"

"If attacking its hide doesn't work…" I shrugged.

"Right."

Michelle didn't look eager to attack the inside of its mouth. Neither was I, but it wasn't like we had much of a choice.

Swooping back in, Michelle grabbed the dinosaur's attention by flitting around its head. The creature opened its mouth to snap at us. I focused on its timing, seeing how long it kept its mouth open, how fast it could snap it shut. It looked like we would only have a split second window here. This creature was fast.

Once I felt certain I had its timing down, I waited until it had opened its mouth again.

"Now!" I shouted.

Michelle created a sword of light, swooped forward, and plunged her weapon into the bottom of its mouth. The blade sank in just like I'd expected. A pained wail escaped the creature as it thrashed its head back and forth, stumbling like it was drunk. Michelle didn't wait for an invitation. She created another golden blade, came in, and impaled it through the roof of this creature's mouth. This time, the attack must have penetrated its brain. The dinosaur didn't wail but tumbled to the ground and didn't get back up.

"I think… that did it," she muttered.

"I think so too," I said.

With the dinosaur dead and no Battle Boars in sight, Michelle and I were free to look for my sword and continue on our way. We still had to escape this place.

✳✳✳

While there was no telling how much time we spent in the cavern, we eventually stepped out of it and into the light. I smiled as rays of light shone upon me. We were in a forested area. The scent of wood and earth filled my nose as hundreds of thousands of trees spread out before us. It looked like this cavern entrance was near the base of the mountain, which loomed behind us like a monolith.

"Finally free," I said as I stretched my arms. My bones popped and cracked with satisfying pleasantness. "I'm so glad we're out of there. If we'd stayed any longer, I think I might have become claustrophobic."

"Don't like dark places?" asked Michelle.

"Not really," I admitted.

Places like that cave reminded me of some of the more brutal missions I'd been on. It was better not to think about those memories.

"We should begin moving," Michelle said. "I think we should consider climbing back up this mountain. I'm sure Christine saw where we fell and is searching the surrounding area. It will be easier for her to spot us from up there."

"Let's start hiking then." I looked at the mountain and sighed. "Looks like we're going to have our work cut out for us."

The mountain we'd been traveling up was much larger than many of the surrounding mountains. There wasn't a trail or path leading up the mountain either, so we had no choice but to forge our own path, which meant climbing steep slopes, walking across ledges, and occasionally flying higher when Michelle's wings weren't tired. Since there was no nighttime, I didn't know how long it took to reach the top, but I think we managed to climb up to the peak in less than a day.

I took in a deep breath. The air up here was frigid and thin, making it hard to draw in any oxygen. During my military training, we'd been sent into the mountains for this very reason. Training at a higher altitude helped build our lung capacity.

"I don't see any ships," I said as I looked in the sky.

Michelle frowned. "Neither do I."

"What do you think we should do?"

I waited for Michelle to answer, but she didn't. Her gaze was drawn toward something in the distance, something behind me.

"Brrrrrrryyyyyyyy…"

I heard the noise several seconds after Michelle did and turned around.

"Aaaaaaaannnnnnnnnnn!!!!"

I was just in time to see Adina flying forward before she slammed into me.

"Oooof!"

My lungs were deprived of oxygen as I hit the ground hard, a crying succubus on top of me. Adina was rubbing her tear-covered face against my chest, soaking my clothes.

"Bryan! Bryan! I'm so glad you're okay! I was… I was so worried about you!"

With a sigh, I reached out and began rubbing Adina's head, caressing her hair. She wasn't the only one who was happy. I'd been worried she might have been dead this whole time. Seeing her alive and whole, and looking for us on top of that, made me feel relieved.

"I'm glad you're okay too. I was worried when you got hit with that Roc's attack."

"What happened after we fell?" asked Michelle.

Adina sat up, still straddling my waist, looked at Michelle. "After you and Bryan disappeared into the mountain, Christine and I killed the roc. It was already injured thanks to you two. Then we began searching for you. We couldn't figure out where you were because the area you disappeared into had collapsed. Christine suggested searching for an entrance, but we didn't find anything. I was actually just coming back from the other side of the mountain when you two appeared."

If Adina and Christine managed to kill the roc, then they must have gained a lot of experience points. That roc had nearly beaten all four of us. It must have been at a level close to Asmodeus himself.

Climbing off me, Adina grabbed my hands and helped me stand up. She took a few steps back, wiped her eyes, and smiled at us both.

"I am glad you're both safe. Anyway, Christine is flying around in her skiff. Our ship is parked not far from here. Let me take you there. We can wait for her to return and begin our journey again."

Michelle and I both agreed with her. I was about to start moving, but Adina and Michelle quickly stopped me.

"What is it?" I asked.

"You can't fly," Adina said. "So let me carry you. It will be faster that way."

"I… I guess I could do that," I replied reluctantly.

"What's wrong?" asked Adina, tilting her head.

"N-nothing." I looked away. I couldn't tell her that the idea of being carried around by a woman was embarrassing.

Adina didn't seem to understand what I was thinking, but she shrugged and scooped me into her arms. I felt like a princess being carried off by a gallant prince, or a newlywed bride being carried by her husband. And yes, it was extremely embarrassing.

CHAPTER 11

Blue Haven was a city built in the Rift Plains by people who had come there from Earth. I didn't know who exactly had built it, but I knew why. Protect the rifts that led into the human realm. Perhaps that was why this city had a more modern aesthetic to it than other cities like Valhalla.

All the buildings looked like they had been taken from an urban development plan on Earth; everything from their shape to the materials used in their production came from my old home.

I looked at one building we were walking past. It seemed to be a general store of some kind. The building was made from red and black bricks, with a glass window display for people to peer through without entering, almost as if the owner was trying to entice people before they debated whether or not they should go in. A flat roof made me think there was probably a door leading up to it. I could see several power boxes up top as well, along with what I guessed was an air conditioning unit.

While this building was only one story, there were many that were two, three, and even four-stories tall. There weren't any skyscrapers or exceedingly large buildings. I wasn't sure if that was by design or due to lack of materials. My understanding was that not many people on Earth knew about the Rift Plains—relatively speaking—so those who did may not have been able to bring in enough raw materials and the necessary equipment to build taller buildings.

I also didn't think they needed to. Like I said, there couldn't have been more than maybe a couple thousand people who knew about the Rift Plains.

"Where are we going?" I asked Christine as she led us through the city, though I guess I should call it a town instead. The population didn't seem large enough to call it a city.

"We're going to an inn," Christine said. "I've only been to Station 13 once, so I don't know much about it. There's a chance this will be the last time we can get a good night's rest."

The woman had a point, so none of us questioned her further as she led us into what seemed like a bar. It was a modern-looking place. The outside didn't look much different from any restaurant on earth, and the inside was pretty much identical to any pub I'd visited. Low lighting. An atmosphere that made me think there should have been a lot of people smoking cigarettes as they played pool. There was a bar located in the middle. Several people were already seated at the stools lining the bar and drinking. A number of tall tables were arrayed around the room, and there were also booths. The wooden floor creaked as we entered.

Quite a few heads turned as we walked further into the bar. They studied us for a minute, their focus on Adina, Christine, and Michelle, but they eventually turned away like we weren't worth their time. I was glad for that, as I didn't need any trouble.

There was no one who took us to a seat, so we just sat down where we wanted. The booth we'd chosen was located close to the entrance. Sitting on the table was the standard setup you'd expect from a restaurant. There were menus available, salt and pepper, packets of sugar and sweetener in a jar. I almost felt like I was back on Earth.

"This is one of the few restaurants in the Rift Plains," Christine informed us as she grabbed a menu. "The owner is a friend of mine. He stumbled upon a rift while searching for me. Afterward, he realized there was money to be made and established this restaurant. Since Blue Haven is surrounded by more rifts than normal, it's become a popular stopping point for people."

"All this seems pretty new to me," I mumbled. "I had no idea it was even being built."

"That's because you haven't left Valhalla since you arrived here," Christine said.

"I guess so."

"Hey… I can't read this menu," Adina suddenly said. "What's it say?"

She pointed to a menu on the table in front of her. I leaned over to see what she was pointing at.

"That's a chili cheeseburger," I answered.

"Is that good?" she asked.

"Chili cheeseburgers are delicious," I said.

"For some reason, my heart feels inflamed at the sound of that," Michelle said with a grimace as she placed a hand against her chest like she could already feel the heartburn. "It does not sound pleasant."

"You'll probably want a salad," I told her. "I'd recommend the Italian vinaigrette for you."

"Then that's what I'll get," she said.

We discussed the food a bit more. Adina was curious about everything, partly because she couldn't read it, but also because the menu had pictures. Valhalla did not have anything like this. In fact, most pubs and restaurants in Valhalla did not even have menus. You ate whatever they were making that day, which was often dependent on what the hunters had caught.

Adina ended up going with a jalapeno burger when I told her it was spicy. I, on the other hand, went with chili cheese fries. Michelle chose the Italian vinaigrette and Christine selected a regular double cheeseburger. She was also the one who placed our orders, traveling up to the bar and letting him know what we wanted.

Our meals were delivered in about fifteen minutes, longer than I expected, but I could tell this place was understaffed. There was a window that granted us a view of the kitchen. It looked like there was only one chef working there.

Conversation was a little sparse as we ate. However...

"W-what is thish?! Ish sho deliwishous!"

"Adina! Don't speak with your mouth full!"

"Michelle! Michelle! You have to try this! It might be the most delicious food I've ever had in my entire life!"

"You know I don't like spicy foods, Adina. It's not going to appease me like it does you."

"But…"

"Please don't force your food on me."

Adina was trying to convince Michelle to try her food before she polished it off, but the archangel didn't want anything to do with her friend's jalapeno burger, which was two beef patties, cheese, fried jalapenos, and fried onion rings, all shoved between two buns lathered in a spicy chipotle dressing.

As we enjoyed our meal, another group of people entered the restaurant.

"Goddamn, I am beat. Guess that's what happens when you work hard."

"You? Work hard? Don't joke around with us. You mean hardly working. We all know you barely did anything. I was the one who pulled all the weight on that last mission."

"Sounds like you were having a pleasant dream."

"Shut your face!"

I looked up to see who had walked in; it was a group of men. Judging their age was difficult, but none of them had any gray hairs or wrinkles on their faces. I judged them to be in their early to late twenties. Among them was a familiar face.

He was a good two heads taller than me, with a head of blond hair immaculately combed to one side. His bright blue eyes, trim beard, and powerful physique made him something of a sophisticated pretty boy. Back in the military, this man would always sleep with a variety of women while he was on deployment.

At present, he was wearing high-tech armor that made him look like a space marine getting ready to march into enemy territory. It was black and white, with glowing lines running along the surface. The gun in his hand was a rifle unlike anything I'd seen outside of science fiction. It was large, powerful-looking, and had an alien appearance. He'd probably gotten it from one of the realms he'd been to.

"Elric?" I muttered in shock.

He must have heard me. Elric turned in my direction and froze.

"Bryan?!"

His shout caused his companions to look in our direction, and while some of them looked at me, most of them looked at the company I was with. Elric didn't pay them any mind as he grinned and walked up to us.

"Well, I'll be damned. I didn't expect to run into you after you disappeared on us. Where've you been?" he asked.

"Valhalla. Home of the Norse," I said.

Elric snorted. "Which Valhalla are you talking about now? Also, it's good to see you three are doing well. Adina, Michelle... Christine. Never expected to see you with Bryan too."

"And why wouldn't I be with him?" asked Christine with a dangerous smile. I could sense nothing good from it, but I didn't know what she intended until she opened her mouth again. "We're all sharing a bed now. It's only natural I'd be with him."

"Ha ha ha! Yeah, I know! Bryan, you old dog! I still cannot believe you stole such a beauty right out from underneath my nose!"

Elric laughed and slapped me on the back several times, causing me to grunt. He'd gotten stronger. I didn't know if this was an avatar of his or if he'd traveled through the rift like I had, but he must have had a pretty high level by this point.

"I didn't seduce anyone," I muttered. "It just sort of turned out this way."

"So you say… but isn't this how you ended up sleeping with most of the women back on Earth? It just kind of happened? That's what you usually say." Elric grinned at me. "There's no need to be modest, you stud you."

I sighed and withheld a wry smile. Elric was something of a comrade in arms who had also served in the military with me. That said, I wouldn't call us friends. He was a bit too flamboyant for me to get along with him, and he had this shifty way of talking that made me suspect he had ulterior motives for everything.

I learned that he and his team—the people behind him—had just come back from fighting off an infestation of insectoid monsters trying to break into the Rift Plain. It was part of a joint effort headed by a man calling himself Orthrus. Kinda pretentious of him to name himself after the two-headed dog from Greek mythology. Anyway, there were apparently several dozen other teams like his fighting on that world.

"We're planning to go back. How about it? Wanna tag along?" he asked.

"Sorry, but we have our own mission here," I said.

Elric shrugged. "I figured as much. Well, if you ever change your mind, just stick around here. We all periodically come back when we need a break from the fighting."

"Sure," I said and waved him off.

Elric joined up with his comrades over by the bar. As he left, Michelle decided to satiate her curiosity with a question. "What did he mean when he talked about you seducing women in your old world?"

I glanced over at the archangel to find her frowning at me, her pout somewhat adorable, though I knew now wasn't the time to comment on it. She also seemed to have gotten the wrong idea.

"After Chris died, I tried all kinds of things to avoid the pain that came from thinking about him. Drinking didn't work. Drugs just made it worse. I eventually discovered that sex offered me a temporary reprieve from my nightmares. When I slept next to another warm body, I could forget about how my friend had gotten killed and just enjoy the experience." I could see my words making her angry, so I quickly continued. "But it wasn't like I seduced women out of habit. Whenever I met someone, I'd normally just talk to them, and it would sometimes end with the woman inviting me to her home. I never had a reason to refuse, and it often helped me, so…"

"So you were using sex to run away from your problems," Christine said.

I smiled, but it felt strained. "Pretty much."

"And what about now?" asked a curious Adina. "Are you using us to run from your problems?"

"Of course not." I shook my head. "Thanks to you and Michelle, I've learned to accept that part of my life."

Adina's vibrant smile reminded me of this one character from a cartoon I used to watch. I'd long since forgotten the name of that cartoon, but the heroine was a very naive and innocent girl with a pure and refreshing smile, just like this one.

"I'm glad to hear that," Michelle said, reaching out to place a hand over mine.

"What about me?" asked Christine, pointing to herself.

"You came after they helped me," I said immediately.

"Wow. How harsh."

Adina, Michelle, and I laughed at the petulant pout on Christine's face.

***

We didn't stay in Blue Haven for long, just one night, and then we left early the next morning.

I stood on the bow of the ship as Adina and Christine took turns steering. According to Christine, the rift that would take us to Station 13 wasn't far from Blue Haven, but it was located high in the air.

Knowing that Station 13 was a space station made me wonder whether our ship would be safe. It might have been years since I'd been to school, but even I remembered learning that space was a vacuum containing low density particles, predominantly a plasma of hydrogen and helium, along with electromagnetic radiation, magnetic fields, neutrinos, dust, and cosmic rays. The reason space was dangerous was because our human bodies could not exist for long in a vacuum. If the freezing temperatures didn't kill us, then the lack of oxygen would.

Our ship was not airtight. If we went into space, that was it. We'd be done.

As I worried about this, the rift we planned on traveling through appeared above us. I grabbed hold of something as Adina pulled us into a steep incline. She angled us straight toward the rift and drove through. As we passed, as I felt the tingle from traveling through a rift, I shunted all these worries from my mind.

This was it.

This was the start of our next adventure.

Or it would be a very quick death.

***

The death I had been worrying about never came. On the other side of the portal was a large docking bay made entirely of metal and thick windows that probably weren't made from normal glass. Beyond the windows lay an expanse of stars and a gigantic planet with an asteroid ring like the one around Saturn. Inside the docking bay were ships of all shapes, sizes, and types.

I think what really impressed me were just how many different kinds of ships were present here. There were the ships I'd expected to see, the high-tech ones that were fully enclosed so they could travel through a vacuum, with flashing lights and powerful thrusters, but they were not the only ships present. Several looked like ours. Wooden boats with wings sat between the more science fiction-y ships. There was even one ship that looked like a skiff made of cogs and gears. It was a downright odd sight.

"Wow… look at those ships!" Adina said as she came up alongside me. "What kind of ships are those? They look so weird."

"I couldn't tell you." I shrugged. "But they are definitely more advanced than our own vehicle."

"I'll say. They're so cool."

Our group unloaded from the boarding ramp and came upon a man who'd been standing next to it as though waiting for us to get off. He was rather portly. A large gut hung over his belt and caused his shirt to stretch, but he seemed confident and there was a blaster hanging at his hip. His outfit was kind of rumpled. It reminded me of an old military uniform, though his had been heavily modified.

"Welcome to Station 13. Before I can let you proceed further, I'll need your names, the name of your ship, and you'll have to pay a docking fee of one thousand Republic Credits."

I had no idea what a Republic Credit was.

"If you don't have Republic Credits, we can exchange what you have currently for them, though be warned that any other type of currency is not worth much here," the man continued. I guessed a lot of people who didn't have Republic Credits came through here.

Christine stepped forward and pulled several chits from a pocket in her vest. She was currently dressed in all black; black pants, a black shirt, and a black kevlar vest. Her sword was still strapped to her back, but now she had a pair of blaster pistols holstered on either thigh.

I wanted a weapon like those now.

"This should be enough to cover us," she said.

"Hmm. Yes, this is enough. Now I just need your names and the name of your ship."

Since I was technically the captain (though I never felt like one), I told him our names and the name of our ship. He wrote them down in his tablet. Adina and Michelle looked fascinated by it. They'd never seen this kind of technology before, and while I had since I watched a lot of science fiction movies in my youth, seeing it in real life was odd.

Once our names were in his database, we were allowed to leave. There were several exits leading to other parts of Station 13. Adina, Michelle, and I just followed Christine as she took a lift to the second floor and walked out of a sliding double door.

I soon discovered that this space station was built like a several wheels with spokes extended from them and connected to a massive cylinder in the center. We were on the second to last wheel, which was also the wheel that contained the docking bay. The other wheels contained residential districts, businesses, government facilities, and so on. The reason it was called Station 13 was because there were thirteen wheels.

We walked down a long hallway that was almost entirely transparent. We had to stop when Adina and Michelle turned to stare outside, their eyes wide. Considering their origins, it was doubtful they had ever seen a sight quite like this.

"So beautiful…" Adina murmured.

"I agree. It's very pretty," Michelle said.

"You've never seen this before? Not even in Heaven?" asked Adina.

Michelle shook her head. "Heaven is a paradise amongst the clouds. It is a realm that exists between earth and the cosmos. Of course, we have a great view of the stars, but we do not live among them."

Christine and I let them stare for a while, but we eventually ushered them through a door on the other side, which led into an elevator. I let Christine take complete control. She seemed to know what she was doing as she pressed a button that made the doors shut and the elevator begin moving, much to the shock of Adina and Michelle.

"W-w-what is this?! Are we moving?!"

"I don't think I feel very good anymore. Is it just me, or do the walls appear to be closing in on us?"

Neither of them seemed to enjoy the ride. Adina clung to my arm and Michelle looked like she might have a panic attack. It was fortunate the ride didn't last long. When the door opened, the two of them were quick to rush out, Christine and I following along at a more sedate pace.

"Station 13 is just a small part of this realm," Christine explained to us as we walked down this other tube, which led to Spoke 6. "It serves as a stopping point for people traveling across this realm. There is no central government or unifying authority here, so it's very lawless. It's the perfect place for a person like the Information Broker to do his business."

No central government did not sound good to me. I wondered how the peace was kept, but I guess the only peace to be found here would be through the barrel end of a firearm.

Spoke 6 appeared rundown compared to the docking bay, with rust clinging to the hallways and floor, stains coating some of the buildings, and ragtag people dressed in all manner of filthy outfits.

I'd been expecting it, but the people we passed weren't all human. Some of them had green skin and six eyes, others were nearly ten feet tall and possessed arms and legs that looked as long as I was tall. There was a couple of people walking in one direction with heads that resembled squids. Exiting from a building was a man… no, it was a woman. A woman with a face like a pig, three tits, and hands with fingers two times longer than a human's. I could only see a few humans within this throng of people.

"What a bizarre place," Michelle said as she moved closer to me.

Adina grabbed my arm. "I'm not sure I like this place."

"It's definitely not a place I'd want to live," I agreed. "We're also drawing attention."

Just as everyone around us drew our attention, we had also become the center of attention to everyone we passed. Humans seemed common enough, but it was anyone's guess as to whether these people had seen an archangel and a succubus. Every person we walked by stared after us.

"All the more reason we hurry this up," Christine said as she led us through the crowd. "Come on, you three. My contact told us to meet him at a bar called the Space Cowboy."

"Odd name for a bar," I said.

Christine shrugged. "This is an odd place, in case you couldn't tell."

Our travel was stopped when several people stepped in front of us. They were a mixed race of aliens I'd never seen before, none of them human. As Adina and Michelle moved so they were standing back to back with me, I noticed that they weren't just in front of us; they were on our left and right too.

We were surrounded.

"Can I help you?" asked Christine.

The person who stepped forward was about the same height as me, had long and proportionately thick fingers with an opposable thumb on each hand. His fingers were tipped with talons. While he was humanoid, he did not appear human. A set of mandibles surrounded his mouth, he possessed no hair, and his waist was far thinner than a human's. It looked like he had less ribs than a human too.

"I ain't never seen women like those two before." He pointed at Adina and Michelle. "You humans can go, but those two stay."

It took me a moment to figure out what he wanted, but I soon understood they were basically telling me to leave Adina and Michelle here. You didn't have to be a genius to know what he wanted.

"You don't mind if I do the honors, do you?" I asked Christine.

"Not at all. In fact, if you didn't, I'd be very disappointed in you," Christine said.

I smiled.

"Hey! Are you listening to me?!" the strange alien… whatever he was, shouted. He took a menacing step forward. "Leave those two here and get lost, or I'll—"

Before the man could even finish his sentence, I had pulled my sword from its sheath, channeled mana through my weapon to activate Fireblade, and impaled him through the face. I could already tell showing mercy to this man would just invite an attack later. People like him never let things go, and according to Christine, a lot of people who remained here were criminals anyway.

Someone who would tell me to leave my companions behind was definitely no benevolent saint, that was for sure.

I don't think his companions were expecting me to straight up kill their leader, so it took them a moment to respond. In that time, Adina, Christine, and Michelle attacked them as well.

Adina slammed her fist into the face of a pig-like man. Her attack blasted him off his feet and sent him crashing into a wall, which dented around his body. I couldn't tell if her attack had killed him. Even if it hadn't, he would not be getting up.

Two golden swords appeared in Michelle's hands as she darted forward, spun around, and swung, taking the hand of an insect-like alien who'd been reaching for his blaster. He screamed in pain and stumbled back. Said scream was cut off when she removed his head with a deft stroke of her blade.

Unlike me, Adina, and Michelle, Christine unholstered her blaster pistols and began firing. Red beams blasted from the barrels. Her aim was impeccable, striking her opponents. Not all of them were clean hits. In fact, a lot of them struck the armor covering these people and were harmlessly deflected. Only a few actually brought any of these people down.

I suddenly felt something slam into the back of my chest plate. A powerful heat spread through my back and made me cry out. Turning around, I noticed a man holding a rifle of some sort and aiming it at me. With a grimace, I shunted aside the pain and darted forward, zigzagging left and right to present a harder to hit target.

My hope that the man would panic didn't happen. He calmly moved his gun to follow me and pulled the trigger. A green energy beam flew at me, but I was already ducking, sliding along the ground on my knees. He tried to turn his gun on me again. I was too close, however, and I didn't hesitate to kick his legs out from underneath him. As he fell to the ground, I stood up and impaled his throat with the Meteor Sword.

The battle had become a chaotic mess now, and quite a few of the people who'd been surrounding us, curious watchers who wanted to see how this would play out, screamed and ran away. It seemed most of them weren't the rough and tumble type. Maybe they were refugees who simply had nowhere to go.

I looked over to find Adina and Michelle fighting their own battles.

Michelle had decided it was better to fight up close where their guns would be useless. She was keeping herself in the center of the fight, constantly moving as she swung her blades. Perhaps because she didn't want to hit anybody uninvolved, she did not use Dance of a Thousand Blades, sticking with pure melee combat.

Having adopted a similar approach, Adina was getting in close to her opponents, but she was not moving around like Michelle. Her method of attacking was far more brutal. Chestplates dented under her incredible strength. Faces caved in when she punched them. I watched as one squid-like creature with tentacles for a mouth pulled out a strange sword with a laser-edged blade and tried to swing at her. She grabbed his forearm, crushed it in her grip, and then tore his arm off. As he released a watery scream, she used his arm as a bat and blasted him off his feet.

Several more enemies surrounded me. I counted three. One was tentacle-faced, another had the head of a pig, and the last one was a skinny giant with a smooth cranium and no nose. All of them were holding ranged weapons. Blasters or a pistols.

I leapt into the air and used Double Jump, avoiding their first volley of attacks. They didn't seem to understand what had happened. That one second of confusion was something I used to my advantage, coming down toward the giant and swinging my Meteor Sword as I spun around. With Fireblade activated, I severed the giant's head from his shoulders. The wound also cauterized so no blood spilled as his head rolled across the floor.

Landing on the ground as his body hit the floor, I darted away from the other two as they fired again, missing me by a hair. I turned around and dashed toward Pig Head. He panicked when he saw me closing in, causing his blaster bolts to go wide. One of them did clip me in the shoulder. I grunted and spun around, but I kept my balance and continued to charge, closing the distance in seconds and killing the man via Death by Piercing.

After seeing his two comrades die, Tentacle Face lost his confidence, turned around, and began running. I thought about killing him. I didn't in the end. Killing someone who didn't intend to fight any longer didn't sit well with me. Of course, if he came back and tried to harm my companions again, I'd show no mercy, but that was for the future.

Adina, Christine, and Michelle were done with their battles as well. Adina was sporting several burn marks from where a blaster bolt had hit her, but she didn't seem too bad off. It looked like her body was resistant to blaster bolts. Michelle and Christine were in the best condition. I couldn't see so much as a scratch on either of them.

"Is this common here?" I asked.

"You mean getting attacked by random thugs?" asked Christine. "It can be. I imagine these people were slave traders, or maybe they were working for one of the two big factions here on Station 13."

Station 13 was controlled by factions through use of force. It seemed violence was how everyone ruled in this place. Those with power pushed around those without it, and those without it either complied or were killed by those who had it. This place embodied the philosophy of survival of the fittest.

I was never a fan of this Darwinian evolutionary theory.

CHAPTER 12

I soon learned the Space Cowboy derived its name from the glowing sign above the entrance. It was a man dressed in pants, futuristic metal boots with spurs, a duster, and what appeared to be a prosthetic arm that transformed into a gun. At least, that was what I was getting. The sign was a uniform color, showing nothing more than the silhouette of the figure I guessed was the "space cowboy" this place was named after.

The inside also had what I'd call a western aesthetic. As we stepped into the bar, the wooden floor creaked beneath us. A strong scent filled my nose, alcohol and sweat, causing it to wrinkle. Low lighting gave the bar a dark and gritty tone that perfectly matched the rough and tumble patrons seated at the old-fashioned wooden tables. A bar sat in the room's center. It, too, had the same old-school quality like everything else.

Directly contrasting with the western touches was the robotic bartender standing behind the counter and the holographic screens floating overhead. I looked from the bartender to one of the screens, which was showing what I thought was like horse racing... if the horses had two heads, flames sprouting from their eyes, and reptilian appearances with six legs each. Many of the patrons were hollering at the screen. My guess was they had placed bets on who would win.

Only a few people paid attention to us as we wandered further into the room and found ourselves some seats in an empty booth. Christine had selected one that would grant us a view the entire room.

"Do you know who we're looking for?" asked Adina as she cuddled into my side. Michelle shook her head when she saw this, but I think all of us had already accepted this was just how our succubus friend acted no matter the situation. I took comfort in the fact that she never changed.

"I don't have the foggiest," Christine admitted with a dry smile. "The person who first contacted me wore a full body cloak with a hood and a mask, and they had a synthetic voice changer. Not only could I not see what they looked like, I couldn't tell if they were a man or a woman."

"They could have been gender fluid," I said.

Christine blinked. "Gender what?"

"... Never mind."

Christine stared at me for a bit longer before shrugging her shoulders and continuing where she left off. "All I know is what my contact told me: wait at the Space Cowboy between twelve hundred and twenty hundred hours. My contact would arrive at that time, every day for one week, six weeks after I left Station 13 for the first time. If I didn't show up for that week, my contact would assume I wasn't interested and stop coming."

"How long has it been since you left the first time?" asked Michelle.

"It's been six weeks and two days," Christine said.

Which meant her contact should still be coming to the bar every day.

I looked around the bar again, observing the people who were already drunk and screaming, either jubilantly or in anger at the screen. There was a human man in a cowboy hat with a mug of some frothing green liquid spilling from the sides. Definitely not ale. I also saw what I believed was a woman, but her species reminded me of a toad. Her face was like that of a frog. Next to her was another of those squid-faced men.

It didn't look like any of these were the contact, who I suspected would be wearing a full-body cloak like last time. People like that never liked having their identities exposed. That was part of their cloak and dagger appeal. Something like that.

"I'm thirsty," Adina said.

"I'll get us some drinks." Christine stood up. "You three wait here."

"What else would we do?" I asked.

"Smart aleck."

With that parting shot, Christine walked over to the bar, leaned against the table, and ordered something from the robot bartender. I watched as metal arms gleaming dully in the light moved with expert precision. I had no idea what she had ordered, but the drinks she came back with were very colorful—as in, it looked like someone had liquified a neon sign and filled our glasses.

"Be careful. This drink is strong," Christine warned us as she set a glass in front of each person.

"Oh, I don't drink…" Michelle tried to say, but Christine was having none of that.

"Come on, even Jesus Christ drank wine," she said, rolling her eyes. "A little alcohol isn't going to kill you."

Michelle still didn't look convinced, but then she stared at her glass with uncertainty. Adina was sniffing hers. She reminded me of a mouse, her small, cute nose wiggling. After a moment, she took a tentative sip and licked her lips. Her eyes brightened and she took another sip. At that moment, Michelle, having finally gotten over her reluctance, grabbed the glass and downed the whole thing in a single gulp.

"Whoa, girl! I said to be careful!" Christine said.

"Hic… careful shmareful… I'm always… alwaysh being… careful… about everything…"

"Are you drunk already?! After one glass?!"

"You did say it was strong," I pointed out.

"Not that strong!" Christine snapped back.

Michelle really was drunk after just one glass of… whatever this was. Her cheeks were flushed a startling shade of red, eyes swirling around in their sockets, and a stupid smile on her face. I'd never seen a smile quite like this before. Even when she was delirious from multiple orgasms, the most she would do was smile contently.

"Hic… Bryan… Byraaaaan!" Michelle leaned into me and batted her eyes. It was… disturbing. "Do you find… do you think I'm… um… hic… attra… attrotive… do you think I'm pretty?"

I really didn't know how I felt about a drunk Michelle, but since she asked, I answered.

"I think you are very pretty."

"Hee-hee. Hic. I think you're pretty too."

"That's nice."

"Bryan… I wanna have sex…"

"I'm not sure that's something you should say in public."

"I like sex."

"So do I, but again, we're in public—and why are you taking off your clothes?!"

"Because it's… hic… it's hot… I'm so hot, Bryan. I need… hic… clothes off."

"No, you don't. Put them back on."

Michelle had just begun removing the straps to her shirt, which would have been a huge problem for me, and so I quickly pulled them back up. At the same time, I decided that a drunk Michelle was more trouble than she was worth. Maybe it would be fun if she got drunk in the safety of our home. However, I did not want any of my girls stripping in front of any man besides me.

I know that made me greedy. I was okay with being greedy and hypocritical.

Perhaps the alcohol had finally hit her fully, because Michelle leaned into me, resting her head on my shoulder as she closed her eyes.

"Bryan… I really… really love you…"

I froze. Then my heartbeat picked up. That attack had been completely unfair. I'd heard that some people become more honest when they were drunk, but this went beyond anything I'd ever seen. And I had seen a lot. My buddies in the military could put away booze like nobody's business.

Except Chris. He'd been a lightweight.

"Drunk Michelle is funny," Adina said as she sipped her beverage. Unlike Michelle, whose cheeks so red they gave lobsters a run for their money, she looked fine.

"I disagree," I said. "Drunk Michelle is going to give me ulcers."

"I think she's amusing," Adina said.

"I agree," Christine added with a chuckle.

I glared at them both, but then the snoring Michelle began sliding down my body. I shifted and wrapped an arm around her waist, adjusting her so she wouldn't fall face first into my lap. Michelle mumbled something under her breath and snuggled closer to me.

"You look like you're having a good time," a voice suddenly said right behind us. I was about to turn, but the voice spoke again. "Don't turn around. Don't make any sudden moves."

"Are you gonna say you have a gun pointed at us next?" I asked.

The voice chuckled. "Cute, but no. I would just rather we do this business transaction like this."

A frown appeared on my face as I listened to the voice, which sounded like it had gone through a synthesizer. It was impossible to tell this person's sex from their voice.

"Hello again, Arcanum," Christine greeted as she sipped her beverage.

I had to stifle a groan. Arcanum? Really? Wasn't that just the Latin word for mystery? And why was someone using a Latin word in a science fiction setting? I suddenly felt like I'd stepped into a poorly written novel.

"Greetings again, Christine," Arcanum said. "I see you brought your friends."

"And I've returned within less than seven weeks, as promised."

"Indeed."

"Are you the one who has the information we need?" I asked.

"No, but I am the one who can help get you the information you want." The person behind us paused. "Of course, that is only if you're willing to pay the price."

Of course the information we wanted wouldn't come free. I hadn't been expecting it to be free to begin with, but it was really annoying to know we'd have to put up with this secrecy for a while longer.

"What's the price?" asked Christine. "I don't have much on me..."

"Don't worry." The person chuckled. "The Information Broker doesn't want your money. Generally speaking, he trades information for more information. However, there currently is no information you have that he doesn't already know."

I was tempted to speak out, to make a snide or sarcastic remark, but I knew that might hurt the process. It certainly wouldn't help. Keeping my mouth shut was a chore, but I did it anyway.

"Then what's he want?" asked Christine.

"A favor."

Before either of us could ask what this person was talking about, a gloved hand covered in a cloak appeared between me and Adina. It set an object on the table and retracted. I really wanted to turn around and look at the person, but I resisted that impulse and instead glanced at the object he'd set on the table.

It was not very big. I'd say it was about the size of my fist, but it was also flat and had a small lens-like film in the center.

While I had no idea what it was, Christine waved her hand over the film part, and I nearly jumped when two figures suddenly appeared above the object. They were both figures about a hundredth the size of a person. One of them showed a human man with broad shoulders, a spacesuit, and a rifle slung over his shoulder. The other showed one of those creatures that had a mandible over its mouth.

"He wants you to deal with these two people," the contact said.

"And who are these two?" asked Christine.

"The human is Johnathan McCloy. He's the head of the faction called Cerberus. The druruian is Sauruss. He's the leader of a rival faction called Hydra. These two factions are currently the two largest on Station 13, and they both make their home on Spoke 7..." The contact paused. "Of course, being the two largest factions and having decided to make the same Spoke their home base means a lot of friction has occurred between them. It started off with some small-scale fights but has quickly escalated into large-scale violence. Many have died, and many more will die if something isn't done."

"And so you want us to kill the faction leaders," Christine said. "To cut off both snake's heads, if you will."

The sound of rustling clothes behind me made me think the contact was shrugging their shoulders.

"Station 13 doesn't have its own military force or even a security force, and we can't ask the other factions to team up and help. There's far too much animosity between the factions to make them cooperate. The Information Broker believes the best way to deal with this is to have an elite task force enter their headquarters and take out both faction leaders. Do that, and the information is yours."

I didn't like this at all. For starters, I had no idea what kind of forces these two factions were comprised of. What were their numbers like? Their weapons? Did they only have small firearms and rifles, or were they also in possession of giant robots that could kill a human simply by stepping on them? What level were their forces at? I knew nothing.

"Can you provide us with information about these two factions?" I finally asked, unable to contain myself.

"All relevant information can be found on the datacard I gave you." More rustling. I could tell the contact had stood up. "I'll meet you here once you've killed Johanathan and Sauruss. If you manage to. Good luck."

Without even giving us time to accept or deny the offer, the contact's presence seemed to disappear. I turned around, but of course, there was no one there.

✷✷✷

Michelle was still passed out and snoring in my ear as we left the bar and made our way to a hotel or inn to spend the night at. Because she had big angel wings that made it impossible to carry her normally, I'd slung her arms around my neck, grabbed her thighs, and carried her piggyback. The only issue with carrying her like this was the way our armor ground against each other. I couldn't say I was a fan of the grating sound emitting from it.

The inn that Christine led us to was, according to her, one she'd used previously when visiting. It was not what I'd call the best inn in town. The walls had some black marks that looked like carbon scoring, the entrance interior was fairly bare, and the only person present was a drurian man sitting behind a counter.

I let Christine handle everything. We were in unfamiliar territory and I didn't have any of the currency used in this realm. She spoke with the inn staff, paid for our room, received a key, and led me, Adina, and the conked-out Michelle toward a hallway in the back.

Our room was on the second floor—room 256. It was not a very big room. The carpeted floor looked a little worn, there was very little furniture, and I only saw one bed. What's more, the bed was much smaller than the one we used in Valhalla. Would we even be able to fit on it? While the room was threadbare, I suppose I should just be thankful there was no weird smells or anything.

I set Michelle into the bed, on her back, and made sure her head was turned just in case she vomited. It sounded dumb, but it was possible to die from choking on your own puke. When you passed out from drinking too much, your body was unable to wake up even when you were in danger, which meant it was very easy to die.

While I set Michelle down, Adina wandered over to the dresser, the only other piece of furniture, and leaned against it. Christine crossed her arms and leaned against the wall.

"So what's our next step?" I asked, sitting next to Michelle and stroking her hair.

"Not much to do but do as the contact says," Christine said, shrugging.

Adina scowled. "I don't like this. That man... er... woman? Whatever. That person didn't even give us a choice."

"That's how the Information Broker's contacts work." Christine wore a dry smile, showing she didn't much care for their modus operandi either but had accepted it. "They contact you out of nowhere, tell you that if you want the information you seek, you will do as they say. Failing to follow their instructions means not getting the information you want."

"I still don't like it," Adina growled, but then she sighed and brushed her hair over her shoulder. "But I guess we don't have much of a choice. So, how should we go about killing these two?"

"The first thing we need is intel." I stopped running my hand through Michelle's hair and turned to the other two. "We can't do anything if we don't know what we're up against. Let's check that datacard the contact gave us."

Christine pulled the datacard from her pocket and came over to the bed. Adina followed behind her. The three of us formed something of a triangle between us as she activated the datacard, which projected a large screen that was written in...

"Huh. That's in English," I muttered.

"Yeah." Christine nodded. "Apparently, English is the language here. I think it's because this is an alternate reality version of our world... or a future version of it."

"Interesting."

I read the information on the card, which currently told us about Johnathan McCloy, the leader of Cerberus. He was a 45-year-old ex-military who'd abandoned his comrades in the line of duty and received a dishonorable discharge. Left with nowhere to go, he drifted around the galaxy and eventually wound up here, Station 13, where he used his knowledge of military tactics to overwhelm the other factions and gather more followers.

"It looks like he has a 230,000-strong force," I muttered. "Their armaments mostly consist of carbine blasters and rifles, but they also have a variety of explosives, and they even have an army of LSM-44 war droids... what are those?"

"They're large humanoid warmachines," Christine answered. "They're about two times bigger than a human. They don't have hands, but numerous weapons can be attached to their arms. That's all I know about them. I only recognize what they are because I've seen a few of them while I was here last time."

Then it was as he thought. This Johnathan possessed giant fighting robots, and not only that, but his force was 230,000 strong. That was just great. I could already see this mission going FUBAR before it even began.

"Let's look at that other guy," Adina suggested. "What was his name? Taurus?"

"Sauruss," I said.

"Yeah. Him."

Christine pulled up the information on Sauruss. He was a drurian, which was the name of his species. They were a hardy species from Logalem. The datacard didn't contain any information on the drurian home planet, but it did say the species was very warlike and their planet was run by a military dictatorship.

Sauruss was a drurian who led a former rebel faction against the current regime and lost. Forced to flee his home planet, he traveled the galaxy as a mercenary to make a living. Like all people who were looking to disappear from the authorities, he drifted to Station 13, where he established his own faction in the hopes of raising an army to travel back to his home planet and destroy its current regime.

The data within the card didn't go into Sauruss' motivations or anything specific like a personality profile, but it did tell about his forces, which were comparable to Johnathan McCloy's.

"It looks like Sauruss doesn't have any war machines like the LSM-44, but he does have more troops and they are better equipped than Johnathan's," I said with a frown.

"These two are both very warlike, but they have vastly different philosophies when it comes to how to conduct a war," Christine told me, still holding the datacard aloft. "Johnathan believes in the path of annihilation. He uses strategies that seek the immediate destruction of an enemy's combat power by wiping out their armed forces. He doesn't have the patience for long-term strategies and prefers to just blow up his problems."

"How very American of him," I said with a chuckle.

Christine grinned before continuing. "Sauruss is much more cautious. He's a long-term planner. He uses the exhaustion strategy."

"That's a strategy where one military force tries to gradually erode an enemy nations will or means of resisting. It's used when someone is pursuing an indirect objective, using military power not against the enemy's army, but against the things that makes him capable of fighting at all," I explained to Adina, who didn't know military strategy. "A good example would be if someone was fighting against an island nation. Rather than try to battle their armies, they will starve the population by waging unrestricted submarine warfare and sinking all the cargo ships bringing supplies to and from the enemy's home island."

"That's a rather vicious way of fighting," Adina muttered. "I imagine the people on the receiving end of that would suffer much more than if you just outright annihilated them."

"I suspect Sauruss is using this tactic because he doesn't want to destroy other factions but absorb them," Christine said. "While Johanathan came into power by bringing over deserters and fellow disgraced military officers, Sauruss gained power by absorbing other factions into his own through exhaustion tactics."

"Sounds complicated." Adina crossed her arms and furrowed her brow. "I hope you two don't mind if I leave all the planning to you. I'm not so good at strategy."

"We know," Christine and I said at the same time.

Christine and I discussed our strategy for several hours and concluded that before we could make any plans, we needed to gain more information. We knew what their forces were like, and we even knew about their chain of command, but there was a lot we still didn't know, like the layout of their base, the current deployment of their forces, and what kind of personalities their targets had.

Early the next morning, as we were pouring over the information we currently had again, Michelle woke up with a low, pained groan. I looked over to the bed where Adina and Michelle were sleeping. It was only big enough for two, so me and Christine had slept snuggled on the floor. At present, Adina was clinging to Michelle, who was staring at the ceiling with a confused and agonized expression.

"Good morning." I stood up and made my way to the bed, where I smiled down at the archangel. "How do you feel?"

"Like I'm going to die," Michelle muttered.

"Hangovers will do that to you," I confirmed with a nod.

"Do you have any water?"

I looked at Christine, who said, "All the water here is filtered, fortunately, so you can just get some from the tap."

Those were the words I needed to hear. There was a small bathroom off to the side, and while it didn't have much, it did possess a few cups in the cupboard beneath the sink. I filled one cup with water and gave it to Michelle, who downed it and asked for another. She only stopped after chugging down six glasses.

"Feel better?" I asked.

"No," Michelle admitted.

"We'll get you something greasy for breakfast to help absorb the alcohol in your bloodstream," I said. "Sorry about what happened. If I'd known you were such a lightweight, I wouldn't have let you drink whatever that concoction was."

"I-It's fine." Michelle blushed and looked away. "Just promise me you'll forget about what happened yesterday."

"Sure."

I highly doubted I'd ever be able to forget what happened the previous day, but I'd at least pretend I did if it would make her feel better.

We caught Michelle up on what transpired yesterday, informing her about our task, the forces we would be fighting against, and our plans going forward. Michelle listened with furrowed brows and a small frown.

"I can't say I approve of what we are doing." She sighed and ran a hand through her hair. "That said, I do understand that we have little choice in the matter… and it sounds like this Jonathan and Sauruss are not good people. I suppose this could be considered retribution for their crimes against others."

Glad to have Michelle onboard with us, I asked Christine to grab some breakfast. She knew her way around this station better than any of us.

Adina woke up during the time Christine was gone. She still seemed groggy as she sat next to me and leaned her head on my shoulder.

Christine returned around half an hour after she left, carrying a bag filled with something that looked like white cubes. She said it was food. I didn't believe it. I tried one, and it didn't taste like food. It was more than a matter of the food being bland. It was completely tasteless.

"This is awful," Adina muttered after popping one of the cubes into her mouth. Her face immediately contorted as if she was in pain.

"I agree that it's incredibly bland," Christine said as she ate without complaint. "However, these cubes are actually some of the most nutritious foods you'll ever eat. They have the perfect combination of carbohydrates, fat, proteins, and all the vitamins and nutrients your body needs."

"And all it took to make such a healthy food was completely eradicating its flavor," I mumbled as I ate another cube. They honestly weren't much different from some of the military rations I'd eaten before. The biscuits contained in some of the rations we had were tasteless too.

Michelle didn't speak a single word, but the look on her face as she ate alongside us said enough. That said, while she obviously didn't enjoy this food, if something so tasteless could be called such, the food did help her hangover. It must have been those nutrients Christine mentioned.

After breakfast, it was time to get down to business. We had some intel to gather.

CHAPTER 13

Just because I understood the importance of gathering accurate intelligence, that did not make me good at information gathering or recon. In fact, those were the two things I was worst at in the military. I was always the guy they delivered intel to. The one they told who to kill and then pointed me at them like a loaded gun. Even basic reconnaissance was something I sucked at.

But that was what I found myself doing for the next week.

Cerberus and Hydra both made their base of operations on Spoke 7, known for its urbanized zones and residential districts. I heard from some residents that Spoke 7 was originally going to be where full-time employees of the company who created this station were going to live.

Station 13 was, believe it or not, created by a company called AmuTech. They were a mining company that expended large amounts of capital on this station to mine the asteroids surrounding the Saturn-looking planet down below. Unfortunately, they had spent too much money, discovered the asteroids didn't have any valuable metals to mine, and went bankrupt as a result. Station 13 was abandoned.

At some point, criminals and refugees began coming here to escape the law or get away from whatever war had displaced them. More and more people arrived, and it was eventually made habitable again.

Of course, because of how many criminals made this place their safe haven, it had now become a den of scum and villainy. Only the refugees who couldn't afford to leave stuck around. Those more fortunate had already long since abandoned this place.

In either event, Spoke 7 was made to be permanent living quarters, which meant a good deal of the spoke was housing and development. These houses did not look at all like the cul de sacs on earth. They looked more like apartment complexes. Each building contained several housing units for the people living there.

Spoke 7 was sectioned into 24 quadrants. Cerberus was located in quadrant 17, Hydra in quadrant 3. They were basically on opposite sides of the spoke, and the area between them was the battleground upon which they waged their war.

Every quadrant except 17 and 3 were considered a no man's land. The people who lived there had evacuated a long time ago, not that I could blame them. It wasn't a pretty place. The scent of burning flesh and blood had permeated the spoke. It wasn't unusual to find one or more corpses just lying in the open where they'd been slain, their bodies stripped of whatever equipment they'd been carrying. A few of the older corpses were rotting and smelled truly awful.

I'd spent an entire week scouting this place out by myself, sending the images back to Adina, Christine, and Michelle via some new recording equipment we'd bought.

We had decided I would go alone because we didn't want anyone knowing I had backup right now. This was being done on the off chance someone from either Cerberus or Hydra discovered me. It was a necessary precaution.

Fortunately, after an entire week of scouting, reconnaissance, and mapping the place out, we'd finally gathered enough intel to begin constructing a plan.

***

A battle was taking place in quadrant 11. I stood on a metal walkway located several dozen meters above and one kilometer away from where the battle was taking place, Adina by my side.

We were no longer dressed in our fantasy armor and sexy succubus outfit respectively. I had donned the sort of high-tech armor gamers might expect from a space marine. The armor was made of a synthetic alloy that deflected blaster fire. The black and white outer shell appeared glossy, which Christine told me was because it had been painted with an absorbent compound that made it heat resistant and negated electric damage. I still had a sword strapped to my back, but a pair of blaster pistols were holstered at my sides.

Adina wore similar armor but meant for women. The chestplate conformed to her physique with near perfection, showcasing her large chest in the most appealing way possible while emphasizing her slim waist and wide hips. It looked heavily modified. Christine's and Michelle's armor did not emphasize their breasts like hers did; theirs were more gender neutral, leading me to believe Adina had chosen this specifically for the sex appeal. That was a succubus for you. She did not have a sword, but hanging from a bandolier was a blaster rifle. It was a repeating blaster rifle that could apparently fire 50 blaster bolts per second.

"It looks like the battle has started," Adina said.

"So it has," I agreed.

"Are we gonna intervene?"

"Not yet. I'd like to wait until I can determine who the victor will be. Once we know which of them is on the losing side, we'll step in and turn the tide."

"Got it. Also…"

"Yes?"

"Do I really have to wear this?"

I removed the binoculars from my eyes and looked at Adina in her new outfit. We had been forced to modify the armor to accommodate for her wings and tail, which made her look odd, I had to admit. I'd never seen a succubus wear armor before, or at least armor like this that wasn't bikini armor. It looked out of place on her, perhaps even out of character.

"Yes, you have to wear it."

"But these clothes aren't sexy at all!"

I actually disagreed. Adina might look uncomfortable, but I thought she still looked plenty sexy. It wasn't all about revealing clothes. A woman could be just as sexy in full body armor, but I knew that wasn't something Adina wanted to hear, so I kept this opinion to myself.

"I know, but that armor is necessary." I held out my hand and smiled when she took it. "Not only will they help us blend in—to some extent—they will also protect us from blasterfire. Trust me when I say we're going to want that protection. Getting hit with a blaster bolt is no fun."

"Ha… well, if you say so," Adina said, not looking pleased.

I turned my attention back to the battle now that Adina had been placated. The two forces were firing at each other between a pair of buildings. Each building was several stories large, featured numerous halls and walkways, and were all hard angles and straight edges. Some people were battling on the flat roofs. They would snipe the people from below. At the moment, it looked like Cerberus was overwhelming Hydra. They had brought out one of their SML-44 war machines, which was laying suppressive fire.

The SML-44 was a boxy cockpit that stood on two thick legs, had arms jutting from either side, and attached to the arms were a pair of large repeating blasters capable of spraying blaster fire like rain. Sitting on either shoulder were a pair of missile pods. Even as I watched, nearly two dozen missiles were launched from those pods, producing plumes of smoke as they flew forward and slammed into the ground near a group of members from Hydra. The missiles lit up the atmosphere as they exploded. Several people were sent flying, their bodies black and burnt as they struck the ground, already dead.

For a moment, I was certain Cerberus would be the ones to overwhelm Hydra, but then something unexpected happened.

A group of four repelled down from a walkway high above the battlefield. One of them landed on the SML-44, while the others landed around it. My eyes narrowed as the one on top placed something on the SML-44's head and activated whatever it was, then hopped off. Blue arcs of electricity soon erupted from the SML-44. Each arc cascaded around the machine. Almost as though it was alive, the machine shook and spasmed as smoke poured out from cracks in the casing. It toppled over seconds later.

"Was that an EMP?" I asked.

"EMP? What is that?" asked Adina.

Still keeping my eyes on the battle, I answered her. "It stands for electromagnetic pulse, though sometimes it's also called electromagnetic disturbance. It's a short burst of electromagnetic energy. It's used by many militaries back on Earth to damage or disrupt machines and any equipment that uses electricity."

"Uh-huh…"

I knew Adina didn't really understand what I was telling her. She still didn't know a lot about technology or machines. The ship we had used to travel here was the only thing she understood, and all she understood about the ship was how to pilot it. She didn't care about its inner workings.

"Just know it's like lightning magic, but it's not aimed at people. It's used to disrupt machines… like our ship."

"Okay. That makes sense."

"And with that attack, it looks like the tides have turned."

Just like I said, the tides had gone from Cerberus having an overwhelming advantage thanks to their SML-44, to Hydra having the advantage with their superior equipment and tactics. The group that had destroyed the war machine were already behind their allies' lines. Meanwhile, the Hydra members were traveling slowly forward as they fired at the Cerberus members.

As someone from Cerberus went down in a smoking heap, a hole punched through their chest, I realized Hydra had more than just what we saw on the surface. There was at least one sniper attacking from a distance. I swiveled my binoculars around and sought out the sniper, who I finally discovered hiding on the seventh floor of a building several dozen meters from the main battle.

"All right. It's time to go." I put my binoculars away and looked at Adina. "There's someone attacking from a distance. He's in that building over there, seventh floor. Take him out first, then meet up with me. I'm going to help out the Cerberus members."

"Got it!" Adina looked fired up now that we were doing more than just standing around and observing. She leaned forward and kissed me fiercely on the lips. I thought I could sense her fighting spirit through her kiss. With a grin, she winked at me and flew into the air. "I'll be back!"

I shook my head and smiled as Adina took off, traveling incredibly quickly despite her new and somewhat heavy armor.

I didn't stick around to watch her go. Rushing along the walkway, I quickly found a set of stairs, raced down them, and reached the street.

I could no longer see the battle, but I didn't need to. While recon was not my forte, I had a great sense of direction, and I already knew where the battlefield was.

Bursting out from between a set of buildings, I found the members of Cerberus being harassed by Hydra's members. Nearly a dozen of the fifty strong had already been killed, gunned down by the superior weaponry of their enemies. Now that I was closer, I could see these two groups were comprised of a combination of humans and aliens. The only way I could tell who belonged to which faction was their armor. Cerberus wore red armor. Hydra's armor was a poisonous green.

This was it.

Mission start.

I rushed out into the crowd of advancing green armored men and attacked the one nearest me. He didn't even have time to turn around before my sword sliced through his neck, separating his head from his shoulders. As the head rolled to the ground, the body continued moving for several more steps, then slowly tumbled to the ground, blood spurting from the severed stump.

Several people noticed my actions. I wore a grim smile as they turned to me and attacked, pulling the blaster from my waist and shooting one squid-faced alien in the face. My blaster fire struck him in the eye. He jerked back and fell down.

I raced forward, holstering my pistol as I zigzagged back and forth across the street, avoiding a hail of blaster bolts. Several bolts struck my chest. It was fortunate Christine had the foresight to buy us armor. The blaster fire was repelled, and while the force stalled me, I continued moving and eventually reached the Hydra members.

With a battlecry, I swung my blade, glowing red as fire wafted from it, and watched in satisfaction as it cut through the armor. This high-tech armor might be great at deflecting blasterfire, but it couldn't deal with a magical attack like Fireblade. No blood sprayed from the wound I carved from the pig-faced man's left hip to his right shoulder, but the smell of burning flesh did fill the air as the wound cauterized. The man squealed and went down. Meanwhile, I was already moving.

My sudden appearance caused the Cerberus members to stand around in confusion. They didn't seem to know what they should make of me, evident by how they had stopped attacking.

"What are you guys doing?!" I shouted at them. "Don't stop firing!"

My words jolted them into action. They took aim with their repeating blaster rifles and unloaded a torrent of red blaster bolts into the Hydra forces, downing several of them in half as many seconds. Fortunately, they had pegged me as an ally and avoided firing on the areas around me.

I found myself locked in combat with one member of Hydra who seemed better at melee combat than the rest. It was a drurian. He'd already discarded his blaster rifle and was wielding two daggers. Sparks flew as we swung our weapons without relent. He really was quite good. He used both blades to block my larger, heavier weapon, and then tried to make me lose balance by pushing my sword wide so he could close the distance and attack before I could recover.

Maybe if I hadn't been using a sword for over six months now, his attack would have worked.

I backpedaled as he came in, spun on the balls of my feet, and swung from the ground upward, my sword cutting diagonally through the air. He tried to block the attack. However, he could only use one dagger thanks to the angle, and my sword weighed far more. The drurian was knocked back. As he stumbled, I came in and used Death by Piercing to impale him through the chest. He died instantly.

After finishing off the drurian, I looked for the next enemy to kill, but then I caught something in the skies above me and looked up. It was Adina. She flew toward the line of enemies several meters from my position, striking the ground so hard the street was upended and a shockwave raced over the vicinity. So powerful was it that even I was nearly blown back. If I hadn't hunkered down and protected my face, I was sure I'd have been knocked off my feet or clipped in the head with flying debris.

The people who'd been in the center of Adina's kamikaze-like attack were nowhere near as lucky as me. Some of them had been ripped apart. Most were simply blown back several dozen meters. A few struck a building, blowing a hole clean through it, while others flew through the air, hit the ground, and rolled across it like ragdolls. I could only whistle. Adina had just taken down nearly one dozen enemies by herself in less time than it took to blink.

Guess that was a level 84 succubus for you.

After her attack ran its course, Adina leapt into the air, flew over to me, and landed.

"How was that?" she asked.

"Perfect." I gave her a thumbs up. "Let's join up with Cerberus now."

With so many members of Hydra gone, the members of Cerberus were invigorated and renewed their attack. More and more green-clad individuals went down in a hail of blaster fire and explosions. In the center of this battlefield were Adina and I. We attacked side by side, mowing down the remaining Hydra members until the other faction decided retreat was their only option.

A cheer went up among the Cerberus members. Adina and I smiled at each other, high-fived, and walked over to the group of red armored humans and aliens.

"Thanks for your help back there," said a drurian man. Come to think of it, I hadn't seen a female drurian yet… or I didn't think I had. I wondered if that meant there were no drurian women, or if they were just more scarce on Station 13. Wait! Maybe they didn't have a sex? What if they were asexual like marbled crabs?!

"You're welcome," I said as Adina hugged my arm and smiled. "I'm Bryan Jenson. This is my wife, Adina. We saw you were fighting against Hydra and decided to lend a hand."

"My name is Grian. I'm guessing you two have something against Hydra?" The drurian introduced himself.

"You could say our grudge against them runs deep," I said, forcing a bitter and making my face look enraged. It wasn't hard. I just imagined all the injustices of the world and let the anger flow through me. Adina had a more difficult time. She wasn't a very good actor, but the way she pursed her lips seemed to convince Grian that her anger was real.

"I guess that means we have a common enemy," Grian said. "You two should come with us. I'll introduce you to our leader. I'm sure he'll be pleased to have allies as strong as you two."

∗∗∗

Adina and I soon learned that Cerberus' base was not located inside of an apartment building in quadrant 13 but underneath the ground in a hidden basement level. The entrance was located in plain sight. Getting in required an activation device that Grian had in his possession. He pressed a button on his wristband, which caused a section of street lift up like a ramp, revealing an entrance that he led us and the rest of his battalion into.

We traveled through several gray hallways, down an elevator, and eventually entered what appeared to be a war chamber. People sat at computer stations. It looked like they were monitoring various quadrants and communicating with other teams out in the field. Standing in the center of this group was a man.

It was a bit weird of me to say this, being an American, but this man looked like he embodied the American ideal. He was tall with broad shoulders, and had a masculine face surrounded by bright blond hair. His strong jawline and defined chin complimented his blue eyes. His body was covered by armor that looked like a spacesuit. A duster had been thrown over it. While the duster looked out of place, I couldn't lie and say it didn't make him appear unique. He looked like a space marine cowboy.

As we walked into the room, the man turned around and spotted us. His eyes lit up when they landed on me, and he paused for a long time on Adina, but he soon turned his attention to Grian.

"It's good to see you, my friend," he said, coming over and clapping Grian on the back. "I was worried when we received your distress call. I was preparing to send reinforcements."

"Thank you. I appreciate that you value me so much." Grian didn't look like he much cared for the man's friendly shoulder clapping, but he didn't do anything to stop it. "I'm not sure those reinforcements would have arrived in time. We were lucky Adina and Bryan here arrived in time to help us."

"Yes, I saw them through the security cameras." The man turned to us and gave a friendly smile. Once again, I noticed his eyes linger longer on Adina than me, but I ignored it. "Thank you for lending us a hand. I appreciate it."

"It's no trouble at all," I said with a smile that I didn't really feel.

Fortunately, the man didn't seem to notice. "My name is Johnathan McCloy. I'm the leader of Cerberus. I saw you two fighting. You're both incredibly skilled and powerful individuals. I've never seen anyone with your powers… or your appearance." He glanced at Adina's wings, horns, and spaded tail, then looked back at me. "We could use powerful people. I don't suppose you'd have any interest in joining us?"

"That depends," I said carefully.

Johnathan raised an eyebrow. "On?"

"On whether or not you can help us get revenge on Sauruss."

My words caused whatever worry Johnathan might have had to slowly dissipate, the tension in his shoulders easing. His smile seemed even more natural now.

"I'm guessing you two have something against Sarauss?" He raised an eyebrow.

"That fucker and his faction killed our only daughter," Adina snarled, and even I was a little taken aback by the viciousness in her tone. There was so much vitriol it was hard to tell it wasn't real. I think what shocked me the most was how genuine it sounded. Like I said, Adina was a bad actor, or I thought that. Could I be wrong?

Grian and his squadron took a step back from the woman as her wings flared and her tail stood on end. An unusual pressure erupted from her. I recognized it as magical energy, but magic didn't exist in this realm, so no one seemed to understand what this sensation pushing down on them was. Even Johnathan looked taken aback.

Johnathan proved himself adaptable when he recovered quickly and put on an expression of remorse. "I am sorry for your loss. Fortunately, we have a common enemy. I'd like nothing better than to annihilate Hydra and kill Sauruss with my bare hands. Sadly, that's not possible right now. His forces are comparable to my own, and he's incredibly cunning. We've been at a stalemate for nearly six months now."

"We came here to offer our assistance," I said. "We'll do whatever it takes to destroy Hydra and Sauruss."

"Good. Good!" Johnathan looked overjoyed, his eyes bright and vibrant. "Like I said, we could use powerful people like you. Grian. Show these two to a room they can stay in. We'll convene a war council meeting in a few hours, so rest up now while you can."

"Yes, sir." Grian saluted smartly before gesturing for us to follow him.

The barracks were located deeper underneath the ground. I wasn't sure where this was in correlation with everything else, but it required us to take another elevator, which led into a winding hallway that contained identical doors.

"This room is empty." Grian pressed a button on the door that caused it to open. "It used to belong to a member from my unit, but he was killed during today's battle. You can use it for now. I'll have someone come soon to remove his personal effects and deliver clean sheets for you."

"Thank you," I said.

"We appreciate your help." Adina smiled at the man,

I didn't think a drurian would find Adina attractive because she was so human, but Grian seemed to become bashful when she smiled at him. He turned his head and scratched his cheek.

"Y-you're welcome. Anyway, rest up. We'll call on you when something comes up that we can use your assistance on."

The man walked stiffly off, which caused Adina to giggle… which only served to make him walk that much faster. As he disappeared around a corner, we turned and entered the room.

It wasn't a very large room, but it was more than enough for two people. There was a single bed. It was just a twin, which meant Adina and I would be sleeping in very close quarters. *Very close.* I was okay with that. There was also a closet that could be opened by pushing a button on the wall, a bathroom, and a dresser built into the wall. Everything was very high-tech. Even the dresser opened with the push of a button.

"That was a nice touch back there," I said as Adina walked over to the bed and sat down. She grimaced for a moment, and I wondered why until I joined her and realized the mattress was stiff. "You really looked angry when you mentioned our 'daughter.'"

"Thanks." Adina grinned and gave me a victory sign. "I was thinking about Naamah, Eisheth, Agrat Bat Mahlat, and Asmodeus at the time."

"Ah..."

That made sense to me since those four were Adina's most hated enemies. Just thinking about them brought about a sense of rage in her. I was not the least bit surprised that she could put on a face like that now.

"What should we do now?" she asked.

I wrapped an arm around her shoulder and pulled the succubus close. She leaned in, head coming to rest on my shoulder, wings folding around us, and her tail curling around my waist.

"Now our job is simple," I said. "We have to help Cerberus and ingratiate ourselves to Johnathan so he will begin to value us more than anyone else. We can plan what our next step should be after that."

Adina nodded. Together, the two of us sat in silence, until a young petty officer came with a clean set of bedsheets. I'll never forget the blush the poor boy had when Adina thanked him.

CHAPTER 14

Have you ever woken up to find someone sucking your dick like a popsicle? It was a pleasant experience. A soft tongue gently glided along your shaft, sending tingles down your spine and leaving a wet trail in its wake. That softness was electric. It made the entire body come alive.

I awoke with a soft groan and looked down to find a pair of mischievous eyes staring back at me. Adina extended her tongue as she kept her eyes locked on mine, traveling from the base all the way to the head. Once there, she engulfed the tip, swirled her tongue around my cock head, and then moved down.

Another stifled groan escaped me. I reached out and grabbed her horns. There was no need for me to actually do anything. I just needed something to hold onto as Adina continued moving until all of my dick was in her mouth and even her throat. Even now I wasn't sure how she did it, but she was the only one among my lovers who could fit the entirety of my cock inside of her.

Deep throating was an interesting experience, something none of the women I'd slept with on Earth could do. Maybe I was just unlucky on Earth. I'd seen some women who would make a video of themselves deep throating a banana on social media. Porn stars could also do it. But I had never personally witnessed someone who could deep throat. The last girl on Earth who tried had gagged and come back up, coughing and sputtering. I'd felt so bad for her that I apologized on reflex.

Adina was nothing like those women. The skills she displayed at sucking me off were better than anyone else I knew. It wasn't long before I released a groan, shooting load after load of cum down her throat. Only after I'd finished did she let go, and despite the fact that I had already cum, I was still quite hard.

"Thanks for the meal," she said before sitting up and moving until she was straddling my hips.

She rubbed her hairless mound against me, grinding up and down. Not only was the feeling sensational, but the sight of her plump limps and hard clit as she ground herself against me was by far one of the most arousing things I'd ever seen.

I placed my hands on her hips. I didn't do anything else, letting Adina take the lead and decide what she wanted for herself. Sometimes this woman enjoyed letting me do all the work. That said, there were occasions where she preferred having complete control. Given my wake up call, I already knew which case this was.

After what felt like hours of excruciatingly pleasurable torture but was probably less than five minutes, Adina lifted her hips and guided my shaft into her tight passage, moaning as my cock spread her lips apart and filled her insides. I had to suck in a deep breath. The pleasant sensation of her warm, tight channel wrapped around my dick nearly made me lose control.

"Being inside you is the best," I murmured.

"Ha… ha… isn't it, though?" said Adina with a twinkle in her eyes.

She rocked her hips back and forth. I gritted my teeth as the desire to cum hit me hard, unwilling to let myself lose control so soon after entering her. Another moment passed. Then she raised her hips and moved them down, raised them again and moved them down. She soon worked out a steady rhythm.

She placed her hands on my chest, pushing her breasts together, making them standout. I was mesmerized by her perky nipples. They seemed so cheerful to me that I just wanted to reach out and pinch them. Sweat formed on her skin, glistening, silky, intoxicating. The sound of her ass smacking my hips echoed around us, mixing with Adina's moans and my grunts.

"Ahn. Haaa. Ah. Hnnn!"

Adina gasped when I surprised her by thrusting my hips just as she was coming down. She pitched forward, the arms holding her up growing weak. As her breasts smashed against my chest, Adina grabbed fistfuls of my hair and kissed me hard. Her kiss was heavy and passionate. It was fire and power. Strength and vigor. I could do nothing but surrender to it.

Even though she was no longer sitting on me, she continued to move her hips. She was even faster than before. I knew from the way her body was gyrating that she was close to cumming. I wondered if I could stave off my own impending orgasm, but I understood my own body better than that. My balls were tightening. It wouldn't be long now.

I felt Adina tighten around me. Not only did her insides constrict around me like a boa, but her thighs had grown taut, her buttcheeks clenched, and her entire body was trembling as she came. I was only able to last a second longer before cumming the second time that morning.

"Ha… ha… ha…"

As Adina took rasping breaths of air, pressed her sweaty face against my chest, and tried to recover, I hugged her close and luxuriated in the feeling of oneness.

It had been two weeks since we joined Cerberus. We'd gone on several missions during that time and quickly made a name for ourselves. Our strength and pristine mission success rate had propelled our standing with Johnathan McCloy to new heights. I didn't know if he trusted us yet, but I knew he valued our abilities.

"Hee-hee."

I looked down at Adina as she giggled to herself and felt my lips curl.

"What's so funny?"

"Nothing." She nuzzled her cheeks against my chest. "I was just thinking about how I have you all to myself right now. It's kind of nice."

There was some truth to her words. When we lived in Valhalla, I was shared between her, Christine, and Michelle (though Christine was often gone for long periods of time), which meant we didn't always sleep together. It had been just the two of us these past two weeks. And she had been taking advantage of that. There had not been a single night where she and I didn't have sex. I didn't wake up a single morning without her riding me to an orgasm. It was only now that the two of us were alone that I realized just how salacious succubi truly were.

If I was an ordinary man, I'm pretty sure she would have sucked me dry by now.

I was honestly a little surprised she hadn't.

"Don't get too greedy." I bopped her on the head. "You know you're going to have to share once we join up with the others."

"I know, and I don't mind. You know I love Michelle and Christine." She raised her head to rest her chin on my chest, eyeing me with that grin of hers. So carefree. So easygoing. "But nobody said I couldn't take advantage of the time I've been given with you."

"I guess you bring up a good point. It is nice being able to spend so much time together."

Reaching out to stroke her cheek, I admired her beautiful face and gorgeous raven tresses. Adina's bright eyes bored into me as she crawled up my chest, grabbed my face, and once more began kissing me. I could do nothing as her tongue plunged into my mouth, as she began grinding her body against me once more. This was definitely not going to end with a single round of sex.

Knock. Knock. Knock.

Though I had been known to be wrong on rare occasion.

Adina scowled and glared at the door, which almost made me chuckle. I slipped out from underneath her, put on a pair of boxers, my pants, and pressed a button on the wall. The door slid open as Adina wrapped a blanket around herself, the outline of her wings stretching the fabric even as they folded into her back. It gave her a hump that made me think of a movie I'd seen a long time ago about a hunchback who lived in a bell tower… what was it called again?

The person on the other end was the drurian, Grian. He looked ten seconds away from saying something, but he stopped when he saw my state of undress.

"Can I help you?" I asked.

"I… uh… something came up," he said, recovering. "Commander McCloy has asked for your presence. Adina's too."

I nodded. "We'll be there in a moment. Just let us get dressed. You kind of interrupted us while we were in the middle of something."

Drurian's could not blush because their skin was harder and didn't have blood vessels like a human's, but I could tell he was embarrassed by how he looked away.

"R-right. I'm sorry about that. I'll let the commander know you'll be up shortly."

"Thanks."

I closed the door as Grian marched off on stiff legs that looked like wooden planks. As the door shut, I turned around to find Adina leaping out of bed and scowling as she placed one hand on her hip.

"Looks like the fun is over," she said.

"Seems that way." I nodded before gesturing for her to follow me. "Come on. Let's take a shower before meeting with Johnathan. I'd rather not smell of sex during what sounds like it could be an important meeting."

✳✳✳

Johnathan McCloy was located in the command chamber. That was where he could be found most often. I'd never seen him take to the field before, and I never saw him around any other parts of the base. It made me entertain the idea that he slept, ate, and even took his baths there.

It was an absurd notion to be sure, but I couldn't help but think that way.

"I'm glad you two could make it. I heard you were tied up by some, ahem, adult matters." Unlike the easily embarrassed Grian, he gave us a knowing grin and winked. The look didn't last long before it was replaced by something more grave. "Sorry to take you two lovebirds away from your private time, but a situation has come up, and I could really use your help."

"We figured as much. It sounds like there's a problem," I said.

"Calling it a problem might be understating matters. Follow me."

Johnathan gestured for us to follow him as he turned around, and who were we to disobey a direct order from our *supreme* commander? We followed him as he walked over to a workstation. The person sitting at it froze a moment, but only for a moment.

"Show us the video feedback from the security camera in Quadrant 5," Johnathan commanded.

"Sir."

The station worker, an older man whose bald head was shaped like a cueball, typed into his monitor and an image suddenly appeared on the screen. I recognized the urbanized zone as one of the many quadrants in Spoke 7. Since all quadrants looked the same, it was impossible to know which, but Johnathan had said Quadrant 5.

In either event, the video feedback quickly began replaying. It jumped forward to several hours. The station worker watched carefully, then began replaying it at a specific point in time.

What we saw was a battle.

"One of our patrols went behind enemy lines because we'd heard a rumor that Hydra gained a new secret weapon," Johnathan began, his tone grave. "While they were coming back, they encountered a patrol and were forced to engage."

"I'm guessing they were wiped out?" I asked.

"They were, but not by an enemy patrol."

With those ominous words hanging in the air, we watched the video as members of Cerberus fought members of Hydra. It was a classic situation I'd seen often in urban warfare. Two forces were hiding behind cover, shooting each other from a distance, laying down suppressive fire as they changed locations to gain a tactical advantage over the other.

Just when I was wondering what had Johnathan so spooked, it happened. A figure flew down from above, landing behind a Cerberus member and slicing his head clean off with a glowing golden sword. This person was a woman with angel wings on her back, wore the poisonous green armor of a Hydra member, and had a beautiful shade of silky blonde hair.

It was Michelle.

Adina let out a little gasp, and while I was sure Johnathan would just assume it was from surprise at seeing someone drop from the sky and remove someone's head like that person was made of paper, I still gave her a reproachful look.

"When our squadron didn't return, I had Tim here hack into the security cameras and scour the video feed to find out what happened," Johnathan told us. "As you can see, this woman showed up out of nowhere and decimated our troops. The whole battle happened so fast no one was able to send a request for help, and none of our men were left alive."

The video continued to play, and indeed, Michelle killed each member of Hydra in a matter of moments. She danced around their gunfire and used her golden swords to cut through their armor. While the armor of this high-tech realm could indeed block blaster bolts, it could not block a sword made from divine energy. Not only did she wield her two swords like they were extensions of her own body, but she created dozens of swords and sent them flying at her enemies.

Most of her opponents died before she closed the distance to engage them in melee combat.

As the screen went black, Johnathan turned to us. "I'm sure you can see how grave a threat this woman is."

"We can," I said as Adina nodded.

"We need to get rid of her before she becomes a hindrance to our plans."

"And I'm guessing getting rid of her will be our job."

"I'm glad you catch on so quick."

We had been out of contact with Christine and Michelle for so long now. This wasn't because we couldn't contact each other, but because we were maintaining radio blackout. It was safer for all of us if we didn't make an attempt to communicate during this time. We could not afford to have either Johnathan or Sauruss find out we were on the same side.

"We'll definitely do what we can," I assured him.

Adina finally spoke up. "Do you have a plan to lure her out?"

"I do." Johnathan confirmed with a nod, and I resisted a scowl when I saw him rake his eyes over Adina's breasts and thighs. Eyes up, buddy. "I'm gathering a large force to assault Quadrant 4 today. It will be the largest force ever gathered since this war began. Two thousand members of my army will be heading out along with half of my SML-44s."

Adina whistled as I said, "That's quite the force."

"That just goes to show you how great of a threat this woman is," Johnathan said with a shrug.

***

Explosions rent the air and sent bodies flying. Blaster bolts whizzed by, burning the atmosphere as they blasted holes into armor. Screams of agony, of rage, of hatred echoed from down below. Spoke 7, Quadrant 4, was in complete chaos.

Adina and I were not a part of that chaos. We observed the situation from above, looking down through our binoculars as thousands of people in either poisonous green or blood red armor viciously fought to annihilated the other side. For some reason, I was reminded of Christmas. A Christmas horror movie.

"Looks like Michelle hasn't shown up yet," Adina muttered as her wings fluttered impatiently. "Where is she?"

"Be patient," I said. "We can't expect her to show up right away. If everything went according to plan, then she and Christine should have become important members of Cerberus by now. They won't send her out immediately unless it becomes clear they need to."

"They sent her out to deal with that small squad," Adina countered.

"Doubtful," I said. "More than likely, Michelle made the decision herself to let us know about her successful infiltration."

"You and your stupid logic."

I snorted as my lover, unable to come up with a viable argument, resorted to acting childish. But it wasn't like I didn't understand where she was coming from. I was also eager to see Michelle and Christine again. I missed them.

The battle below was becoming more pandemonic by the second. Bodies were piling up as they were taken down with a combination of blaster fire and hand grenades.

I noticed that no one here seemed to have any special powers like we did, which meant this realm probably relied on a different leveling system. No one had magic. What they had was techniques and equipment upgrades. A good example was Grian, who had a skill called Sniper Shot, which caused his perceptions of time to increase, making it seem as if everything was moving slower. I didn't know if Johnathan also had any special skills—I assumed he did—but he did have his duster, a pair of modified pistols, and a massively overpowered repeating blaster.

"I see her!" Michelle suddenly shouted as she pointed at a speck in the distance.

I aimed my binoculars at the speck, and sure enough, what appeared in my vision was Michelle. Her two wings flapped as she soared through the sky. Her armor was… hideous. Poisonous green did not look good on her. But that was a secondary concern.

"Let's wait until she begins attacking," I recommended.

"Kay!"

It was easy to tell Adina was excited as we waited for Michelle to arrive. She and the archangel were great friends by this point. They got along well, watched each other's backs, and while they did bicker, I never had the sense that it was out of malice. I didn't know how sisters acted, but I imagined it was something like that.

Michelle came closer and suddenly swooped down to begin attacking the Cerberus members below us. Her first attack was the skill Dance of a Thousand Blades, which created hundreds of golden swords that fell from the sky like rain and impaled numerous Cerberus soldiers. After that, she landed lightly on the ground, raced forward, and began decimating an entire squadron by her lonesome.

That was our cue.

Adina grabbed me under the armpits and flew up. We kept Michelle in our sights and descended. The woman was just in the process of slicing through a man from his right shoulder to his left hip when Adina let me go, allowing me to land right in front of her. The archangel's eyes widened with surprise and delight, but neither of us gave any other indication that we knew each other.

I didn't attack with my sword, choosing to raise my pistol and fire at her instead. Michelle flapped her wings and darted away. While she avoided by attacks, she could not avoid Adina, who plowed into her like a ferocious tigress defending her territory. Michelle had no choice but to block Adina's attack with the flat of her blade, but that sent her flying backward. She flew even further than normal because she was in the air and had no traction.

Acting as if she was being overwhelmed, Michelle took off through the skies and tried to gain distance, but Adina and I followed her. While the succubus took to the skies and began "attacking" with "ferocious" and "deadly" attacks, I took careful aim and shot at Michelle with my pistol. None of my attacks hit. Of course they didn't.

My aim was always just slightly off, making it look like they would hit, only to miss because Michelle had moved just in time to evade.

It was a hard act, a deadly deceit. There was a very real chance we could kill Michelle if we weren't careful and vice versa, but all of us knew each other well enough by this point to make our fight look deadly. We trusted each other enough to perform this dangerous dance.

With Adina attacking from above, Michelle was forced back to the ground. It looked like we had cornered her. Michelle's back was to the wall. She could no longer retreat, couldn't take to the skies, and couldn't proceed forward without going through me.

All according to plan.

Just when it seemed as if we had the upper hand, something powerful slammed into me. I felt a brief moment of pain as I was clocked upside the head and stumbled away. Michelle used that time to attack Adina, swinging her two swords with incredible finesse, though the attacks were avoided when the succubus flew backwards.

I no longer had the time to pay attention to Adina and Michelle as a fist flew for my face. Tilting my head, I reached out to grab the extended forearm, spinning around and hoping to throw the person who tried to punch me over my shoulder. It didn't work. The person who attacked me grounded themselves and prevented me from lifting them.

I let go and jumped away before they could attack again. Spinning around, I came face to face with a muscular blonde woman decked out in green armor similar to Michelle's. There was a white stripe on her shoulder pads that differed from the archangels. I believed it somehow denoted this woman's rank.

"You took your sweet ass time getting here, Christine," I said, trying not to grin.

"Bryan, it's good to see you." Christine smiled at me seconds before aiming her rifle and opening fire.

The weapon she had was a repeating blaster, which could shoot a hailstorm of projectiles, about fifty every second. It was a lot like the machineguns in my world, except this sprayed blaster bolts instead of led.

I raced around a wall and hunkered down as the woman unleashed her load upon me. None of her attacks had hit, but I think I was honestly lucky this time. Was this woman trying to get me injured?! I knew we needed this to be authentic, but come on!

Once she realized her weapon was useless, Christine ran forward. I listened to the sound of her footsteps. She was getting close. Closer. Closer. I took a deep breath and counted down to five inside of my head, and then sprang out from behind the wall and kicked her blaster out of her grasp. As the weapon clattered to the ground, I unsheathed my sword and attacked.

I wasn't the only one with a sword. Christine unsheathed her blade and attacked me as I charged in. Her overhand slash was powerful. I could feel my knees buckle as I blocked it, which made me wonder if she'd risen another level or two, but I shunted those thoughts aside as I angled my sword to deflect her attack instead of taking it head on. Moving back two steps, I waited for her to bring up her blade, and then attacked with my own swing.

Sparks flew as our weapons clashed for a second time, and this time, we didn't remove them but began pushing against each other, as though to overpower the other. Our faces were now so close we could feel each other's breath. It was the perfect chance to speak.

"You were successful?" I asked.

"I was." Christine replied. "You?"

"Yup."

We pushed once more and leapt back at the same time. I went on the attack, swinging my sword from my right hip. It was blocked when Christine angled her blade to accept my attack, flicked her wrist, and pushed my weapon wide. She tried to counterattack with a thrust, but I sidestepped it before she could impale me through the chest.

I felt almost like we were sparring back on Valhalla, but this was no mere spar. The slightest mishap could result in injury or death. We had both accepted this, but that didn't mean I wasn't worried.

Our blades locked again.

"Have you learned anything?" I asked.

Christine subtly nodded. "Sauruss plans to attack Johnathan's supplier. We learned that Cerberus is getting a large-scale shipment of SML-44s. Sauruss thinks Johnathan is planning something big, so he plans to personally take charge of this battle, so you know it's going to be an important mission. If you can convince Johnathan to join them, I think that will be our best bet to finish them both at the same time."

I didn't nod as we backed off again, but I acknowledged her words in my own way. Now we needed to keep fighting until someone sounded the retreat.

High above us, the battle between Adina and Michelle was picking up. Adina was firing off energy blasts from her fists. Each blast looked like a giant fist-shaped sphere of pink fire, which detonated in the air as they met Michelle's flying golden swords. Each time the two attacks met, an explosion so brilliant it reminded me of fireworks filled the sky.

To avoid making it look like I wasn't trying, I activated Fireblade and attacked with an overhand swing, which Christine blocked by activating her own special skill. Her blade glowed a bright white color. It was more like an overlay of energy than flames. Our swords clashed, but no sparks flew this time. I strained my muscles and tried to overpower her. However, while I was stronger than most people, I had nothing on this woman, who was at level 90 last time I checked. She quickly pushed back, throwing me off balance and going on the attack.

I avoided her first slash by jumping backward. Her second came in like lightning, a powerful thrust that I narrowly dodged. Rather than let herself be taken by surprise, she moved as if she'd been expecting me to avoid her attack, spinning on the balls of her feet as she swung even from this disadvantageous position.

Sweat poured down my back. My breathing came out in heavy rasps. A harsh sting from several areas where my face got nicked by Christine's sword bled.

There was no time to focus on anything other than my battle with Christine, but I really hoped the death toll would rise enough that Cerberus and Hydra decided the battle was no longer worth it and the damned order to retreat. The only problem was I didn't know how long it would take before both forces decided enough was enough.

As the fight continued between me and Christine, more small cuts appeared on our arms. We were doing our best to make our fight seem real without outright killing each other, but the longer our battle went on, the harder it became to avoid injury. Our bodies tired. We became sloppier.

I think it was fortune that a loud buzzing sound filled the air. That was Cerberus's signal to retreat. Had it come any later, one of us might have been heavily injured.

Leaping back as I pulled out my pistol, I fired off several shots that Christine dodged and raced backward. Just then, Adina swooped down and picked me up under my armpits. I looked down to see Michelle do the same thing to Christine and try to give chase, but I fired warning shots to ward them off.

"Looks like… everything went according to plan," Adina said, breathing labored.

"Yeah. I also got some good intel. You?" I asked, looking up.

Adina had several burns on her arms, legs, and neck, but she looked like she was in good shape, albeit tired.

"I think it turned out well," she said after a moment. "Michelle and Christine have infiltrated Hydra and are getting closer to Sauruss, but they haven't earned his trust yet. He values them, but he seems suspicious too."

"I guess that can't be helped. I heard Sauruss was more cautious than Johnathan."

"Hmmm."

Silence came between us. Down below, our army was retreating under the blaster fire of Hydra. Several people went down as they ran away, shot in the back by a group who had no intention of giving them any reprieve.

We had failed our mission, which marked this as the first failure in our list of missions for Johnathan, and I was okay with that.

***

"So, you couldn't kill that winged woman?"

"I'm afraid not. She had a colleague who attacked me when we were fighting. Adina was forced to fight her by herself, which resulted in draw."

"Ha… well, if that isn't just the bitch's tits."

Johnathan sighed as I gave him a debriefing of what happened during the fight in Quadrant 4. I had, of course, only given him the basic rundown about how we'd found Michelle, fought her, cornered her, and were interrupted by Christine. I said nothing of how Christine and Michelle were my lovers, or that we hadn't actually been trying to kill each other. He had no need to know that.

"I'm sorry for failing to kill her," Adina said, her head bowed. It made her look remorseful, but I knew the truth. She was looking down so no one would see her smile.

"No, it's fine." Johnathan waved her apology off and tried to smile. "You two have been doing a great job out there, so we grew reliant on you, but I guess even you're not invincible. This woman and her partner were able to match you in combat. That's no small feat. However, it's not like they emerged victorious either. It was a draw. That means when you two fight them next time, it will come down to skill and luck."

I didn't think we'd be fighting them again at all. Our next plan was to have the news that Sauruss was going to attack Johnathan's next shipment leak to Cerberus, convince Johnathan to confront Sauruss in person, and kill them both at the same time, but make it look like they had taken each other out. That would be the best way to take care of these two and not deal with any backlash from their underlings.

Of course, getting the knowledge that Sauruss would be personally taking charge of the attack on Cerberus's shipment was up to Christine and Michelle. Not me. All I could do was wait for something to happen.

I really hated waiting.

CHAPTER 15

The days passed quicker than I expected. After the large battle between Cerberus and Hydra, neither side attacked the other for a good while. That was not to say small skirmishes didn't happen. However, there were no large-scale battles like the one from before. Fights that broke out were always between small squads.

Before I knew it, another week had passed.

I was beginning to grow worried. According to the information Christine had provided during the fight, a large shipment of SML-44s should be coming in soon, and Sauruss planned to attack the shipment and steal all of the equipment for himself. Even if I didn't know when it would happen, I imagine it should happen soon. How else could Sauruss know about it? And yet, we hadn't heard a word about him attacking or even planning to attack a shipment yet. Had Christine and Michelle failed in their mission? I hoped that was not the case.

To get my mind off my worries, I decided to check my level, which I hadn't done in a long time, and I realized that my level had actually risen a bit since we'd come to Station 13. I think it was from all the people I had killed. Nobody here was above level 60 except for Johnathan, who was at level 70. Sauruss was probably at the same or a similar level. While killing people several levels below you didn't net as many experience points, I'd still killed so many people that I'd gone from level 72 to level 76.

Name: Bryan Jenson

Class: Magic Swordsman

Magic: Red

Level: 76

Attack: 240

Agility: 200

Defense: 200

Mana: 200

Total Status Points available: 0

Special Skills:

Thousand Cuts+17

Whirlwind Slash+10

Death by Piercing+8

Fireblade+17

Helm Splitter+1

Total Skill Points Available: 0

I made sure to allocate my skill points appropriately and also upgraded my special skills. Because my Attack stat had reached 240 points, I gained the ability to learn the special skill Helm Splitter. It was an attack that broke through any and every form of armor out there to deal incredible physical damage.

That was what the skill said anyway, but it wasn't like knowing Helm Splitter automatically made me able to use it. First, Helm Splitter was still in its infantile stage with only a single point allocated to it. This meant there was a high-rate of failure when using Helm Splitter against an armored opponent. Right now, I could probably break through leather armor, but the armor used on Station 13 was far beyond my ability to break. Well, I was certain my physical strength would make up for how weak this skill currently was.

Adina had also leveled up. She was now at level 85. While gaining a single level didn't seem like much, I had to take into account the fact that she was a full nine levels higher than me. It became downright difficult to level up the higher you level was. That she leveled up at all by killing level 60 grunts was honestly a miracle.

My worries about Johnathan not getting the news that Sauruss was planning to attack his next shipment proved to be unfounded. I would have sighed in relief, but I had no idea that an even bigger problem was looming on the horizon.

Grian came by again, telling us Johnathan wanted to speak to us.

"He says something urgent has come up and would like your presence in the command room."

"All right," I said as I stood by the door. "Just let us get dressed. Fortunately, we were already in the process of doing just that. It shouldn't take more than a minute."

"That's fine. I'll wait here and escort you when you're ready."

I tilted my head and frowned a bit when I saw how… stiff Grian looked. He shifted his gaze to the side when he noticed my hard stare, as though avoiding it. This didn't seem like he was feeling bashful or anxious. This was something else.

"Everything okay?" I asked.

"Everything is fine," he said.

Since I couldn't see any reason for his behavior, I shrugged and went back inside of my room. Adina was already dressed in her armored suit. I went over to where my suit was stored in the closet and put it on. I also grabbed my sword, slung it over my shoulder, attached my pistol to my hip, and I even placed a few hand grenades onto my belt. I'd never used hand grenades before. They normally required a Skill to use well, and I had no hand grenade skills, but I could still throw them.

Once Adina and I were dressed, we left the room and followed Grian as he directed us to an elevator.

The ride up was… awkward. Adina was hanging off my arm and looked like nothing was bothering her, but Grian was shifting on the balls of his feet. He seemed nervous. Maybe even frightened. We didn't speak as the elevator ascended, and soon we were being led into the command chamber.

I immediately noticed there were a lot more people in the command chamber than normal. They weren't the average station workers who sat behind consoles and communicated with others. Dressed in full battle armor and holding rifles in their hands, these people stood silently off to the sides. Were these the people who would be involved with whatever operation was underway? Or was this something else?

"Adina. Bryan. Glad you two could make it," Johnathan said with a smile as he gestured for us to come over. "Another situation has come up."

"Is this why there are so many people present?" I asked as we walked over to the man.

"Partly," Johnathan said. His words were evasive, but he quickly began talking again before I could question him. "We recently received some information that Sauruss was planning to attack my latest shipment. The one I've got coming in this time is big. It contains nearly five hundred SML-44s."

"That's almost half your current force of SML-44s, isn't it?" I asked.

"That's correct." Johnathan nodded, his expression grave. "This is also why it's imperative we stop Sauruss from attacking that shipment. He plans on stealing my equipment and using it for himself." He paused. "Not only did we get word that he plans to attack our next shipment, but we also learned that Sauruss is planning to take part in this mission himself. I guess he wants to make sure things go smoothly."

I tried to keep myself calm, but I could feel excitement bubbling inside of me. This was the moment we had been waiting for.

"What do you plan on doing?" I asked.

"Well, we obviously can't do nothing. We need to intercept Sauruss and his group before they can attack our shipment. However, we're also at a bit of a loss as to how we should do this. Our intel states Sauruss is planning to make this a major offensive. He's bringing a lot more forces to bear than he ever has before, even during our last big battle." Johnathan paused to stare at me, and there was something in that stare that made me unnerved, though I shoved that feeling aside. "What do you think we should do?"

It seemed odd that he was asking me for advice. Was this a test? Was he trying to see if I could create a good plan? I wasn't sure, but something told me that what I was thinking was not what he had in mind.

Still doing my best to shove the strange feelings I had to the side, I said, "The only way to avoid having our shipment stolen is to meet force with greater force. We can gather a force that's equal to whatever they have, but we can also use the SML-44s currently in our possession."

Johnathan nodded as if he was onboard with the idea. "Anything else?"

"I also think you should be the one to lead us," I stated. "If Sauruss is going to be there, this may be the chance all of us have been looking for to end this battle in a single, decisive victory. And the one who should lead us to victory can't be anyone but you."

A smile appeared on Johnathan's face. "You've got quite the way with words. I'm surprised a military man such as yourself can be so charismatic. Most members of the military can only follow orders."

"It's former military," I admitted. "But how did you know I was in a military?"

Placing his hands behind his back, Johnathan stood with his feet shoulder width apart, back completely straight. It was a common pose among military men. This was a pose I stood in often back in basic training, where our instructors would yell in our faces. It brought back nostalgic memories.

"I, too, was once a member of the military," Johnathan said. "I belonged to the United Navy Space Fleet of the Earth Union. Our training doesn't appear to have been much different. You've got the same bearing and general mannerisms as a man from the military. I recognized it the moment you walked through those doors for the first time."

So that was it. Well, it wasn't like I shouldn't have been able to figure that out. I'd already known Johnathan was ex-military, but I'm sure I would have recognized his military background even if I hadn't been made aware beforehand.

"Anyway, you do bring up a good point. Perhaps I should lead the charge this time. A leader shouldn't constantly command from behind. It's important that my men see me fighting alongside them."

I nodded along with everything he said, trying hard to make it seem like I actually agreed with him and wasn't just interested in getting him outside of this base so I could kill him and make it look like he and Sauruss killed each other.

"However, before that, I want you to see something else we found that you might be interested in," Johnathan said.

"What is it?" I asked, and while I couldn't explain why, I had a very bad feeling, like bugs settling in the pit of my stomach.

"I wanted to show you this."

Johnathan pulled a device from a pouch at his hip. It was one of those datacards, the kind that the contact used when showing us the information about Johnathan and Sauruss. He waved a hand over the card. It lit up with a brilliant blue glow, then projected in image in thin air.

The image was of a ship, a very familiar ship. I should recognize this ship. It was the one I traveled here on with Adina, Christine, and Michelle.

The sinking feeling grew worse.

After the image appeared, it began moving, showing me this was actually a video recording... or a holographic recording, I guess. It showed me, Adina, Christine, and Michelle walking off the boarding ramp together and talking to the dock master. Christine paid the fee and then we all left together.

Suddenly, Grian's strange behavior this morning made sense.

A series of clicks and whirring noises alerted me and Adina to the soldiers surrounding us, their guns glowing vibrantly as they charged them up and took aim. I counted 50 in total, including Grian.

"I always thought there was something odd about you two," Johnathan said with a strange smile. "You're both so powerful. There's not a single person on Station 13 who can match you in raw physical strength and ability—except for those two. It made me suspicious. That's why I had my men check the security cameras outside of Spoke 7 to see if they could find any information on you. Imagine my surprise when I discovered that you and those two you fought were not only acquainted but seemed awfully close."

This was not good. I'd completely underestimated Johnathan. Maybe it was because he was a deserter, the kind of person I subconsciously held in contempt for abandoning his post, or maybe there was another reason. Either way, I had never once considered that he would be smart enough to look up information on me and Adina like this.

Now he knew we weren't on his side, all the work we had done to ingratiate ourselves to him had gone up in smoke within a split second, and I wasn't quite sure how we'd get out of this situation.

"Any last words?" asked Johnathan.

"Just two," I said. "Adina! Floor!"

Adina reacted so quickly it was almost like she'd read my mind. Her right fist contained glowing blue energy as she slammed it into the floor. Metal squealed and people screamed as the floor was torn apart right underneath our feet. A hole nearly a dozen meters in radius spread out. We dropped through it. The drop below wasn't far, but nobody except me and Adina had been prepared for it, so while we landed on our feet, they landed on their asses.

"Let's go!" I shouted.

Truth be told, I would have liked to kill Johnathan before we left, but he and his soldiers were already recovering and aiming their weapons at us.

I swung my sword and activated Whirlwind Slash, cutting through several soldiers, armor and all. As blood sprayed from their wounds, Adina fired off several Energy Blasts that exploded against soldiers further away. We opened a path as Johnathan retreated to a safe distance and began shouting orders as he fired on us.

"Shoot them! Open fire!"

Blaster bolts whizzed by our heads, struck the ground and walls, releasing intense sizzling sounds as the metal interior became blackened with carbon scoring. Adina and I didn't move in a straight line. We darted left and right at random to present a harder-to-hit target before eventually turning a corner.

"What now?" asked Adina.

"Now we escape. This mission has failed," I said.

It sucked, but missions sometimes went awry. To be honest, I'd been thinking this mission was coming along a little too easily, but I guess that just meant it was saving all our bad karma for this one moment. Now all our planning was in ruins. We would have to find another way to kill Johnathan.

"Attention everyone!" a voice suddenly shouted from speakers in the wall. It was Johnathan. "This is an emergency situation! Adina and Bryan are traitors who tried to kill me! They were thwarted and are now running free in our base! I want all hands armed and searching for them! Shoot to kill!"

Well, shit. The situation had just gone from bad to worse.

The announcement had caused nearly everyone in the base to arm themselves and attack us on sight. We ran in every direction we could. However, it soon became apparent when we ran into several ambushes that they were tracking us. This base had security cameras installed inside just like Spoke 7. More than likely, Johnathan was tracking our movements and directing his forces to ensnare us.

"There are more coming!" Adina shouted as several dozen men in combat suits charged from around a corner.

"Mow them down!" I shouted back.

Adina flapped her wings and lifted into the air as the soldiers opened fire. I managed to avoid being hit by throwing myself against the wall. Meanwhile, Adina returned their fire with a volley of Energy Blasts, powerful bursts of blue energy coalesced into a sphere that exploded against their chests, destroying their armor and demolishing their bodies. Many of the attacks she launched crushed their rib cages or made their heads explode. The iron scent of blood became thick.

With the enemy in disarray, I rammed into their forces with reckless abandon, swinging my sword in a horizontal arc that cut through a man's trachea. Blood gushed from his wound like arterial spray, but I was already moving on, my sword igniting in flames as I used Fireblade to cleave through someone's chestplate. There was only a moment of resistance before my blade cut through the synthetic armor and bit into hard flesh. The man screamed as he went down.

A click alerted me to danger before the sight of a man with his hand on a trigger did. I was too far away to attack him, and he had me dead to rights.

Just as I was about to dodge, Adina came screaming in, her foot careening off the side of the man's head. I almost flinched at the loud crunch that echoed down the hall. The soldier's face had collapsed on itself.

After she sent the soldier flying, Adina landed on the ground and began systematically demolishing everyone with her incredible physical strength. She sent one man flying with a punch to the chest, his armor dented and cracked. Another had his face caved in as he was lifted off the ground when she hit him with a snap kick. Several people tried to open fire, but she took to the air and avoided the worst of it before landing back on the ground and taking her pound of flesh from them. The woman was like a force of nature.

God, I loved her.

We somehow managed to fight our way to an elevator, and though it probably wasn't the smartest idea, we climbed inside. We needed to ascend to the first basement floor in order to leave this place. This base also didn't have any stairs in this area. The elevator was our only way up.

"This feels weird," Adina murmured.

"Weird how?" I asked.

"We're being chased by people who want to kill us, but here we are just standing inside an elevator as it slowly moves up to the first basement floor. I can feel my sense of urgency diminishing in here."

"I understand how you feel," I said.

The elevator was indeed moving slowly. Actually, wasn't it moving slower than normal?

I looked up to see what floor we were on and realized the elevator had actually stopped at basement level 3. It only took me a moment to realize what that meant, and in that moment, the elevator doors opened.

And revealed several dozen soldiers aiming their rifles at us.

"Damn it!"

We only had a moment to press ourselves against either side of the elevator as the soldiers opened fire. I gritted my teeth as blaster bolts whizzed past us and struck the wall, burning it until it was black, then red. The wall melted through. That would have been us if we hadn't moved in time.

"What now?!" asked Adina.

"Let's get onto the roof!" I shouted.

I used Fireblade to cut a hole through the roof and leapt up. The elevator shook as I landed on it. Unlike the elevators back on Earth, this one used magnetic propulsion instead of a pulley system, so we unfortunately couldn't just cut a metal chord and expect it to fall. Adina landed on the roof barely a second after me.

"Adina, smash this thing apart," I said.

"I can do that."

With a grin, Adina channeled more mana into her fist, blazing energy igniting around it. She brought the fist down. Energy exploded as she used Energy Blast to punch a large hole into the elevator, which went through the roof and floor. The elevator shook and rumbled. Her attack had destroyed the power source that kept the magnets working. Without that source, the elevator was bound to fall.

Adina grabbed me and held me close as she flapped her wings, rising into the air as the elevator fell down with a squeal, disappearing into the depths of the base. Several soldiers appeared in the now open entrance and tried to shoot up at us, but Adina was already out of their range. She quickly ascended to the first floor. I used Fireblade to slice the door open.

Because we wanted to avoid having holes blasted through our chests, we didn't just fly straight into the hallway. She floated over to the side and pressed her back against the wall. I used my Meteor Sword to peer around the corner. There were indeed several dozen soldiers waiting for us.

"What should we do?" asked Adina.

I thought hard about what we needed to do. Our first priority right now was escaping from this base. Our second priority was losing our pursuers. Our third priority was hooking up with Christine and Michelle and creating a new plan to deal with Johnathan and Sauruss. Right now, we could only focus on priority one. Nothing would happen if we didn't get out of here.

The biggest issue was breaking through this group and making it to the exit. I didn't think we'd be able to escape unless someone was willing to draw the attention of everyone here, allowing the other person time to escape. It was a cliché plan. However, it was cliché because it often worked.

Of course, there was only one person I would allow to do this.

"Adina, I want you to follow behind me for now," I said. "We're breaking through this group."

"Sounds good to me!"

I was sure Adina would have been cracking her knuckles if she wasn't holding me.

We counted to three before Adina threw me into the hallway. I hit the ground, rolled forward, and brought my pistol up as I came to my feet. I fired off several shots. Most went wide. However, everyone in the hall dove out of the way, which gave me time to remove a hand grenade and lob it into the air. While it was flying, I aimed at it and fired, striking the grenade and causing it to explode.

The grenades used in this realm were not the traditional M67 fragmentation grenade I was used to. They were small cylinders about two inches in length. Rather than explode and shoot high-velocity shrapnel at people, this produced a powerful explosion of plasma. The resulting explosion was devastatingly effective, especially against shielded infantry.

In this confined space, it was even more effective.

The explosion caused the hallway to warp, expanding outward like a balloon. I was far enough away that all the blast did was push me back, but the people who were in the center of that impact were annihilated down to their atoms. The ones who weren't in the epicenter of the explosion but still near it had their faces and armor burned off. Most of them died from shock.

"Come on!" I shouted to Adina.

There were still a few stragglers who'd managed to avoid being caught in the blast. I slid my sword along the throat of one such person, who was far too shocked to do anything else. Adina broke the skull of another one. Together, we pushed through the straggling defenses and journeyed deeper into the first floor.

As we continued running, I located all the cameras inside and shot them. While it had been awhile since I fired a gun since coming to the Rift Plains, it was nice to see I hadn't lost my touch. I used to be a crack shot when I was in the SpecOps. My ability to shoot a target from two hundred yards with a 9mm was something I'd been proud of back then.

We didn't immediately head to the exit but instead ran around and caused as much of a ruckus as we could. We killed, we shot up security cameras, and we destroyed a variety of rooms. It was just too bad I didn't have any talent as a hacker. If I did, we probably could have programmed some of the SML-44s to attack the people in this base.

Even though chaos reigned, it would eventually calm down. The longer we fought, the more organized the forces arrayed against us became. It wasn't long before they had pinned us down in a hallway.

"What now?" asked Adina as she and I stood with our backs against the wall, figuratively and literally.

"Now?" I took a deep breath. "Now, I am going to distract these guys by charging right down their center. I want you to use that distraction to escape. Get in contact with Christine and Michelle. Let them know what happened and try to find me. If you don't find me, assume I've been captured and come rescue me."

It was a testament to her faith in me that Adina didn't immediately argue against me staying here to draw attention away from her. I appreciated that. At the same time, I could see in her displeased expression that she was not happy about this arrangement. Sadly, there was nothing I could do.

"Promise me you won't die," Adina said.

I smiled. "I have no intention of dying. Just make sure you rescue me if I get captured."

"Fine." I wasn't quite prepared for Adina to grab my face and pull me into a kiss. It didn't last long, but it was hard and passionate, and I was left breathless when she pulled back. "Good luck."

"You too."

As Adina took off down the corridor, several people shouted to open fire, but I stepped around the corner at that moment and opened fire on them. I also tossed my last grenade. As the ensuing explosion killed even more people and burned just as many, I raced forward and began attacking with reckless abandon. My goal was to draw attention to me. I needed to be flashy.

I made liberal use of Fireblade and Whirlwind Slash. My sword tore through armor like it was butter and my special skill allowed me to attack many people at the same time. Six people died in my first attack, which combined Fireblade and Whirlwind Slash to create something similar to a firestorm. I think there was actually a skill called that. Sadly, I didn't know it.

Several people came at me from the front. This hallway was wide enough for three people to stand shoulder width apart, but that was not enough for someone to slip past me. One of the men charged in for melee combat. He raised his combat knife and slashed down. I met his attack, sparks flying, and disarmed him with a flick of my wrist. As his knife clattered to the ground, I impaled him through the throat.

No one else seemed interested in attacking me at close-range. They held back, aimed their rifles, and opened fire. One of the blaster bolts struck me before I could avoid it. The attack glanced off my armor. I spun from the force, dodged several more bolts, and jumped to run along the wall, waiting until I had closed the distance before kicking off the wall and landing before another enemy.

The drurian I attacked went down when I bisected him, my sword carving a line through his flesh. I kicked him in the chest as he died, sending him into one of his friends and knocking them both down. That only bought me a bit of time. I fired my pistol from the hip, shooting two people in the face, watching as the plasma burned through their heads. However, even though three people had just died, there were still plenty more enemies.

I didn't know how long I'd been fighting for, but I knew it was time to leave. After running one more person through with my blade, I took off down the opposite direction as Adina, and the squadron of enemy soldiers followed me, screaming in rage. I had killed several of their people. I had betrayed them. I was sure their anger at me blinded them to everything else.

Since my goal wasn't to escape but draw attention away from Adina's escape, I didn't travel in the direction of the exit and instead took numerous random turns. I shot out the cameras every time I saw one. I hoped this would cause even more confusion among their ranks. If they couldn't figure out where I was, then they hopefully wouldn't figure out Adina was no longer with me—at least, not until it was too late.

After what felt to me like several hours, I decided it was finally time to secrete myself away. The halls didn't have any vents, but I traveled into one of the rooms and found a grate that led into a ventilation shaft. I guess even high-tech facilities built on space stations required ventilation. My only concern was people would know I'd gone into the vents because I couldn't put the grating back in place, but the vents did branch out in many different directions, so I hoped it would be awhile before anyone found me.

I was pretty exhausted by this point. Crawling around inside of a vent only made me more tired and cranky. I really wanted to get some sleep. Would anyone find me if I decided to stick around in this vent and get some shut-eye? I didn't know, but I dismissed the thought because I didn't want to risk it.

After traveling for who knew how long, I eventually found what appeared to be a hidden hallway. I think it was a rarely used maintenance corridor. The blue lighting was low and made it hard to see, but at least I wasn't blinded by darkness. Slipping out of the vent after I cut through the grating, I landed on the floor in a crouch and began walking in some random direction.

This corridor was larger than I expected. It could probably fit six people standing shoulder width apart. My thoughts on how this was a maintenance corridor felt more believable now. I could already imagine various pieces of machinery and repair equipment being transported through here and affecting whatever repairs were needed to keep this base functional.

I was pretty sure Adina had escaped by this point. There was always a chance she hadn't, but given her strength, I couldn't see anyone being able to stop her—unless Johnathan deployed the SML-44s, but even those might not be enough. I'd seen that woman tear apart several dozen centimeters'-thick metal with her bare hands.

Ding. Ding.

A noise caught my attention as I traveled, causing me to twist my head and look around. I soon discovered figures walking out from the depths of the corridor. They weren't human. Each one was about two times taller than myself, walked on tree trunk metal legs, and had a wide array of weapons attached to their arms and shoulders. The glowing red visors embedded into the thick and sturdy bodies glared at me.

"You don't know how much trouble you've caused me," a voice issued from a speaker on the leading SML-44.

I shrugged. "I don't particularly care about how much trouble I've caused."

"No, I guess you don't… but you will."

"That so? You gonna kill me?"

"I wish I could, but it seems you have some connection to Sauruss. I can't afford to kill you until I know what you know."

It seemed Michelle and Christine being in Hydra made Johnathan think I was somehow involved as well, like a double agent or a spy sent to infiltrate his ranks. Nobody who led a faction like this could miss on the opportunity to gain some intel on their enemies. It was the paradox of keeping a dangerous person prisoner. It would be better to just kill them, but what if they knew something vital to your survival? If you just kill them, you might lose out on that key bit of information that could help you live another day.

"Well, that sounds unfortunate," I said.

"It is very unfortunate… for you, that is," Johnathan said.

A second after he finished speaking, the SML-44 fired something from a barrel underneath the main canon on its right arm. I didn't know what it was. It struck me faster than I could blink. The world spun wildly for a brief moment, and then everything went dark.

CHAPTER 16

I regained consciousness but didn't open my eyes right away. Everything came back to me in a rush, and I knew I'd been captured by Johnathan and his faction. The fact that my wrists were restrained behind my back and I was sitting in a hard chair merely provided more evidence to support my thoughts.

Keeping my breathing and heart rate from rising as I woke up was not easy, but it was something I had been trained in. There were devices on Earth used to monitor pulse and heart rate. It would let people know when someone woke up. I was sure there was something like that here, so I did my best to make it look like I was still unconscious.

The hissing sound of a door suddenly sliding open echoed around me. Footsteps came next. I tried to listen while maintaining my unconscious state as whoever entered sat down somewhere in front of me.

"There's no point in pretending anymore. I already know you're awake."

It was Johnathan, and it sounded like my act hadn't fooled him. I guess they had even more advanced technology here than on Earth. They must have known the moment I woke up.

"Good morning, Commander." I raised my head and made a big show of yawning.

Johnathan looked amused. "You're certainly nonchalant for a man who's been captured."

"Am I? I guess I'm just used to this kind of thing."

"You get captured a lot?"

"More than you'd think."

Technically, I'd only been captured once in my entire life. Namaah had captured me and then tossed me in prison, where I was tortured by Meliperum for information on Earth. That had been some of the worst torture I'd ever experienced. Meliperum had been brutal. Even now, I sometimes felt phantom pains from when she'd torn into me.

Now that I was no longer pretending to be asleep, I observed my surroundings. The room was a perfectly uniform shade of gray, except for the window on my left. It took up an entire wall. I was sitting on a metal chair, my hands cuffed behind my back, legs cuffed to the chair. I attempted to move, but the chair was bolted to the floor. Guess that option was out.

"I'm sure I don't need to tell you why I'm here," Johnathan said.

I shrugged. "You want information on Sauruss."

"So you already know. That will make things easier." Johnathan's amiable expression evaporated as he stared at me with a hard glint in his eyes. "Tell me everything you know about Sauruss. His strengths. His weaknesses. How he planned to kill me. I want to know all of it."

"Then I'm afraid I'm gonna have to disappoint you." I smiled at him, cheerfully, happily, mockingly. "I've got nothing to say."

"So it's to be torture then?" asked Johnathan. "You could avoid that if you just tell me what I want to know."

"Sorry, but unlike a certain someone who abandoned their post, I don't betray my comrades."

My words must have really set him off. I didn't even have time to blink before Johnathan stood to his feet and punched me as hard as he could. It wasn't a quick jab either, but one that he had put all of his weight into. My head cracked back as my vision whited out. It was a good thing Johnathan's level was much lower than my own. While the punch did hurt, it was nothing compared to when Meliperum had gouged out my chest.

I shook my head to clear out the cobwebs, then smiled at him. "You hit like a ninny."

"You're a funny guy." Johnathan snarled as he decked me in the face again. I didn't so much as grunt as my head once more whipped back. "But being funny won't get you anywhere here."

"Oh, I don't know." I chuckled when he finished punching me. Blood welled up in my nose and trickled down my nostrils, but I snorted it out. "I think it's given me plenty. Seeing you so enraged is prime entertainment if you ask me."

Johnathan gritted his teeth, but he soon calmed down. Well, shoot. I'd been hoping to enrage him more. So long as he was angry and not thinking, I was the one in charge of this interrogation, but he seemed to have caught on.

"I guess you leave me no choice," Johnathan said with a sigh.

He snapped his fingers and several people came in. I didn't recognize any of them, but that was no surprise. This was a faction with several thousand members.

They were wheeling in a trolley that floated a couple dozen centimeters off the ground. That was some high-tech, sci-fi stuff. I turned my head to watch as they moved behind me and began undoing the bolts on the chair.

For just a moment, I thought about trying to escape, about breaking free of these cuffs, killing Johnathan, and fleeing during the chaos. I only entertained the idea for a moment. Maybe I could kill Johnathan now, but I didn't think I would escape. There was also no guarantee I could kill Johnathan since my armor and weapons had been confiscated.

I was doing this mission because we needed to in order to gain information on Michelle's home, but I was not so set on completing it that I was willing to die.

The soldiers finished undoing the bolts and set me on the trolley. I was pushed out and led down a hallway, through a series of thick blast doors, and into a room that made me think "sci-fi torture chamber." There were no chains, no tools covered in blood, but there was a large device like a bed with straps. Well, I called it a bed, but that was only because it was lying horizontally across the ground. It didn't look that comfortable.

"Strap him in," Johnathan said.

They undid the cuffs around my feet and hands, and for another second, I considered making a break for it. Several things prevented that. Namely, the soldiers who had accompanied us here. There were at least six with their rifles trained on me. I wouldn't be able to escape before they pumped me full of holes.

"This is your last chance," Johnathan said. "Tell me what I want to know."

"And? Let's say I do tell you, will you let me go?"

"…"

"Thought not. Do your worst."

I knew how interrogations like this worked even before traveling to the Rift Plains. Once a prisoner no longer had any use, once you had wrung out everything you could from them, the prisoner was always disposed of. That went double for someone dangerous. In fact, the more dangerous the prisoner, the quicker their captors wanted to kill them.

"Fine," Johnathan muttered before glancing at one of the men. "Do it."

I didn't know what was going to happen, so I braced myself for anything, but as the man holding a strange device in his hands fiddled with it, I realized that nothing could have prepared me for this.

A scream tore from my throat before I could even realize what was happening. Agony raced through my body. It felt like every nerve ending had suddenly come alive with pain. Pain. Pain. Pain. That was all I felt. It was like my entire body had become a receptacle for pain. Even if I wanted to keep myself from screaming, I was unable to even think about that as I screamed at the top of my lungs.

And then it was over.

"Ha… ha… ha…"

"Hurts, doesn't it?" Johnathan asked, a sympathetic expression on his face. "You know, when I was in the military, they used this device on me. You say I abandoned my post, but that wasn't the real story. I was a simple commander stationed on an inhospitable planet with hostile natives. At the time, our facilities were being overrun, a bioweapon had been let loose, and my men were dying in droves. I took all the soldiers who still lived and fled the planet. I wasn't about to let my men die in vain. And what did I receive upon returning to the United Earth Navy? Court martial and dishonorable dismiss. They said I abandoned my post, and sure, maybe I did, but it was going to be lost anyway. I just made the most logical choice to save as many people as I could."

I wasn't sure why he was telling me this. His past meant about as much to me as the dump I'd taken this morning.

"And? What's your point?" I asked, having been given enough time to recover.

Johnathan shrugged. "I guess I don't really have a point. Maybe I just wanted to mention it because you were also once in the military. Now, are you going to tell me what I want to know?"

"If you suck my dick, I'll consider it," I shot back.

"I thought that would be your answer," Johnathan said before nodding at the man who controlled this torture device.

My screams once more echoed around the room.

***

Time had an odd habit of blurring together when you were being tortured. It was impossible to tell how much time had passed as every second not spent experiencing excruciating agony was spent unconscious. Maybe days had gone by, maybe only a few hours had passed, and maybe it had been months. I really didn't know.

That device they used was an impressive piece of work. While I wasn't sure how it worked, I understood the general principle behind it. This thing worked by connecting to the nerve endings and making them send a message to your brain that you were experiencing the most incredible pain imaginable. It didn't actually hurt you in the literal sense, which made it easier to keep prisoners alive. The only thing they had to worry about was someone dying of shock.

I was made from pretty tough stuff, so they didn't worry about me dying.

Every session often ended with me blacking out. When I woke up again, I would be lying inside of a cell and unable to move for several seconds. Once I woke up, they would feed me those terribly bland food cubes, let me take a shit, and then I'd be right back on the torture device.

"Ga... ha... hurk..."

"You really are resilient," Johnathan said after what felt like hours of being tortured. "Do you know how much time has passed since we began? I suppose not. Let me tell you that it's been a considerable amount of time, and yet, despite how long we've been at this, you've refused to budge even an inch. You have my respect."

While the man said he respected me, I thought he sounded very angry about something. His tone was biting and cold. There was also an impressive snarl on his face. Had my silence really pissed him off that much?

I cracked a grin at the man, even though just moving my mouth hurt like a motherfucker. "W-what can I say? I've always been a stubborn bastard."

"You are indeed, but in this case, that is not a good thing."

Perhaps he could tell I was not interested in talking yet, because he immediately had his soldiers turn on the torture device again. My body shook and jerked, spasming as pain flooded my body once more.

I think I blacked out. When I came to, I was being dragged down a hallway, my feet trailing against the floor.

I think the fact that I woke up so soon meant I was getting used to being tortured. Whether that was a good thing or not was something I couldn't figure out quite yet.

I wanted to use this chance to break free from my captors, but while I might have been awake, I didn't have the strength to actually move. Thus I had no choice but to let them drag me to my prison cell and toss me inside. I grunted as my face smacked against the floor. The sound of a door slamming shut echoed behind me, but I hardly paid attention as I forced my stiff muscles to move, flipping over onto my back and staring at the ceiling.

"God, this sucks," I muttered as, unable to maintain consciousness, I passed out again.

When I woke up again, it was because of a loud blaring in my ears. I blinked several times and resisted the sudden urge to vomit. An acrid scent reached my nose as I pressed my palms against the ground and sat up, ignoring the way my body screamed in protest. I realized the scent came from my pants. The liquid had dried, but there was a stain there.

Great. I'd pissed myself. It must have been when they were torturing me.

Wincing as I strained my muscles, I wobbled to my feet and tried to stumble toward the door, but the world tilted backward. Instead of moving toward the door, I found myself sliding down the wall.

The blaring continued to echo all around me. I remembered hearing this once before, when Adina and I had caused a ruckus in the base. Since Adina had escaped and I was still locked up, I concluded that someone must have entered the base and been discovered. Was it Adina? Had she come to rescue me?

A new noise soon mixed with the alarms: the sound of explosions and screams of pain. I lifted my head as the door opened and three women walked in. I recognized all of them, of course, and I couldn't help but crack a smile when I saw them.

"Hey, you three."

"Bryan!"

Adina and Michelle shouted my name at the same time and raced forward. Christine hung back and guarded the door as the archangel and succubus knelt beside me. Michelle reached into a pouch on her hip and removed a vial filled with red liquid. A health potion. She uncorked it as Adina tilted my head, making it easier for the blonde woman to tip the liquid down my throat. I coughed, but Adina helped me swallow it by massaging my throat.

"T-thank you," I said, already feeling a bit better as the warmth spread through my body.

"Are you okay?" Adina asked with concern. "I'm so sorry it took such a long time to get you."

"How long has it been?" I asked.

"Two weeks," Michelle answered. "Adina came to us about a week ago. We found her being chased by Johnathan's men and disposed of them. She told us about what happened, so we brought her to Sauruss. It took a lot of work to convince Sauruss that Adina hadn't been sent as a spy. After that, we kept trying to appeal to him to launch an attack on Johnathan's base, but he wouldn't budge."

With Adina and Michelle's help, I was able to stand up. I raised my arms and clenched them into fists. Health potions certainly were amazing. My body had already recovered most of its vitality.

"What changed his mind?" I asked.

"Adina helped him successfully capture Johnathan's latest shipment of SML-44s," Michelle said. "In fact, I'd say she was instrumental in the success of that mission."

"That explains why Johnathan was so mad when he was torturing me last time," I muttered with a sigh.

"You three can talk about this later," Christine said as she peered out of the hallway. "Let's get going."

"Wait. Are you three the only ones here?" I asked.

"Of course not," Christine said. "After successfully stealing Johnathan's latest shipment of SML-44s, we were able to convince Sauruss to launch an attack on this base. More than seventy-five percent of Sauruss' forces along with the SML-44s he commandeered are attacking at this very moment. We merely used this opportunity to rescue you."

"Is Sauruss here?" I asked.

"He is."

Christine led the way outside of the prison cell and into the hallway. This prison was much different than the ones I was used to. There were no prison bars, just doors that led to rooms similar to mine. We raced down the hallway, wary of attacks, but perhaps because this base had other things to worry about, no one came to attack us.

"In that case, let's end this mission now," I said.

"How?" asked Christine.

"We'll blow up this entire base," I said as we turned a corner. There was no one down it, so we quickly ran. I could hear more explosions in the distance and realized there was fighting elsewhere.

"This base uses a plasma core for energy. If we destabilize the core, we can blow the base sky high."

"Are you sure that's a good idea?" asked Michelle. "Won't it damage the Spoke?"

I shook my head. "These Spokes are made from a heat and plasma resistant alloy and won't be destroyed from mere explosions. At most, it will destroy this base and maybe the surroundings within a several kilometer radius."

While Michelle didn't look convinced, Adina and Christine both expressed their agreement with the plan. Majority vote decided it.

"Before we blow up this base, I want to make sure we kill Johnathan and Sauruss," I said.

"It would be better to make sure they are dead than to just assume they died in an explosion," Christine agreed.

"I also have to pound him one for hurting you," Adina added.

As we left the prison behind, we came across several battles taking place. Sometimes it was in the middle of a hallway, and we had to backtrack to avoid being caught up in it. Other times the battle would take place in a large room. There were many warehouses and docking bays for various vehicles and cargo ships. It looked like Sauruss' forces had decided to take control of these areas first so they could acquire Johnathan's equipment.

The first thing we needed to do was find my armor and weapons, which we sadly couldn't find. This place was just too big. We didn't even know where to look.

I took the women up to the command center. As we arrived on the floor with the command center, we found several soldiers in red and green armor already locked in combat. It looked like the members of Hydra were trying to force their way into the command chamber, while Cerberus members were defending it with their very lives.

"I don't think we're going to be able to reach the command center like this," Adina said.

"I think you're right." I grimaced. "Let's backtrack and try to think of something else."

Still doing our best to avoid getting caught up in a battle between the two opposing forces, we moved through the halls, ducked inside of rooms, and crept our way toward the barracks. Just as we were turning a corner, a group of men in red armor skidded to a halt in front of us. The man in the lead was none other than Grian. His eyes widened when he saw me standing before him.

"You're—"

I gave him no chance to speak. Darting forward, I ducked low and came up with a palm strike uppercut. My palm struck his jaw and lifted his body into the air. Spinning on the balls of my feet, I raised my left foot and slammed the sole of my bare foot into his armor. The armor cracked as he was sent sailing into one of his comrades. They both went down in a tangle of limbs.

"Leave Grian alive, but kill the others!" I told the women.

They all nodded.

Adina darted forward and slammed into one of the soldiers, her fist shattering the armor and punching a hole clean through his chest.

She removed her hand quickly, spun around, and launched a powerful reverse heel kick that sent the dead man flying.

Michelle was beside Adina, swinging her twin golden swords without relent, her weapons cutting through armor like it was made of tofu. Two men were killed in just as many seconds. She removed their heads from their shoulders with ease. Adina also killed her second soldier by landing on his shoulders with a high-jump and using her feet to break his neck. I almost flinched at the sickening sound of his neck cracking as his head turned a full 180 degrees.

"I didn't even get to do anything," Christine muttered as she slung her rifle back over her shoulder.

I shrugged. "I didn't do much either."

"You're unarmed. I've got a big gun."

"Point taken."

Grian was still alive. I hauled the man to his feet and slammed him against the wall, pressing my forearm to his neck underneath his mandible. Choking noises echoed from the man as I applied more pressure.

"Brya—hurk! Bryan! I… I had nothing… to do with… urk!"

"I don't care about whether or not you were involved in my torture," I said, cutting him off. "Tell me where Johnathan is keeping my equipment."

"I… don't…"

"Don't tell me you don't know." I cut him off. "Even if you're not completely sure, you must have some idea."

Grian remained silent for a moment, and I began applying more pressure to his throat. He choked and relented.

"Okay! Okay!" I eased off. Grian's mandibles opened as he gasped for breath. "I… I don't know if they will be there, but if I was him, I'd keep your equipment in my room. I'm sure they will be in his quarters."

"Thank you," I said with a smile and finally removed my hand from his throat. "Get going. I suggest you leave this place."

"You're… not going to kill me?" he asked.

"Do you want me to?"

Grian shook his head.

"Then leave. Now."

Grian didn't hesitate to run off, leaving behind his comrade's corpses behind. The man wasn't a coward, but he didn't actually have any loyalty to these people. He was in it for the money and prestige. Now that it looked like Johnathan had taken a major blow he might never recover from, the man was abandoning ship.

Such a mercenary lifestyle.

"Thank you for not killing him," Michelle said. "I know there are times when we must kill people, but I do not approve of killing in cold blood."

I shrugged. "There was no reason to. Now let's hurry."

We didn't remain in that hallway for any longer. The four of us traveled down the barracks and toward the commander quarters, which was located one floor down.

Johnathan's quarters were much larger than anyone else's, and the interior was far posher than I'd expect from a military man, even ex-military. Paintings lined the walls, weapons hung from racks, and the furniture was made of wood instead of synthetic materials. I found my sword hanging from a rack and quickly grabbed it. My armor was in a chest. I put it on with Adina's help. Michelle also lent a hand, but I had a feeling she just didn't want Adina hogging all of my attention.

"Now what?" asked Christine.

"Now we find out where Johnathan and Sauruss are," I said. "We kill them, blow this place up, and leave."

***

In order to find Sauruss and Jonnathan, we needed to find a computer that was installed into the base's network, hack into it, and look through the security cameras. That meant traveling back to the command chamber.

The fires of battle still raged everywhere. It seemed even more fierce than it had been seconds ago. Corpses were strewn about the halls, smoke wafting from their bodies. An acrid scent filled the air, burnt flesh mixed with ash, molten metal, and singed ozone.

When we arrived at the command center, it was to find nothing but a pile of red armored corpses and several men in green armor standing around. When they saw us, all of them snapped a salute.

"Madam Christine. Madam Michelle. It is good to see you. I see you've completed your mission," one of the men said. He was a drurian. Actually, I noticed most of these soldiers were drurians, with only a few other species mixed into them.

"We have," Christine said with a smile. "And what of you? Have you completed your mission?"

"Yes, ma'am. The command center is now ours."

"Good. Where is Commander Saurruss?"

"Not here. He left not long ago to chase after Johnathan. The leader of Cerberus apparently made a run for it when it became obvious we would win."

"And do you know where he is?" The drurian shook his head. "That's fine. Let me into the command center. I'll find out where Johnathan and Commander Saurruss went and provide backup."

The drurian snapped off another salute as he stepped away from the door and allowed us to pass. I was really impressed by how much respect these people had for Christine, who they seemed to treat like a goddess of war. They respected Michelle too. However, the quiet archangel didn't have the same charisma as the Earthling with Valkyrie training. The woman was a natural born leader.

Christine went over to one of the control stations, used a device that let her hack into the network, and shifted quickly through security camera views. I watched with narrowed eyes as scene after scene scrolled past at a rapid rate.

"Stop! There!" I suddenly shouted.

Christine stopped the monitor on an image of the power control room. Two people were fighting inside of it, Johnathan and a drurian I took to be Saurruss. It looked like they were in a deadlock.

"How fortunate for us," I whispered.

They were exactly where we needed to go. My guess was Johnathan, realizing he had lost, decided to blow this entire base up rather than let it fall into Sauruss's hands. He would take out this base and his enemies with it. How vindictive. Either way, however, this was a great boon for us. We could kill Sauruss and Johnathan, then set this place to blow up. It would be killing two birds with one stone.

"Let's go," Christine said in a commanding tone that gave me shivers. This woman was sexy when she was acting like a commander.

***

The power control room was located in the last basement level of the base. Getting there required us to take several different elevators—a defensive measure against someone reaching this most important room. It was purposefully convoluted, though now it seemed like making it that way was useless.

After exiting one last elevator, the four of us traveled through a narrow hallway lined with corpses, eventually reaching the power control room.

The door was already busted open. It looked like someone had used an explosive to blow it up. We peered inside and found ourselves staring at a large control room with a large window taking up one side of the room and several control stations that were responsible for the monitoring, maintenance, and power distribution of the reactor.

Beyond the glass window was the reactor, which looked like nothing I'd ever seen before. I'd say it most closely resembled an atom.

A glowing blue nucleus floated in the center of several rings that spun around it at a rate so fast it looked like they were standing still.

In the very center of this room was Johnathan and Saurruss, locked in combat, blades clashing and blaster bolts firing. I had to admit they both had skill. Johnathan was a better shot than Sauruss, but Sauruss was better at dodging and close combat. Even as I watched, Johnathan was backpedaling as he fired at his opponent, who deflected each blaster bolt with his sword.

That sword of his was something I found myself interested in. It looked like a single-edged blade, but running along the edge was an intense blue beam of energy. Plasma? I couldn't tell, but it was able to deflect blaster fire, which was impressive in and of itself.

Of course, the man wielding it was every bit as impressive. The way he danced across the ground, his precise movements as he swung his blade like he knew where Johnathan would fire before Johnathan knew it himself, was all incredible. It was a good thing this man was only around level 70. If he had a higher level like 80 or heaven forbid 90, we would have been in serious trouble.

As if moving on an unspoken signal, the four of us entered the room and moved behind Sauruss. The drurian was taller than any other I'd seen. His body, covered in muscles that made his military training obvious, looked back at us and nodded in satisfaction.

"I see you rescued your husband," Sauruss said. "That's good. And now…" He turned back to Johnathan. "I have the advantage."

Johnathan's face turned red with anger. "Damn you! Fucking damn all of you! I would have owned this station if it weren't for you fucking shit stains! If I can't attain this victory, then I'm going to take all of you down with me!!!"

"No, you won't," Saururss said, calm as could be. He seemed to really believe we were here to help him.

I looked at Michelle, who nodded and glided forward. She moved so quickly Saururss didn't even have time to be surprised when she turned on him. A single swing of her blade cut through his armor. The attack was a horizontal one. It created an incision along his neck. Flesh split and a sickening noise echoed around us as the drurian's head fell to the ground.

Johnathan was so shocked by what happened that all he could do was gape. In that moment, I burst forward at a speed he couldn't keep up with. He tried to backpedal, but he didn't get too far before I thrust my sword forward. The blade, coated in bright orange fire, went through his armor and impaled him in the chest.

"You… didn't work… for Saurruss?" he asked as we stood so close I could feel his breath on my face.

"Nope," I said. He deserved an answer. "I work for the Information Broker."

"Ha… figures… we were… played…"

With a final swing, I removed my blade from his chest and watched him stagger backward. He fell onto his backside, raised a hand to cover his bleeding chest, and looked at me as the light faded from his eyes. I kept a cold look on my face as I watched him fall back. I nudged him with my foot and checked his pulse to make sure he was dead.

"It's done," I said, standing back up and turning to my companions. "Let's set this place to blow up and leave."

Christine knew more about technology than me. I guessed she'd already traveled to many realms with a higher level of tech than Earth. She manipulated the control station that dealt with the distribution of power, and as she did, the nucleus-like reactor began shaking as sparks crackled around it. While she did that, I grabbed the sword Saurruss had been using.

To the victor goes the spoils.

"Okay," she began, stepping back. "I've created a feedback loop within the reactor. All the power going to everything except the elevators and doors is now being redirected back into it. We have maybe twenty minutes before it overloads and blows up. We should be at least ten kilometers away when that happens. Otherwise, we're gonna get caught in the blast."

"Then let's leave," I said.

We didn't stick around inside that control room, traveling down the hall and up the elevator. The ride up seemed slower than before. Did that mean there wasn't as much power going into it, or was this just my imagination playing tricks on me because of my impatience. I found myself tapping my foot against the ground as I waited for the ride to end.

"Relax," Michelle said. "If you're jittery, you're going to make the rest of us nervous."

"Sorry," I said, taking a deep breath and stopping.

The doors soon opened and we stepped out. We managed to reach two more of the elevators needed to reach the top floors. It was only after we ended up in basement floor three that we encountered a problem.

"There are the traitors! Kill them!"

Several people in poisonous green armor opened fire on our group as we were rounding a corner, forcing us to move back and avoid being shot. I was confused at first. Why would Hydra fire at us? But then I recalled the words one of them said. He called us traitors, meaning he must have somehow learned we were responsible for Saurruss's death.

"The command center," Christine and I said at the same time.

"You're saying they used one of those monitors to see us killing Saurruss and Johnathan?" asked Adina.

"Most likely," I said.

"It's the only thing that makes sense," Christine added.

"Well… that's no good," Adina muttered.

"What should we do?" asked Michelle.

"Nothing for it. We have to get out of here fast. Let's just plow through them and hope our superior levels are enough to avoid death," I said.

Michelle didn't look pleased with that idea, but none of us had a choice in how we did this. We needed to get out of here.

While my level was actually the lowest, I still led the charge as I bolted around the corner and raced forward, shooting at the men several meters away. Adina, Christine, and Michelle came after me. While Adina and Michelle flew through the air, Christine hefted her heavy repeating blaster and managed to somehow precisely fire around us, spraying blaster fire into our enemies and softening them up before we crashed into them.

The scent of blood became thick as I sliced into someone's head. My sword became stuck in their cranium. I yanked it out, causing blood to spray everywhere, stepped to the left, and thrust my blade through the throat of another. The squid-faced man gurgled as I removed the blade.

Adina landed on the floor beside me, her fist flying into someone's face, pulverizing their head. The bloody chunks that scattered everywhere was disgusting. However, it had a great effect on lowering the moral of our enemies. Nothing made people more frightened than seeing someone's head explode from a simple punch.

On my other side was Michelle. She landed on the ground, swung the blade in her left hand, and sliced through a man, armor and all. The man went down screaming. She ignored him and swung the sword in her other hand next, this time cutting through the barrel of a gun aimed at her. Before the surprised soldier could do anything, she stabbed him through the chest.

With Christine providing cover fire, the four of us carved our way through numerous groups of people trying to kill us. I liked to say we did a good job. At the same time, as the battles continued, I began tiring. It didn't matter how high my level was. Everyone had a limit on their stamina, and we were quickly reaching ours. My limbs were beginning to feel like lead.

"We'll never reach the exit! Let's head into one of the hangers and take a ship!" I suggested.

Adina, Christine, and Michelle didn't say anything. They were too busy concentrating on staying alive. However, they followed me as I changed direction, racing down a corridor and entering one of several hangers. This one was large enough to contain six ships. All of them were small transport vehicles meant for small-scale operations.

The one I led everyone to was pretty small, about maybe fifteen meters in length and five in width. It looked like a bird. This ship with a tapered nose reminiscent to a beak was called a PTV, short for Penguin-shaped Transport Vehicle. The back was able to carry six people, and there were two seats up front for the pilot and co-pilot.

"Do any of you know how to fly this?" I asked.

"You mean you don't?" asked Christine.

"Course not. I've never flown one before."

She sighed. "You are very lucky. I can fly it."

I pressed a button to lower the ramp. Several people burst through the doors and began opening fire on us as the ramp went down. Christine and I opened up with our heavy repeating blaster and pistol respectively, which didn't stop our enemies from attacking, but it did force them to fight defensively. The ramp lowered in that time and the four of us traveled inside.

Adina took over for Christine to help me provide cover fire as the human woman sat in the pilot seat and started it up. Michelle was standing not far from us. She was unable to sit because her huge wings got in the way.

The engine thrummed with life, a low whine that became louder with every passing second. Adina and I continued peppering our enemies with laser fire. I took careful aim and shot people in the face, but she merely moved her gun from side to side, laying suppressive fire that forced many people to take cover. Once the ship began hovering in the air, I hit the button that closed the ramp.

"Hold on, everyone!" Christine called back to us. "We're getting out of here!"

This docking bay was the kind where vehicles exited from the ceiling. Christine angled us up, which caused the three of us to hang on so we wouldn't fall against the ramp. She pressed a button that released a pair of missiles, which struck the exit and detonated with a brilliant haze of blue. The docking bay doors were turned into slag.

"Here we go!"

I felt bad for Adina and Michelle, who couldn't sit because of their wings. Maybe that was why I also didn't strap in either. The three of us were practically hanging by this point as Christine drove our ship through the exit and entered a tunnel. At the very end of the tunnel was another door, but she merely fired some missiles at that one and blew it up too.

Once she cleared the tunnel and ascended above the buildings, Christine leveled out, and the three of us who were not properly strapped in crashed to the floor. I groaned as I lay on my stomach, Adina and Michelle somehow landing on my back. I didn't say they were heavy. You never told a woman she was heavy unless you wanted to find yourself in the dog house, but dear lord, it felt like my spine was being crushed by a sumo wrestler.

"Could you two… please get off?" I asked.

"Yeah. Sorry, Darling," Adina said.

"I apologize, Bryan. Just… give us a second," Michelle said.

I grimaced as they shifted around on my back before getting up, then sighed in relief when the crushing combination of their both their weights finally left me. I sat up slowly, checking to see if my body was in proper working order. Once I confirmed that I was indeed alive and not paralyzed, I stood up.

Just then, a massive rumbling echoed around us. This vehicle didn't have any windows in the back, so we all crowded around the front and stared outside. I whistled as a massive explosion of light and energy erupted in the distance. That must have been the reactor exploding and blowing the base to smithereens.

"It looks like we escaped just in time," I said with a sigh of relief.

"We were lucky," Christine added.

"So what now?" asked Adina.

"I think we need to see Christine's contact," Michelle said.

"You're correct," I agreed with a nod. "Let's head back to Spoke 6."

***

We found ourselves sitting in the Space Cowboy once more, though we were a lot more worn and ragged than last time. We'd gone straight from Spoke 7 to here. Now I was sitting between Adina and Michelle, who were so tired they leaned against me, resting. I could use some sleep myself, but I didn't want to miss the Information Broker's contact. Christine was sipping some purple concoction on the other side of Adina.

A rustling sound appeared behind us.

"I heard about what happened in Spoke 7. Seems you were not only successful in eliminating Johnathan and Sauruss, but you destroyed their factions as well."

I shrugged. "It was easier this way."

A chuckle. "I'm not saying you did a bad thing. While this will create a huge power gap, the Information Broker has plans to put someone else in power on Spoke 7, so this actually works out better for us than if you just killed them."

"Glad to be of service," I said. "Now, about that information."

At that moment, Adina and Michelle, who'd been quietly relaxing, opened their eyes and sat up. I could sense the anticipation from Michelle. The entire reason we'd come here was to get the information we needed to find her realm.

"I have two datacards here," continued the contact. "One contains information on Michelle's realm, where you can find the rift for it, and what the current situation is like. The other one contains information on Adina's mother. It also has the current location of Asmodeus, Agrat bat Mahlat, and Eisheth. You can only choose one datacard, Bryan. Which will you choose?"

Adina and Michelle froze when they heard what the contact said. He had information on both Michelle's realm and the locations of

Adina's most hated enemies? That was a boon for us. However, his last words about how we could only choose one datacard put a damper on any joy we might have felt. I thought this contact was being unnecessarily cruel to us.

"M-Michelle…" Adina swallowed thickly. "I think… we should get the datacard with information about your realm first. We… that's what we came here for."

"No…" Michelle shook her head. "It is true we came here for that, but you… you've wanted to know where those three are for a long time now. With that information, we can save your mother. We should get the data you need first." Michelle gave Adina an unconvincing smile. "I can wait."

I was really touched that these two cared enough about each other to put off their own desires for the other person, but it really didn't help solve our situation. What's more, I didn't want them making this into an argument.

And yet, just before I could speak, the contact chuckled.

"Relax, you two. I am just kidding."

"Huh?" Adina and Michelle muttered at the same time. I was in much the same boat. Huh?

"You four went above and beyond what was expected of you," the contact continued. "Not only are Johnathan and Sauruss gone, but their factions don't have the strength to recover. The Information Broker already has some of his people in Spoke 7, taking control of the situation. It won't be long before he has complete control there. That's enough for us to give you the information on both Seventh Heaven and The Seven Circles of Hell."

A hand extended from behind us and placed two datacards onto the table. They didn't look any different from the one we received when first coming here, but contained within these two datacards was apparently the information we needed to help Michelle reach her realm and Adina to fight the people who sealed away her mother.

The hand retracted, then the contact stood up.

"Good luck, you four. I look forward to seeing what you do next," he or she said, and with that, the contact was gone.

~Fin

AFTERWORD

I would like to thank everyone who picked up a copy of Swordsman of the Rift 2 and gave it a read. I hope you enjoyed it. If you did, please consider writing a small review on Amazon so other readers can decide whether or not my story is worth reading.

For Swordsman of the Rift 2, I wanted to add more meat into both the story and gamelit elements. You'll notice that I expanded upon the importance of having high stats and how they can be used to learn a variety of skills. I felt like my previous volume was too basic. It didn't have a very in-depth leveling system, so I tried to correct that. I don't know if I succeeded.

This particular story was an attempt at expanding on the Rift Plains and the many worlds that are connected to it. It was a bit hard for me to figure out how I can describe it all since this universe is something Jamie Hawke created. He just invited me to write stories within the universe itself. I did not want to step on his toes. On that note, I'd like to thank him for letting me write stories within his universe.

The Rift Plains is supposed to be a universe that was created after a company's experiment to let people speak with their departed loved ones went wrong. A myriad of worlds were either created or became connected through the Rift Plains. My understanding is that most of these worlds are loosely based on mythology. That was why I decided to have Bryan and the others living in Valhalla, but one that was based around the concept of floating islands like Granblue Fantasy instead of the traditional mythos we know of.

I also decided that the last half of this volume was going to take place on a space station. I figured why limit myself to just mythology? Why not add a more sci-fi setting? I hope everyone liked this idea.

Here are some last minute thanks to the many people who made this possible.

Thank you Abby. She was my proofreader for this volume. I went over her edits and believe she did a superb job.

Thank you DanteWontDie for agreeing to be my artist. The cover is freaking awesome. I have loved his artwork for a really long time. The man knows how to draw amazing T&A.

And thank you, readers. I will always be grateful to the support you show me. I could never have gotten this far without you, and I hope you will be willing to support me again when the last volume of Swordsman of the Rift comes out. Thank you again.

~Brandon Varnell

DID YOU KNOW THAT BRANDON IS CREATING A MANGA ADAPTATION OF AMERICAN KITSUNE ON PATREON? LOOK AT THE NEXT PAGE FOR A SNEAK PEAK!

HAVE YOU EVER EXPERIENCED ONE OF THOSE LIFE-CHANGING INSTANCES? AN EVENT SO MOMENTOUS THAT, YEARS LATER, YOU'RE STILL MARVELING AT HOW IT CHANGED YOUR LIFE?

I HAD ONE OF THOSE. IT HAPPENED A WHILE AGO

EVEN TO THIS DAY, THROUGH ALL THE CHANGES THAT HAVE HAPPENED, THROUGH ALL THE EXPERIENCES THAT I'VE BEEN THROUGH, I STILL CAN'T BELIEVE HOW THIS ONE MOMENT CHANGED MY LIFE FOREVER.

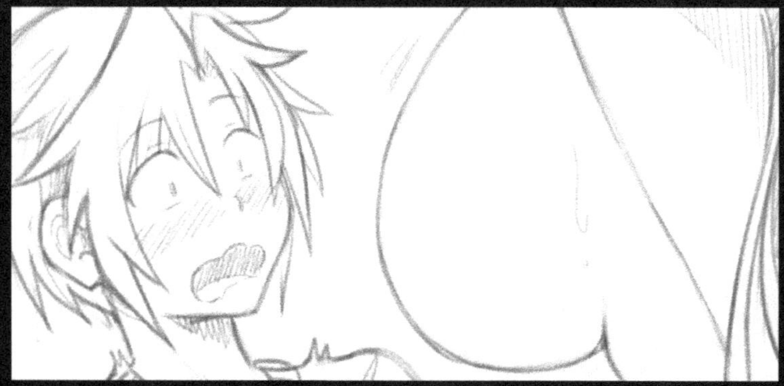

NO MATTER WHAT CAME AFTER, OUR FIRST MEETING IS SOMETHING THAT I'LL ALWAYS REMEMBER.

ESPECIALLY SINCE, AT THE BEGINNING OF THIS TALE, I THOUGHT SHE WAS NOTHING
BUT AN ORDINARY FOX WITH, UNORDINARILY ENOUGH, TWO BUSHY RED TAILS.

LIFE

.

.

.

.

.

.

.

.

.

IT HITS YOU WHEN YOU LEAST EXPECT IT TO.

AMERICAN
KITSUNE

Hey, did you know?
Brandon Varnell has started a Patreon
You can get all kinds of awesome exclusives
Like:

1. The chance to read his stories before anyone else!
2. Free ebooks!
3. exclusive SFW and NSFW artwork!
4. Signed paperback copies!
Er... maybe we don't want that last one, but the rest is pretty cool, right?

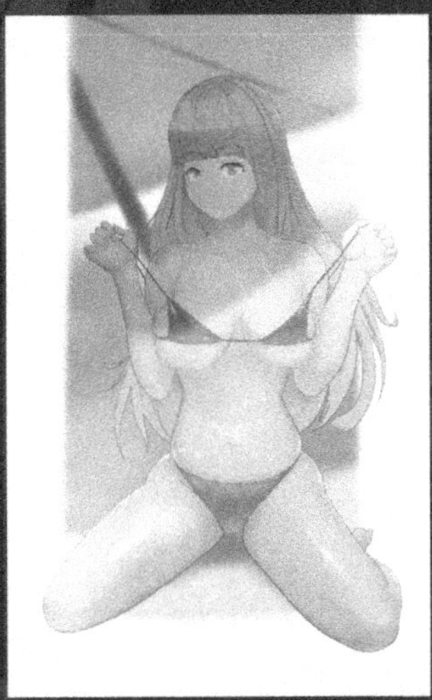

To get this awesome exlusive conent go to:
https://www.patreon.com/BrandonVarnell
and sigh up today!

American Kitsune

Volumes 1-2
available on Amazon and Kindle

WIEDERGEBURT
LEGEND OF THE REINCARNATED WARRIOR

Volumes 1-7
are available now!
A Most Unlikely Hero

Arcadia's
IgnobleKnight
Volumes 1-6
are available now!

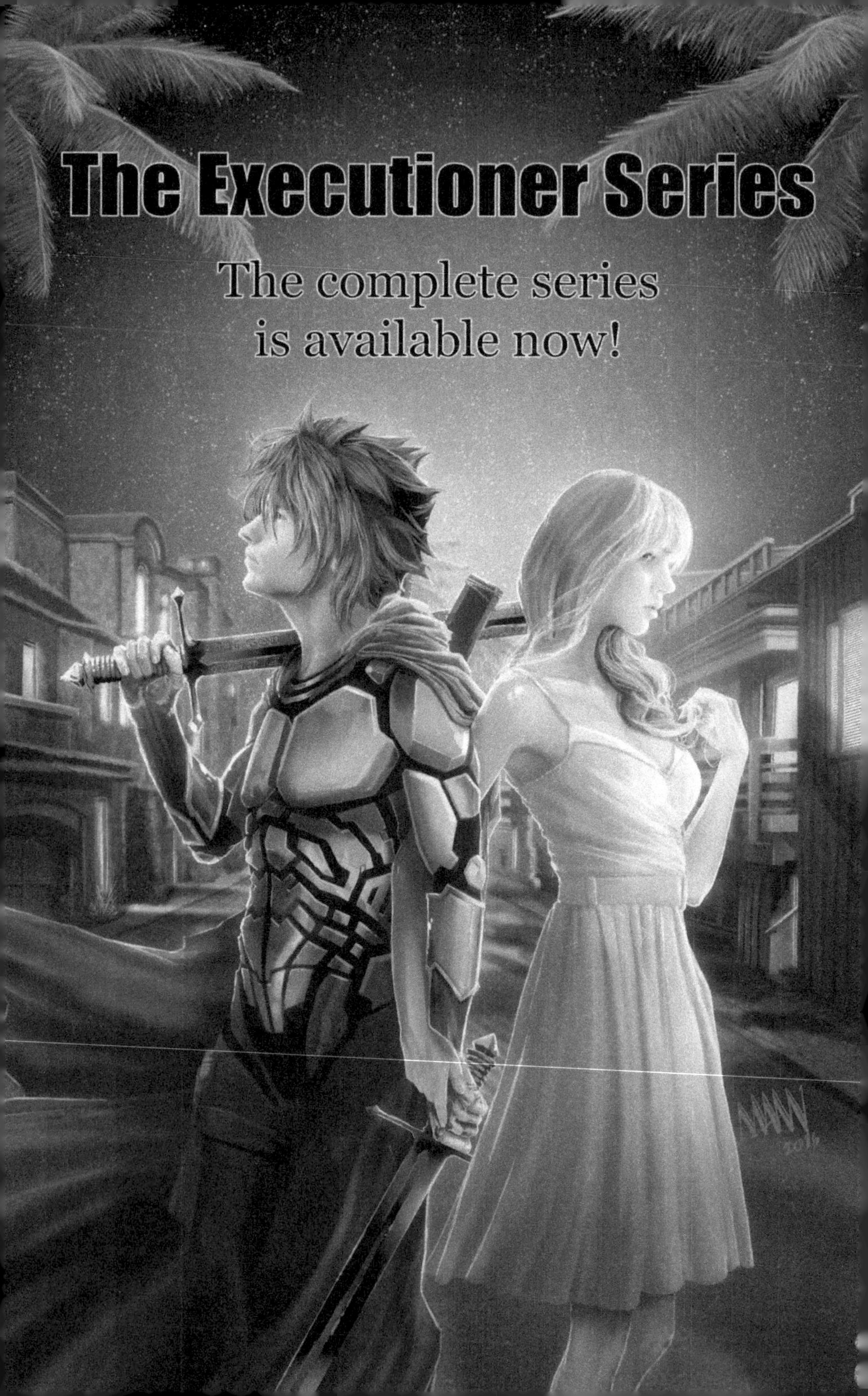

The Executioner Series
The complete series
is available now!

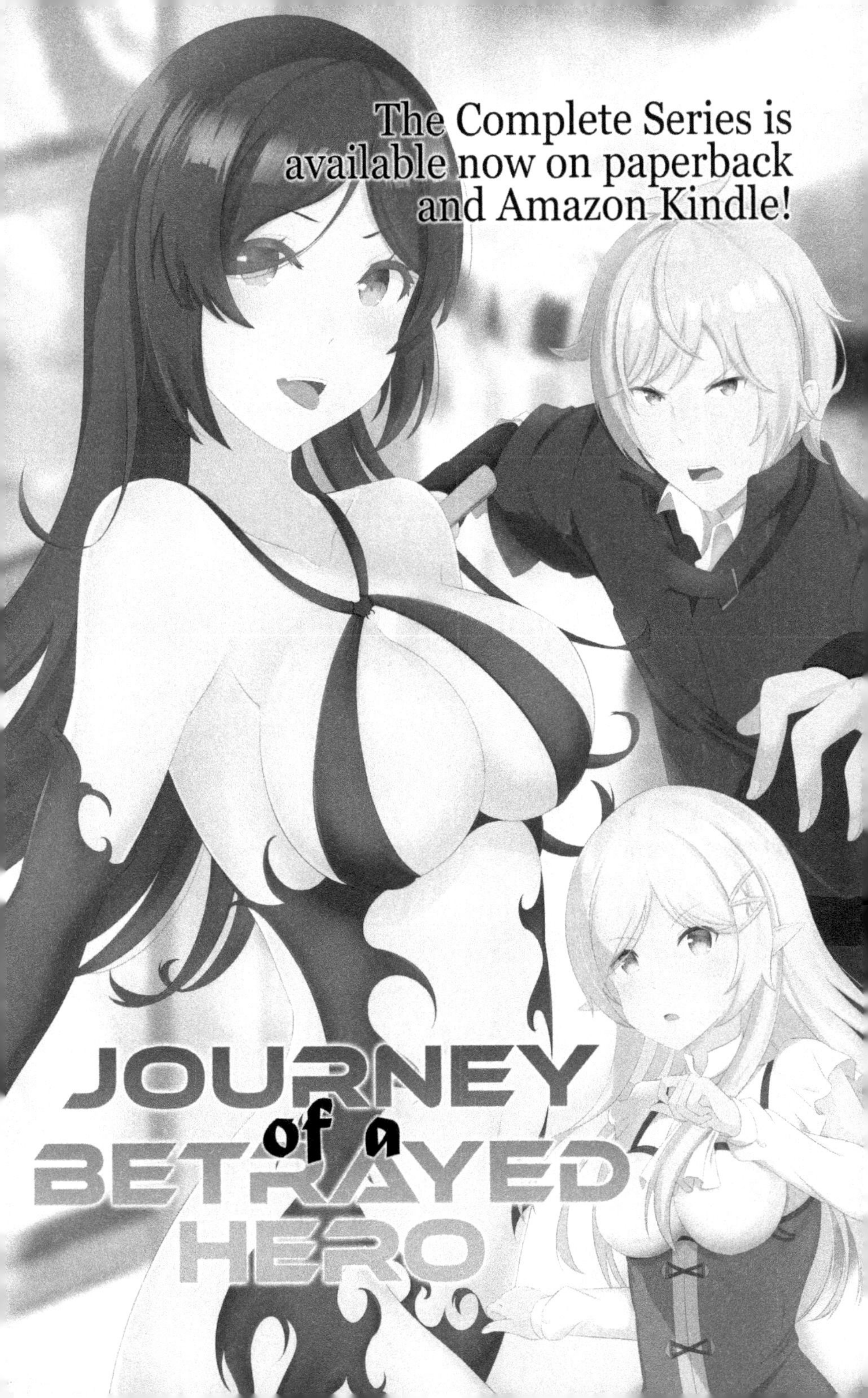

The Complete Series is available now on paperback and Amazon Kindle!
JOURNEY of a BETRAYED HERO

www.ingramcontent.com/pod-product-compliance
Lightning Source LLC
Chambersburg PA
CBHW070828190726
48292CB00006B/2151